9-13

MISTLETOE Memories

4-in-1 Romance Collection

JENNIFER ALLEE, CARLA OLSON GADE,
LISA KARON RICHARDSON, AND GINA WELBORN

BARBOUR
PUBLISHING

'Tis the Season © 2013 by Carla Olson Gade
Mercy Mild © 2013 by Gina Welborn
Midnight Clear © 2013 by Lisa Karon Richardson
Comfort and Joy © 2013 by Jennifer AlLee

Print ISBN 978-1-62416-127-8

eBook Editions:
Adobe Digital Edition (.epub) 978-1-62416-475-0
Kindle and MobiPocket Edition (.prc) 978-1-62416-474-3

Scripture quotations marked KJV are taken from the King James Version of the Bible.

This book is a work of fiction. Names, characters, places, and incidents are either products of the author's imagination or used fictitiously. Any similarity to actual people, organizations, and/or events is purely coincidental.

Cover design by Kirk DouPonce, DogEared Design

Published by Barbour Publishing, Inc., P.O. Box 719, Uhrichsville, Ohio 44683, www.barbourbooks.com

Our mission is to publish and distribute inspirational products offering exceptional value and biblical encouragement to the masses.

ecpa Member of the
Evangelical Christian
Publishers Association

Printed in the United States of America.

'TIS THE SEASON

Carla Olson Gade

DEDICATION

To my Dad, Kenneth Olson, the first man I kissed under the mistletoe. With precious Christmas memories— especially Christmas lights and pickled herring.

Christmas is a season for kindling the fire for hospitality in the hall, the genial flame of charity in the heart.
WASHINGTON IRVING

CHAPTER 1

S low there, boys. Whoa, Hippocrates. Whoa, Galen!"

Annaliese Braun arched back as she drew in the reins with a firm grip. Spooked by a high-pitched whistle, the pair of riled horses continued their unsteady trot. The conveyance shook and the horses lurched ahead. The carriage shuddered beneath her as she tried to maintain control and pull the horses to a stop.

"Ea–sy fellas," Annaliese called out to them, peering at the packed dirt road before her. The carriage felt askew. She leaned over and beheld the large wheel wobbling at her side, looking up in time to see a large branch strewn across the mountain road. The team shifted and with a jolt, angled back. The rear wheels of the wagon slid into the wide gulch at the side of the road. Wet with leaves from last night's storm, the slippery descent tipped the carriage at a precarious angle on the uneven terrain. The carriage rocked from side to side, back and forth, as the horses wrestled to gain footing.

I must stop the horses! Annaliese moved to the edge of the footboard of her father's red landau. As she felt for the tread, her cotton pelisse caught on the side lantern. She steadied the toe of her ankle-boot on the small step and tugged at her

long cloak. As she struggled to free herself, the horses bucked and knocked her onto the damp ground where she landed in a most unladylike fashion. Hippocrates and Galen shuffled about as they dug their hooves into the rocky, leaf-strewn slope.

She looked up at the carriage looming over her, trying to find her voice. The harnesses pulled taut and the wheels rolled forward—toward her legs beneath the coach. Annaliese pushed against the ground trying to move, when strong arms grabbed her by the shoulders, hoisting her from harm's way.

She landed with her back against a warm, thumping, masculine chest, facing the bent knees of buckskin breeches tucked into knee boots. "The horses!" she screeched out. "I am all right, please get them!"

"You are sure?" he asked, with a slight guttural intonation.

"Please, hurry!" *Schnell!*

The man sprang to his feet and climbed up the shallow embankment to the road, running after the confused horses. He took hold of Galen's harness and yanked back. "*Ho. . . halte,*" he called out, working his way in front of the team, bringing them to a stop. Hippocrates tossed his head and blew out reverberating snorts.

The man led the horses to a small glade off the side of the road, drawing the faltering carriage behind them.

Annaliese was taking deep breaths, trying to regain her senses, when the handsome rescuer squatted down in front of her, taking deep breaths of his own. His green eyes, brightened by his ruddy face, gazed at her intently. "Miss Braun, it is good to meet you at last," he said, a subtle inflection of Dutch upon his tongue.

Annaliese blinked. It really was he, and she was not dreaming after all. The man she'd longed to meet, had continued to avoid all summer, took her by the hands and gently pulled her to her feet. She rose, finding herself in such proximity to him that there was nothing else she could say but, "Why, Mr. Yost, how do you do?"

"Stephan, if you please, miss," the Heath House resident carpenter said, taking a few steps back from her. "It is what I am accustomed to." His eyes roamed the top of her head with curiosity. "To answer your question, I believe I fare better than you this day."

From the corner of her eye, Annaliese noted her plaid chin ribbon dangling somewhere in the vicinity of her temple. She winced. "I must be quite a sight." She lifted her hands and felt the disheveled state of her bonnet.

A crooked grin rose above Stephan's cleft chin.

Annaliese withdrew her bonnet of braided straw and gathered taffeta, and her thick plait plopped onto her shoulder. She often wove her unruly locks into a neat coif surrounding the crown of her head, but the pins from the back must have come undone, as had her pride.

She released a deep sigh as she glanced down at the hat, turning it about in her hands. The back was crushed and fall leaves were plastered to it. "Perhaps I should begin a new fashion and leave them." A nervous laugh escaped her lips and she began to pluck the leaves from amongst the small plumes and other trimmings. "I should have thought of it before the resort guests went back to their grand homes in the cities. They could have shared the latest fall headdress with their elegant friends." Enough of her nervous chatter. What

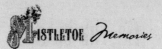

did he know of fashion, with his rugged apparel befitting a tradesman?

Stephan nodded, muffling a laugh, and turned to look at the horses.

As he did so, Annaliese pulled off her soggy chamois driving gloves and discreetly felt the back of her pelisse, finding that the damp ground had saturated the fabric.

"If you are all right, Miss Braun, we should see to the horses and your carriage."

"Yes, of course."

Stephan took long strides up the incline and turned to her, extending his hand. She placed her ungloved hand in his firm grip and he carefully helped her to the road. Then the handsome Dutchman motioned for her to walk ahead of him.

"You may go ahead, thank you." She fanned her warm face with her gloves in the absence of her fan. Who would have ever expected to need a fan on a morning outing in the country in late October? She followed Stephan to the roadside patch where her geldings nosed through wet leaves and nibbled on the spiky grass. Careful to keep her backside away from Stephan's view, she worked her way around the team and wagged her finger at them. "Hippocrates and Galen. You have been most naughty today. There shall be no carrots for you."

Stephan's eyebrows lifted. "Hippocrates and Galen?"

"My father named them after the ancient physicians," she answered. Stephan issued a slow nod.

Annaliese raised her brow and shrugged. Did he understand the logic or simply find their names peculiar?

He cocked his head. "Now tell me, Miss Braun, how did your intelligent horses deposit you and your carriage into that gulch?"

Annaliese swallowed. *Gulch?* It was a gulch all right, and she had fallen straight in. Stephan Yost may have rescued her, but her heart was in the precarious position of rebelling against her plans for the future.

❧

Stephan gazed at the woman before him, her light brown braid framing her brow and flowing rebelliously onto her shoulder, and her long, rumpled, military-style coat dampened by her fall. Yet never had he met anyone so *mooi*—beautiful—in his life. He had admired her from afar, capturing an occasional glimpse of her at the resort. But their paths seldom crossed, he being busy with his first season at Heath House, building and making repairs, and other ventures. She, well, he wasn't sure exactly what she did besides facilitate activities for the rusticators. When he first learned that she was the daughter of the resort's doctor, he was tempted to injure himself so that, by chance, if she assisted her father with his patients, he might gain the chance to meet her. He kept his ears tuned to the chatter of the guests and soon discovered that Dr. Helmut Braun was an esteemed and wealthy physician from New York. The doctor's daughter would never consider associating with an itinerant carpenter.

"It all happened so fast," she said, snapping him back to the present. "The horses spooked and took off, and as they went faster the carriage began to shake. It felt like the wheel started coming undone, and then they almost ran over that downed tree." She pointed at the huge branch nearby. "Then

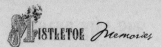

down in the gulch they went. I suppose I really should not blame them. They were as scared as I." She pouted at her dun and bay and caressed their faces. "Isn't that right, Galen? You, too, Hippocrates."

Stephan walked over to the loosened carriage wheel. He knelt and ran his hand along the spokes as he inspected it. "I think I can fix this and get you on the road again. Do you have a toolbox with spare linchpins?"

"We do," she said.

He angled his head toward the downed branch. "First I will clear that from the road."

"*Gut*, we would not want anyone else running into it."

Stephan stood and stretched. "*Gut*, you say. Your German word sounds much like *goed* in my Dutch."

"Yes, it does sound similar. You must find it helpful, being here amongst so many Germans in this area, especially down the mountain in the German Valley."

He nodded. "*Ja*."

"Ja," she said, donning a little smirk that made her cheeks color.

A chuckle rose in his throat. "Will your hooved physicians be all right for a minute while I see to the downed branch?" He patted Hippocrates on the neck, or was that Galen?

"They shall be fine, so long as they are not spooked again. They are normally docile creatures." Miss Braun patted their necks.

Stephan turned and strode toward the road.

"Let me help you," she called, then hastened her steps beside his longer strides.

Though he knew her slim figure would provide no strength

for the task, he did not object to her offer. Her company pleased him. Stephan released a cheerful whistle to an old Dutch folk song, but Miss Braun reached up and clamped her palm over his mouth.

He pivoted toward her, staring at her, not knowing what to make of the gesture. Slowly, he lifted her palm and puckered his lips, about to tease her with another whistle. Perhaps it was some sort of game.

Miss Braun peered up at him with a look of desperation and planted her soft lips over his. He met her wide-eyed gaze of deep azure, trying to gauge when to pull back from this most pleasurable meeting. She withdrew and slipped her hand over his mouth again then placed her finger to her lips. "Shhh. . . You'll scare the horses." She slowly released her hand and winced, her cheeks flushing with color.

"I see," he whispered, nodding. "You do not want me to whistle."

"No." Her lips rounded as she formed the word and she drew in a little breath.

"Then you shall have to employ me to that end." Stephan leaned down and pressed his mouth over hers, enjoying her sweet taste. When she did not resist him, he placed his arm around her shoulders and drew her closer. Her palm rested against his chest and he breathed in deeply. His calloused hand found its way to the nape of her neck and he worked his fingertips into her soft hair. He thought he could hear her sigh, when she quickly pivoted to a sharp sound piercing the air.

He spun toward the loud whistle. A barefoot lad in breeches and a too-small coat stood by the road's edge and placed his fingers in his mouth, about to whistle again.

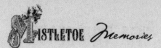

Stephan held up his hand. "Quiet! You'll scare the horses." He looked over his shoulder, seeing Miss Braun hurrying to the horses' side as they became restless. At least they were now tied and the carriage's brake locked in place.

Stephan jogged toward the youth, who was now bent over, hands pressed to his knees, trying to catch his breath. "What is it, lad?"

"*Ich habe gejagt—*"

"Speak English, boy."

"I have been chasing after Dr. Braun," the boy said, with his German accent. "I saw his red carriage *und* whistled, but he hurried on." Ah, so that was what all this whistling was about. The boy must have spooked Miss Braun's horses.

"Sorry, but Dr. Braun is not here. Miss Braun was driving his carriage." Stephan pointed to where she stood holding onto the horses' reins under the shelter of some trees.

The lad looked up at him, his eyes pleading. "But I must see Dr. Braun. *Mein onkel ist krank.*"

Miss Braun came forward and Stephan and the boy walked toward her. "Your uncle is sick? Who is he?"

The boy's eyes moistened. "Mein onkel ist Herr Rolof Schroeder."

Miss Braun pressed her fingers onto the child's shoulders. "*Sprechen sie auf Englisch, bitte.* Where is your uncle now?"

"He is at his mill on the West Springtown Road. *Wo ist—* Where is the doctor?" the boy asked.

"He is at Heath House." Miss Braun glanced at Stephan, worry tensing across her face.

Stephan gripped his jaw. "It won't take long for me to fix the wheel. Annaliese, get the toolbox, please, and make sure the horses' harnesses are secure. Come quickly, lad, and help me move the branch from the road."

"*Danke*," the boy said with a relieved sigh.

"I beg pardon, miss," Stephan said with a grimace, eyeing Miss Braun apologetically. "I believe I called you by your given name in error."

Miss Braun moistened her lower lip. "You may call me Annaliese. If you promise not to call my horses Herr Hippocrates and Herr Galen."

"I shall be sure not to do that. Besides, I intended to call them *Dokter* Hippocrates and *Dokter* Galen." Stephan chuckled.

The youngster grinned and peered up to the tree branches looming overhead. Stephan and Annaliese followed the lad's gaze to the nest of mistletoe wrapped around the branch of the black gum tree. "*Ist sie ihre liebchen*—your sweetheart?" the lad asked looking from Stephan to Annaliese.

The pair spun toward the boy, each protesting in turn.

"*Nee!*" Stephan grunted.

Annaliese hiked her chin. "*Nein!*" What had she done?

CHAPTER 2

How could she. . .why did she. . .? Yet, with her eyes fixated on Stephan's lips, the only solution that had come to mind was to kiss the man to keep him from whistling, lest her horses become frightened once more. And now, Annaliese found herself perplexed by the feelings the kiss had stirred within her. The first humiliating kiss had been unsettling enough, but the one he had stolen from her—that she had allowed him to take—had positively altered her.

Although Annaliese had admired the resort carpenter from afar from the moment he arrived at Heath House, she had suppressed her attraction to him, just as she had the fellows who had shown interest in her through the years. Although she had enjoyed a few brief summer romances, she had long resolved that her contentment in life would come from caring for her father into his old age. Papa had given her so much since her mother died, sacrificing even his own chance at romantic love, or so she thought, for her sake. Love, after all, was not all about romance, it was a greater joy, and calling. Then why had it pricked her heart that Mr. Stephan Yost, the one man she had secreted an attraction for, had not seemed to take notice of her—until now? And here she was rescued by him, kissed by him, and about to travel down Schooley's Mountain with him on an act of mercy.

Annaliese closed her eyes and breathed in the fresh scent

of the tree-lined road. The end of the season at Schooley's Mountain's famous resort had arrived. She'd come down the mountain to deliver some clothing that had been left behind by summer residents to the old stone church. Each year the reverend and his wife were happy to accept the resort's donation and distribute the garments to those in need. Mr. Heath and a worker had loaded the carriage, and she assured them that she was more than capable of making the delivery on her own. Others would be available to unload the items, and it was merely a few miles of travel. Although it had rained the night before, evidenced by the carpet of freshly fallen autumn leaves, the day was brimming with promise. As she had driven past a clearing coming down Schooley's Mountain Road, a grand view of the pastoral Musconetcong Valley opened up before her, and the sun was breaking through the clouded morn.

Now Hippocrates and Galen were ready to go, with another mission ahead—to come to the aid of Herr Schroeder. It appeared that Stephan was almost finished making the wheel repair. The millwright's worried nephew paced about, every now and then hovering over Stephan's shoulder to assess his progress.

Annaliese called to the lad. "Would you like to give the horses some carrots?"

"Ja," he said and came around to where she stood in front of her team.

She unfolded a cloth that she'd wrapped pieces of carrot in and handed them to the boy. *"Vas ist der namen?"*

He took the carrots and offered each horse a nibble. He patted their faces and smiled up at Annaliese. She glanced at

his worn clothing. His breeches were patched at the knees and his vest had a torn pocket. He appeared clean, though his hair was a bit mussed. Then it occurred to her that she shouldn't be making hasty judgments, as she surely was an unkempt spectacle in her own right.

"I am Rory Schroeder. You needn't speak to me in German. I only speak that way when I am upset, like my uncle does." The anxious boy looked back at Stephan.

Stephan rose, wiping his hands on a rag. "Well, Rory Schroeder, we are ready to be on our way." He extended his hand toward the lad. "I'm Stephan Yost, a carpenter from up the hill at Heath House. You have met Miss Braun."

"Yes sir," Rory said, glancing up at her.

"If you take that small toolbox and put it away where Miss Braun tells you, I will take one last look at the carriage and we will go see to your uncle's health," Stephan said.

Annaliese led Rory to the boot at the rear of the landau. After putting the toolbox away, she looked over the edge of the conveyance, at cartons of clothing on the seats and floor. Her mouth twisted as she tried to think of where two extra passengers would fit.

"I can make some room for us," Stephan said.

"Would you, please?" she asked.

"Ja. I can drive if you wish."

"I would appreciate that. I thought perhaps you could take Rory and me to his uncle's, as it is along the way, and then you might go to Heath House to fetch my father. That is, if you can. I have already imposed on you enough this morning." She thought of his rescuing her from being run over by the carriage, his repairing the wheel, his indulging her with kisses. . . .

16

"That is no problem for me, and I am happy to help." He opened the door of the open-topped landau and shifted the cartons of clothing around, making room for the boy in the seat behind the driver's platform. "Climb in, Rory."

Stephan handed Annaliese up to the driver's seat. To his credit kept his eyes upon her face and not the back of her damp pelisse. He then settled in beside her. She turned to Rory and said, "I am praying for your uncle as he waits for us to get to him. I am not a doctor, but I can perhaps lend him some comfort until my father arrives."

"Tell me, Rory, what were you doing so far up the mountain road?" Stephan called back over his shoulder, as he drove the carriage out onto the road.

The boy kneeled and leaned on the back of his seat, facing the front. "Uncle Rolof sent me to the mineral spring to get some healing waters. He has sent me every day, but he is getting worse. I was praying to God when I saw the doctor's carriage up ahead and then it turned onto the post road."

Annaliese tilted her head toward Stephan. "It was a divine thing how this all turned out, though I dare say, I hadn't thought so when my carriage went off the road."

He glanced at her and nodded. "Divine." He looked back toward the road ahead, and she noticed the corner of his mouth curve.

She clasped her hands in her lap and drew them in toward her abdomen, releasing a little sigh. *And all because of a whistle.*

"It is a good thing I whistled," Rory said.

"I guess you have never heard, then, that it is unlucky to whistle in a wind," Annaliese called back to Rory.

"It was not windy. I've never had bad luck with it, though

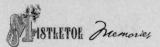

some call whistling the devil's music," the lad said, tugging his floppy hat over his ears. "Can you whistle, Miss Braun?"

Annaliese grimaced. "I don't know, but I shan't risk scaring the horses again."

"I heard that if a girl whistles she will grow a mustache," Stephan called back to the boy.

Rory let out a hearty laugh. "What else have you heard, Mr. Yost? Do you know any stories?"

"Hmm. Let's see. . .I once read about a man who met a strange person in a ravine—" Stephan cast a sidelong grin at Annaliese. "The man was a Dutch colonist of old New York and was traveling through the Catskill Mountains. The stranger asked the man to carry a keg to his village for him. After the man arrived and had a feast, he fell into a stupor and slept for twenty years. When he awoke everything had changed—his wife was dead, his daughter married, and America was an independent country."

"That must have happened before the American Revolution!" Rory said.

Annaliese and Stephan chuckled at the boy's naivete.

"That was the story of Rip Van Winkle by Geoffrey Crayon," Stephan told the boy.

"Mr. Crayon is a good friend of my family, from our hometown in New York." Annaliese turned back to Rory. "I shall tell you a *geheimnis*—a secret. The author is really Esquire Washington Irving, but he goes by another name for his publications in *The Sketch Book*."

"Why does he use another name, Miss Braun? Isn't that lying?" Rory asked.

Annaliese wrinkled her brow. "I think it is like this, Rory.

My horses are named Hippocrates and Galen, but my father calls them '*die docktoren*,' as Mr. Yost has also called them the *docktors*."

"Some people call my uncle Herr Schroeder and some call him Mr. Schroeder. But I call him Onkel Rolof." Rory shrugged and turned around in her seat, seemingly satisfied with her answer.

Stephan cocked his head in her direction and smirked.

Annaliese smiled back, until his gaze fell to her lips. She lowered her lashes and cupped her hand on her cheek, sliding it over to conceal her mouth. She dared glance at Stephan again and saw the crinkles at the corner of his eye. The stubble on his face below the profile of his high cheekbone glinted in the dappled morning sun. His dark blond hair hung past his neckcloth, which was peeking out above the collar of his brown frock coat of worsted-wool. Not a fashionable man, but keenly attractive, no less. Handsome, witty, benevolent, hardworking, gallant—by all means, Stephan Yost was the perfect catch—if she were looking.

—as he was, when he caught her staring at him, and grinned.

❧

Stephan snapped the reins as he ascended the mountain, and Hippocrates and Galen responded in turn. They were making good speed, though he was careful not to exhaust them, as they had a return trip to make to Schroeder's Mill. The "docktors" were a good team of horses, when they were not subjected to the sound of a whistle. But he was glad of that. In fact, he was rather fond of whistling, or rather, of *not* whistling.

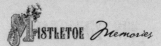

Stephan turned the carriage between the stone pillars marking the entrance to Heath House. He drove down the wide trail lined with colorful maples and junipers, and slowed the team as he neared the clearing of the rustic resort. He scanned the semicircle of cottages with the main hotel at its apex. Hopefully, he'd find Dr. Braun at his own cottage, where he served his summer patients. Stephan drove the landau up to the unpainted clapboard cottage and pulled on the brake. He peered down at the troublesome wheel that, for the moment, appeared stable.

Ephraim Marsh, longtime manager and new owner of the resort, came out of the modest building followed by his father-in-law, Joseph Heath, the former owner of Heath House. Mr. Marsh leaned against the porch rail and grinned. "You look like a dandy driving that fancy carriage, Yost. Say, is everything all right? Where is Miss Braun?"

The front door swung shut behind Dr. Braun as he followed the men out to the porch. Stephan remained in the driver's seat, relieved to see them all. "Dr. Braun, you are needed at once. Rolof Schroeder has taken ill, and your daughter is at the mill ministering to him until you can come."

"I shall get my bag," the doctor said, and entered his cottage again.

"How did you learn of this?" Mr. Marsh asked.

"His young nephew saw Miss Braun driving the doctor's carriage and stopped her," Stephan said.

Mr. Heath cocked his head back. "All the way down the mountain?"

"She had not gotten that far." Stephan looked over his shoulder to the cartons of clothing remaining in the carriage.

"Before she arrived at the stone church, the carriage went off the road—on the turnpike between Springtown and German Valley. I discovered her as I was coming back up the mountain from Swackhammer's forge, where I had gone for a repair this morning."

Dr. Braun returned and looked up at Stephan in alarm. "Was Annaliese harmed?"

"Nee." Stephan shook his head. "The carriage had a loose wheel, which I repaired."

"Danke, danke," the doctor said, and exhaled. He climbed up beside Stephan. "You may continue to drive, as you know the way to Herr Schroeder's."

Stephan looked over at Mr. Marsh. "I shall make up my work later." He hoped his employer would understand.

Mr. Marsh nodded and handed him a bottle of water from the spring, from the resort's ample supply. "Go now. See to Schroeder. When you are through, assist Miss Braun with the delivery to the church to be sure the carriage remains stable."

"*Dank u.*" Stephan gulped some water and set the bottle by his side. He wheeled the carriage around and headed back toward Schooley's Mountain Road. "Come on, boys, you have a patient to see."

Annaliese's father looked straight ahead, observing his team of horses. "I see you've become acquainted with *meine* docktoren, ja?"

"Ja." Stephan chuckled. "Hippocrates, Galen, and I have come to know each other well today."

The physician turned toward Stephan. "Und my Annaliese?"

"Ja, and your daughter." Stephan tightened his grip on the reins. "I had never met her until today, sir, although I had seen

her around the resort."

"Mmm-hmm," Dr. Braun murmured, staring at Stephan with lifted brow. "You are the quiet one. I see you about busy repairing this, building that. How did you find your first season at Heath House?"

Stephan turned onto the main road. "I have enjoyed being here. It is not as pretentious as Saratoga Springs. Though I did recognize some of the guests from Saratoga."

"Ja, some folks are inclined to taking the waters in various locales. It is addicting to some," Dr. Braun said.

Stephan narrowed his eyes, looking at the doctor. "Addicting? Like. . .opium or laudanum? I wasn't aware minerals had those kind of qualities."

"Nein, nothing like that. Addicting in the mind, that is," Dr. Braun said. "Although there are health benefits to the mineral waters, I tend to think it is the fresh outdoor air that does our visitors the most good. I know it has served my daughter and me well for some twelve years now."

"You have been coming here for that long?" Stephan asked.

"Ah, yes," the doctor said. "Annaliese was only a girl of twelve when I first came to be Heath House's physician. I was a recent widower, and it seemed like a wise choice to leave my practice in the city for the summer so that my daughter could enjoy the outdoors whilst I treated patients."

"And has she liked it?" Stephan asked.

"Meine *fräulein* ist not made for the city. At the end of each season I nearly have to surgically extract her from *der* mountain in order to get her back to Manhattan." Dr. Braun chortled. "Und you, Stephan? Do you prefer the mountain air to the city?"

"I do," Stephan said, as the docktors trotted along. "It is more pleasant to work in the country than in the city. I have worked in many places, and I like it here. Yet now that the resort season has ended, I have a limited amount of work to do off-season. I might scout around to see if there is a need for a carpenter in the area."

Dr. Braun crossed his arms, hiking his chin. "May I ask you this, Stephan Yost, have you experience building houses?"

CHAPTER 3

Annaliese enjoyed the magnificent fall foliage as Stephan drove the carriage down the mountain at a pleasant pace. She sat sideways so she might participate in the conversation with him and Papa. Stephan had cleared the seat for her when Herr Schroeder agreed to accept a donation of clothing for his great-nephew. While her father saw to his patient and she remained near to administer assistance, Stephan had helped Rory sort through the crates to find garments to fit him. The boy entered the stone house with clothes piled high in his arms, Stephan following only as far as the door, where he left a pair of boots for the lad. Annaliese had invited him in, but Stephan insisted on staying with the docktors.

"I am so glad to know that Herr Schroeder will be well again soon," Annaliese said. "It was kind of his neighbor to promise to look in on him and be sure he does not drink too much water from the mineral spring."

Stephan looked at Papa. "I thought the mineral waters restored good health to folks and that is why they are so admired."

Annaliese worried her lip, afraid that the answer Stephan was going to receive was more than he was anticipating.

"Only in moderation," Dr. Braun said. "I encounter the same problem with long-term visitors at the resort. When they overindulge in consuming the water from der mineral spring they become prone to a stricture of the digestive system and occasionally develop an intestinal infection. Left untreated, the consequences can be dire."

Stephan scratched the back of his head, clearing his throat.

Papa continued. "The chalybeate mineral springs are beneficial for Herr Schroeder's condition of nephritis—the inflammation of his kidneys—but only in limited measure."

Stephan nodded. "Ben Franklin said, 'Do everything in moderation, including moderation.'"

"Der Good Book also cautions us, 'All things are lawful... but all things are not expedient.'"

Annaliese groaned. "Oh, Papa, only you could find scripture to apply to this malady."

"You do know, liebchen, there is a wealth of medical wisdom found in God's Word." Papa patted his leg to the rhythm of the horses. "My remedy for Herr Schroeder came directly from the Bible. 'Drink no longer water, but use a little wine for thy stomach's sake and thine often infirmities.' Und eat more sauerkraut."

"I did not know sauerkraut was in the Bible." Stephan chuckled. "But I might refrain from telling Mr. Marsh your remedy."

"For der sauerkraut?" Papa asked. "Only if he requires it."

"Nee, the part about not drinking the water," Stephan said.

How Annaliese would love to see Stephan's facial expressions.

Papa waved his hand in the air. "Eh, he knows my ways. Mr. Marsh also knows I encourage his guests to take the

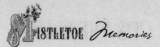

mineral baths at the spring house. *Vergebe mich,* I should not have said that in mixed company." He angled back toward Annaliese. "Your *vater* ist getting *zu alt.*"

Annaliese squeezed Papa's shoulder. At four and twenty, if anyone was getting old it was she, at least from the vantage point of her employer's new bride, Levinia Heath Marsh. Her friend, still aglow in her recent state of matrimony, had teased Annaliese throughout the summer each time an eligible patron of Heath House took notice of her. But Annaliese dismissed each suggestion. Many of those gentlemen were visitors who hailed from the elite society of Philadelphia, New York City, or Baltimore. They would surely dismiss her once they discovered that she had no intent of discontinuing her summer routine at Schooley's Mountain. How could she ever leave her father's side when she was all he had?

"What about your parents, Stephan?" Papa asked.

The question piqued Annaliese's interest, and she anticipated hearing the quiet Dutchman's reply. Stephan had simply appeared at the resort at the beginning of summer—a lone carpenter whom no one seemed to know and who kept to himself, busy at his trade. Word got out at last that the reserved worker had been employed at other famous resorts, yet Levinia had once inferred that his references were far more impressive than that.

"My parents are in the old country. I immigrated with my cousin Hans a few years before the War of 1812. We enlisted, but he. . .he did not survive. I have been on my own since." Stephan snapped the reins.

"Und you decided to stay in America though you have no family here now," Papa said, more of a statement than a question.

"Ja." Stephan said no more.

"Will you return to Heath House for another season?" Papa asked.

Stephan shrugged his shoulders and released an unintelligible grunt.

An awkward pause hovered over them as the conversation came to an abrupt halt. As they rumbled past the crooks and turns in the road toward German Valley, Annaliese became drowsy. She hadn't realized she had succumbed to her fatigue until her eyes sprang open at the sound of the *clop*, *clop*, *clop* of the horses' hooves beneath her as they crossed Neitzer's wooden bridge over the Raritan River. Annaliese patted her cheeks and took in a deep breath. The carriage stopped at the tollgate and Papa paid the two-cent fee before turning onto Fairview Avenue. They had arrived at the old stone church.

❧

Stephan's attention remained unduly long upon Annaliese's pleasing face as he settled her to the ground, having helped her from the carriage. The gentle pressure of her hands upon his shoulders when she leaned on him for support reminded him that he could never allow a woman to count on him again.

Annaliese's clear blue eyes held his gaze as she put her hands by her side. She cleared her throat and glanced down at his hands, still holding her waist. "Thank you, Stephan."

Stephan groaned inside. Every thought, every action in her presence was out of plumb since they'd kissed that morning. He removed his hands and stepped aside. "You are welcome, Miss Braun."

"Miss Braun?" Her cheeks colored and she cast her gaze at

the pebbled ground. Her eyes flitted up again. Did he detect a hurt look from beneath the gentle curl of her long lashes?

"Annaliese," her father called from the door of the church. "Reverend Hendricks has asked us all to take the noon meal with him and Mrs. Hendricks."

"That sounds delightful, Papa." Annaliese tilted her chin at Stephan as she faced him. "I know you have already spent much of your day coming to our aid, but if you would care to remain for the meal, we shall be happy to release you of your obligation to us."

"Miss Braun...Annaliese...I consider you no obligation." He swallowed. "It will be a pleasure to stay for the meal, as it is my pleasure to serve you." He dipped his head, inclining a slight bow.

She offered a shy smile. Where was the impetuous young woman who had silenced him in the glade beneath the mistletoe? The mystery of Annaliese Braun only incited him to want to discover more about her.

Stephan reached into the landau and grabbed a crate of clothing.

"Here, I will take that." The pastor of the Union Church held out his arms.

Stephan passed the crate to the sturdy-looking man. "Thank you, sir."

"Reverend Hendricks, this is Stephan Yost, from up at Heath House," Dr. Braun said by way of introduction.

The reverend nodded, as did Stephan in kind.

"I will gather those loose items after you men take care of the crates," Annaliese said.

"Hand me one, Stephan," said Dr. Braun. Stephan handed

a crate off to him and the two older men went into the church.

Stephan left the largest crate for himself, piled high with all sorts of garments. "I will be back to help you with that," he said, as he picked the crate up and looked at her over his shoulder.

Annaliese went to the carriage and leaned in. "There's not much left. I think I can handle it myself," she called. "I will be right along. Thank you."

Stephan entered the stone building and Reverend Hendricks led him to an alcove where the clothing was to be stored.

"It was benevolent of Mr. Marsh to donate clothing, once again, for those in need. He does so at the end of each season," the reverend said.

"Ja, it is a generous deed," Stephan said. "Do you need me to shift some of those crates around?"

"Yes, please," Reverend Hendricks said. "Perhaps I can find a spare box for the loose items still in the carriage. What are they, shoes and umbrellas?"

"I believe so." Stephan looked toward the hallway. What was keeping Annaliese? "Where is Dr. Braun? Did he go outside to help his daughter?"

"No, I sent him across to the house to let Mrs. Hendricks know that company had arrived." The minister held up a fancy rose-colored gown and grinned. "I am not sure this will be useful to the town folks, but, eh, we never know. Perhaps some young maiden can use it for her wedding."

A twinge of foreboding pricked at Stephan. "I am going to see what is keeping Annaliese."

The minister nodded. "Good, and then you and Annaliese

can join us at the house. 'Tis directly across the way. She will show you."

Stephan stepped through the large door of the church, and his gaze immediately fell to the sight of a growling dog baring its teeth at Annaliese. She stood by the open carriage door, fraught with terror. Her eyes darted to Stephan and he slowly nodded to reassure her. His heart pounded as he searched about to see if there was something he could use to ward off the animal. He could whistle, distract the dog, but he feared that the already agitated horses would bolt. There, a shovel. He eased along the facade of the building and retrieved the tool, which was leaning against the front wall. He then scooped up some pebbles.

The dog's ears pointed up, his haunches rose, and he snarled at Annaliese. Stephan inched toward the animal and, coming around the side, he tossed the pebbles at it. The dog jerked around and barked fiercely.

Stephan gripped the wooden handle of the shovel with both fists, holding it across his chest. He crept toward the dog, trying to get between it and Annaliese. He pushed the shovel toward the animal. "Get! Get out of here!"

The dog lunged at him.

Annaliese screamed. "Stephan!"

A loud whistle pierced the air as Reverend Hendricks came at the dog with a whip and snapped it against the ground. "Down, Luther! Down!"

The dog went whimpering to his master, who leashed him at once. But Hippocrates and Galen hurtled forward, catching Annaliese's coat and gown in the carriage door and knocking her down. The horses stormed down the road in a fury.

Reverend Hendricks restrained his barking dog and Dr. Braun hurried over to Annaliese. Stephan dashed to her side.

"I am well, Papa," Annaliese said as she observed the damage to her calico day gown.

She peered up at Stephan. "Are you all right, Stephan?"

Stephan gazed down at her. "Ja, I am fine." He shook his head, marveling that she thought nothing of herself. His head pivoted in the direction the horses had taken.

Dr. Braun followed his gaze, his palm clamped to his forehead. "*Mein vagon!* Die docktoren!"

Annaliese's eyes became moist as she looked at Stephan. "The horses—"

Stephan tossed his coat over the fence and turned to her father. "I will bring your horses and carriage back to you." And Annaliese.

"Schnell, bitte!" Dr. Braun cried out as Stephan jogged down the road.

Luther barked in the distance.

❧

Annaliese still trembled inside. This day had been one painful, dreadful, or humiliating ordeal after the other. First, the carriage accident, then the kissing incident, Rory's ailing uncle, the dog attack, and now the missing horses and carriage. . .and Stephan. Shouldn't he have returned by now? Perhaps she should go after him. Nein, Papa would never allow it.

"You look very lovely, dear. I thought that gown might fit you well," Mrs. Hendricks said, looking at the rose-hued silk gauze gown she had found for Annaliese lying atop one of the boxes of the donated clothing. "I will do my best to repair

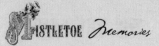

the tears on your own gown and pelisse, but it might require some creative handiwork."

"I appreciate your help, Mrs. Hendricks. You have been most kind," Annaliese said.

The robust woman smoothed her apron. "Why don't you have a seat? I am sure Stephan shall return soon, and then we shall eat. I have prepared a fine stew."

Standing at the window, Papa turned around and announced, "He is back. With the horses."

"God be praised," Reverend Hendricks said, while his wife gazed heavenward, uttering a silent prayer. "My neighbor's son is waiting for him and will help him secure the conveyance and the horses."

"Das ist gut. Danke." Papa exhaled deeply.

Annaliese paced, waiting for Stephan to enter the Hendricks' parsonage. She wished to run outside to see how he fared. How the horses were. If the carriage was all right.

Apparently sensing her apprehension, Papa placed his hand on her arm, staying her. "I will go see."

She resumed her pacing but paused when the door opened behind her. She spun around and saw Stephan at the doorway, with Papa behind him.

Stephan took in a deep breath and stepped over the threshold into the keeping room. "*Hallo!*" His gaze traveled over her, lingering overlong.

Annaliese blushed and offered a demure smile. Oh, if he could see how handsome he looked with his bright eyes glistening, his face colored from exertion.

He raked back his wind-whipped hair and grinned. "You needn't have dressed for the occasion, Miss Braun. Yet, I do say, you look rather fetching in your new gown."

Mrs. Hendricks came to Annaliese's side. "She does look lovely. 'Twas a blessing to find a spare gown with the donated garments, even if it is befitting a ball or a wedding."

"Ja, indeed," Stephan said with a nod. "Though I do not think your carriage is as fortuitous. I explained to your father that the brake is in need of repair."

"Jacob Day, the carriage-maker, should be able to take care of that for you," Reverend Hendricks said. "Though I fear I am responsible, since Luther frightened your team."

Papa waved his hand dismissively. "Annaliese already had a minor accident with the carriage this morning. It could have been damaged then."

"Though we must be sure to let folks know not to whistle around the horses, as it frightens them," Annaliese said to Reverend Hendricks.

"How will you keep them from doing that?" Mrs. Hendricks asked. "Why, anyone could whistle at any given moment."

Stephan put his fist to his mouth and cleared his throat as he cast a stealthy glance Annaliese's way.

Oh, that she could disappear.

"Herr Schroeder's nephew, Rory, whistled while trying to get Annaliese's attention earlier today and frightened the horses, resulting in the accident," Papa said.

"What was so urgent?" Reverend Hendricks asked. "Is Herr Schroeder still unwell?"

"Ja, but I suspect he will recover soon," Annaliese's father said.

"That is good to hear," Mrs. Hendricks said. "The lad

would become an orphan if he lost his uncle."

"Hasn't he any parents?" Annaliese asked.

Mrs. Hendricks shook her head. "Herr Schroeder has raised his great nephew since the boy's grandfather died in the war."

"Rolof's late sister's husband," the reverend said. "Rolof's wife passed away from the influenza a few years ago and he has cared for Rory alone ever since."

"You speak of his grandparents," Papa said. "I assume they raised their grandson until Rolof became his guardian."

"Yes. Luisa Krause, the boy's sweet mother, died shortly after the birth and—" Mrs. Hendricks hesitated and looked at her husband.

"'Tis a shame, the boy never had a father." Reverend Hendricks tightened his lips. "He has taken on his uncle's surname."

The stool Stephan was leaning on suddenly pushed away from him, scraping against the floor, garnering everyone's brief attention. His face grew flustered as he settled the stool.

Papa looked down, shaking his head at the reverend's statement. "That is unfortunate."

Mrs. Hendricks clucked her tongue.

"How old is Rory?" Annaliese asked.

"I would say he is about ten or so," Mrs. Hendricks said.

Stephan's gaze shifted in her direction and she noticed the muscles in his jaw stiffen. Did he not care for the lad? But how could he not? The boy was affable, polite, and even funny.

Reverend Hendricks moved toward the chair at the head of the long table. "Please be seated everyone, and we can continue our conversation over our meal. We shall enjoy the *hasenpfeffer* that my wife has made for our dinner."

"Hasenpfeffer?" Stephan asked.

"Sour rabbit stew," Mrs. Hendricks said cheerfully. "With potatoes and fresh rye bread."

"*Wonderbar!* Annaliese's *mutter* used to make that for me." Papa looked from Mrs. Hendricks to Annaliese as they were seated. "Something gut for the day's troubles."

With the day not yet over, Annaliese could not help but wonder what else this day would bring.

CHAPTER 4

Stephan entered the parsonage with water dripping off his slouch hat and the caped shoulders of the oilcloth coat that he'd borrowed from the reverend. "The *docktor*s and the landau are secured in the barn for the night."

"I did not realize we were expecting another rainstorm," Reverend Hendricks said. "Snow will be upon us before you know it."

"Oh dear, not yet. 'Tis only October. There remains a late harvest still for many to tend to." Mrs. Hendricks took Stephan's wet garments and hung them to dry.

Reverend Hendricks placed his hand on Stephan's back. "Come join us by the hearth, young man, where you can warm yourself."

Stephan sat on a Windsor chair by the large fireplace, facing Annaliese and Dr. Braun, who were seated in the settle, but he doubted anything would remove the chill he had after finding the headstone with Luisa's name on it out in the church-side graveyard. As he stood there in the pouring rain, a torrent of tears streamed down his face. Luisa, the young woman he had once loved—he'd found her at last, but there was no way to redeem the past. She was gone.

Stephan stared into the fireplace as Mrs. Hendricks poked the timbers in the hearth.

"This is a pleasant surprise, to have overnight guests at the parsonage," she said, as several sparks flew up.

"'Tis kind of you to accommodate us on such short notice." Annaliese glanced at her father apologetically, as he dozed against the high-backed settle. "Papa missed his afternoon nap."

Dr. Braun's eyes sprang open. "Who ist napping?"

Annaliese's face filled with mirth and she patted her father on the arm.

Stephan observed the warmth that passed between father and daughter. How he missed his own parents in Holland, though he trusted they were in his eldest brother's good hands. At times he wondered if it might have been best for him to return home after Hans had died, but by then he'd been offered employment by a comrade in New York, and he hadn't looked back.

"Stephan, I understand you are the new carpenter at Heath House," Reverend Hendricks said.

Stephan shifted in his chair. "Ja. It is a good resort, for its rustic charm. Mr. Marsh manages it very well." *Why must people ask so many questions?* Not that he had anything to hide. Not really. Not for certain.

"Folks have been resorting to Schooley's Mountain since the end of the last century. George Washington even stayed at Heath House," said Reverend Hendricks.

"Mr. Marsh preserves the room that the president slept in at the Alpha, the resort's oldest building." Stephan noted Annaliese, sipping her tea, looked like a fine society lady. "Is that correct, Annaliese?"

Annaliese nodded. "The furnishings are just as they were while he visited there, from what I understand."

"It is reported he wrote in his diary that he was not fond of traveling up the mountain in those years before Schooley's Mountain Road became part of the Washington Turnpike," the reverend said. "He called Dutch Valley to Schooley's Mountain a 'hazardous and round about thoroughfare.'"

"Dutch Valley?" Stephan asked.

"The name of this area before it became known as the German Valley," Reverend Hendricks said. "You have not visited my church before. Do you attend elsewhere?"

"I do," Stephan said. "I attend the stone church at Pleasant Grove, on top of the mountain by Heath House."

The reverend steepled his hands beneath his chin. "Ah. Many of the employees of the Heath House and Belmont Hall resorts attend there, whilst much of the German community come here."

"As do Annaliese and I," Dr. Braun interjected.

"Thank you," Stephan said, glancing up as Mrs. Hendricks handed him a tankard of coffee. He turned again toward the reverend, who sat in an upholstered wing chair. "Has your church been here long, sir?"

"Ah, yes. The original church was an old log cabin built in the 1740s. For a long time it was the only outpost for pastors traveling abroad. Folks walked miles, many barefoot, to hear the sermons preached here," Reverend Hendricks said. "They used to heat the building by an eight-foot-square charcoal pit in the center of the building. It nearly smoked the parishioners out each Sabbath, as there was no chimney."

"And the pastor?" Stephan asked.

"He endured it. Reverend Henry Muhlenberg was a hearty and ambitious sort." The reverend folded his hands in his lap. "He was the patriarch of the Lutherans in America."

"He could speak eight languages," Annaliese added.

"Indeed he could, Annaliese, and that gave rise to the hundreds of congregations that he oversaw throughout New Jersey, Pennsylvania, and many other regions. He also had a few sons who became clergy, one of whom became a general in the War for Independence. And his namesake was also a pastor here and is responsible for having built this stone church in 1774."

Mrs. Hendricks, in a nearby chair, looked up from her stitching and clucked her tongue. "You needn't give him the entire church history, dear."

"I find it interesting and like hearing about the buildings," Stephan reassured her. "Your church is a unique structure, as churches go, with its sloping room and no steeple."

The pastor held his palms up. "Nor does it have a chimney, like the log church."

Stephan clasped his hands behind his head and stretched as he observed Mrs. Hendricks rise from her sewing and stoop by a low cupboard of the paneled wall to retrieve a log. He quickly rose. "Here, allow me to do that."

"Thank you, Stephan," she said, glancing toward the window. "The rain might have slowed, but I would like to keep the chill from setting in."

Stephan followed her gaze toward the window. If the rain stopped entirely he might make it back on his own, although it was growing dark—too dark for traveling. "I hope Mr. Marsh has concluded that we had a delay due to the rainstorm."

"I am sure of it," Dr. Braun said. "He knew our destination, and that we would have to remain here if the weather became inclement."

Annaliese smiled at Mrs. Hendricks and set her cup on the side table. "Our fine hostess would never have allowed us to return under such formidable circumstances."

"Thank you, dear. Now perhaps you can help me set the table for our light supper," the minister's wife said.

Annaliese rose from her seat. "I was just now going to offer." She walked across the wide span of the hearth, pausing in front of the log stack. She bent over and retrieved a paper from the floor.

His letter. It must have fallen from his waistcoat pocket. Stephan stood abruptly. "I believe that may be my letter from the Schooley Mount post this morning." He'd hardly had the time to contemplate a response. But now...

Annaliese held the folded paper with the broken wax seal. She turned it over, glancing down at the addresses. "Yes, it is addressed to Mr. Stephan Yost." Her eyes widened. "From... *Count de Survilliers,* Joseph Bonaparte!"

꙳

Annaliese handed Stephan his letter. "Please forgive me, Stephan. I was astounded to behold such a missive, in my very hands."

Stephan nodded as he accepted the letter and slid it into an interior pocket of his waistcoat. "My former employer."

Annaliese tilted her head with curiosity. "Joseph Bonaparte? Napoleon's brother? The former king of Spain?"

Stephan smiled. "I was not a member of his royal court, if that is what you were thinking."

"I thought you worked up at Saratoga Springs?" Papa asked Stephan, although that was news to her.

"I met Mr. Bonaparte at Saratoga. When he saw my

40

carpentry work and learned that I had also worked on the Sans Souci Hotel, he contracted me to work for him. He employed me for the winter at Point Breeze, his estate in Bordentown. It is an impressive property overlooking the Delaware River." Stephan looked at Mrs. Hendricks. She was listening attentively with the others, who were now gathered around him. "I apologize if I am keeping you from your work, Mrs. Hendricks."

"I find this utterly fascinating. Do go on, please," she said.

Annaliese wondered, had Mrs. Hendricks just insisted that he share more? What little Annaliese was learning of Stephan, he did not seem overly forthcoming regarding his private affairs. Perhaps that would change in time, with her, as they got to know each other. She was hoping, after all, for. . .a friendship.

Stephan rubbed the back of his neck and drew in a deep breath. "The estate burned to the ground this past January—"

"Oh, yes. We heard about that, did we not, dear?" Mrs. Hendricks inquired of her husband.

"I understand that the neighbors were able to save some of his valuable belongings," the reverend said.

"He was most grateful for their coming to his aid. He immediately set about rebuilding on his property by converting his brick stables into a new mansion. Mr. Bonaparte contracted me to remain until its completion in June."

"And that is when you arrived at Heath House," Annaliese said, glancing at the floor. She would not want him to think she had been observing him since he had arrived in Schooley's Mountain, although she had certainly taken notice of him.

"Ja. He provided me with an excellent reference for Mr.

Marsh when I expressed my desire for employment at Heath House. He informed me that he was fond of Schooley's Mountain and had almost built his estate by Budd's Pond."

Mrs. Hendricks gasped. "Truly? Could you imagine that?"

"I have heard that he has visited the spring," Dr. Braun said. "Perhaps he will resort to the new Belmont Hall sometime, in keeping with his finer tastes."

Annaliese perched her chin upon her fist, glancing up at the beamed ceiling. "I hear that Belmont Hall is exquisite, but I must say that I shall always prefer the rustic charm of our little cottage at Heath House." She hooked her arm around her father's elbow. "In fact, I wish we could live here all year round."

Papa craned his neck toward her and proffered a grin. "Perhaps you shall receive that wish someday, my Annaliese."

She widened her eyes. "Might you consider it, Papa?"

Her father's palms turned upward and he glanced at Stephan, but for an instant. "Eh, we shall see."

The carpenter's brow drew into a subtle arch before his eyes darted toward hers. "You might ask Mr. Marsh to install a larger woodstove in your cottage, although it would take a bit of work to ready the abode for winter's use."

"'Tis a lovely idea. Although Mr. Marsh would never allow it. The resort will close up completely until spring preparations." Annaliese cast her gaze away.

"Maybe someday you will remove here for good, Dr. Braun," Reverend Hendricks said. "Perhaps when you retire."

"We would love to have you a part of the community year round." Mrs. Hendricks looked from Papa to Annaliese with a smile. She then turned to Stephan. "What about you,

Stephan? Where do you go in the winter months, other than to the grand estate of Mr. Bonaparte?"

Stephan widened his stance, clasping his hands behind his back. "That is yet to be determined. The letter from Bonaparte... His resident carpenter has been dismissed and he desires that I return for permanent employment."

"Do you mean to say that if you take the position we will not see you again at Schooley's Mountain?" Reverend Hendricks inquired.

"That is the count's request," Stephan said, his mouth pulling taut.

Mrs. Hendricks sighed, and sighed again. Her gaze flitted toward Annaliese and back again to Stephan. "You be sure to take the matter to the Lord, won't you, Stephan?" she said, smoothing her hand over her mobcap.

Stephan gave the reverend's wife a nod and looked down at the floorboards. Annaliese lowered her head and felt his gaze wander to her ankle boots, where it rested a moment before traveling to her. Their glances caught, ever so briefly, and a torrent of emotion saturated her with loss, regret, and could-have-beens.

"Come now, Annaliese. Let us prepare the table. It is time to sup," Mrs. Hendricks said. "You men can retreat to the parlor."

As Mrs. Hendricks went to the kitchen, Annaliese gathered the creamware plates from the hutch and set them around the table. The pattering of the rain, falling heavily on the rooftop, harkened to her long-dormant thoughts of discovering love. If ever that were to be, surely she could love someone like Stephan Yost.

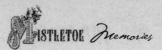

Annaliese turned around to retrieve the bowls and collided with Stephan. She drew in a little breath and was about to say she was sorry, but the words would not form.

Stephan steadied her by his firm grip upon her forearm. As he looked deeply into her eyes, the pressure of his hold lightened. His hand trailed over her wrist and his fingers twirled around hers, sending warm shivers through her. His eyes darkened, and he seemed to breathe in her scent.

And then he released her.

CHAPTER 5

Stephan stood in the frosted yard of the Union Church's cemetery. Speckled with red and gray slate grave markers, some in flowing German script, Stephan stared at the only one that mattered:

In Memory of
Luisa
Beloved Daughter of
Heinrich and Freida Krause
1792~1810
Age 18

Stephan slammed his clenched fist against his thigh. *Nee!* She was too young. Her name should not be inscribed upon a tombstone at all. She should have never carried his child. He should have never left her. She should be alive.

Stephan groaned beneath his breath, "Oh, God. How can You forgive me?" He closed his eyes tightly, and his temples pulsed. He pivoted around and swooshed the air from his lungs into the cold morning air.

"Stephan."

The small cloud of condensation hung in the air between him and Reverend Hendricks. "Luther and I returned from our morning walk and saw you out here." The minister looked down at the headstone. "Did you. . .know her?"

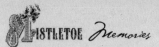

Stephan swallowed the lump in his throat. "I knew her."

Reverend Hendricks shoved his hands into the pockets of his black frock coat, eyeing Stephan with concern. "Did you. . .love her?"

"Not enough." Stephan rubbed his temples.

"You are Rory's father."

"I believe I am."

Moments passed until Dr. Braun's call broke through the silence. "*Guten morgen*, Reverend Hendricks, Stephan. We are ready to depart when you are."

Stephan looked up and saw the doctor on the path in front of the church. "Good morning, doctor. The horses are harnessed to the carriage so we can leave now, if you wish." Stephan looked back at the reverend. He hesitated, not knowing what more could be said.

Reverend Hendricks nodded in understanding. "Perhaps we can continue this conversation another time."

"Perhaps."

Stephan stuffed his hands in his coat pockets and strode toward Dr. Braun, looking down at the crunchy earth beneath his boots as he went. He took a deep breath and glanced up as Annaliese ambled toward her father, looking as crisp as the morning. A bittersweet chill rustled over his skin at the sight of her.

"Good morning, gentlemen," she said, smiling. She glanced about and took in a deep breath of the fresh morning air. "There is something about the air after it has rained. It is like all things are cleansed, made new again."

Stephan could feel his brow lift slightly, affected by Annaliese's optimism. *If that were only true, many things would be different.*

"Each day is a gift," Reverend Hendricks said. " 'It is of the Lord's mercies that we are not consumed, because his compassions fail not. They are new every morning: great is thy faithfulness.' "

"Amen," said Dr. Braun. " 'Tis gut medicine."

" 'Amen.' The word is the same in English, German, and Dutch," Reverend Hendricks said.

"I know we say 'amen' in agreement, but what does the word mean exactly, Reverend Hendricks?" Annaliese asked.

Reverend Hendricks inclined his head toward Annaliese and then glanced around the group as he spoke. "The original Greek word means 'so be it.' " As the reverend spoke the last words, his gaze rested on Stephan.

So be it.

Stephan brought the carriage around, and he and Annaliese and Dr. Braun said their farewells to Reverend and Mrs. Hendricks, thanking them for their hospitality. Onward they went, through the tollgate, over the bridge, and up the turnpike road to Schooley's Mountain. Annaliese sat with a blanket over her lap on the driver's seat next to Stephan, while Dr. Braun sat in the back of the carriage.

"How kind it was of the reverend and his wife," Annaliese said, "to allow us to stay with them overnight. Mrs. Hendricks was even able to repair the tears on the seams of my coat and on my gown. I do say, Papa, it would be nice to have a large home someday, with plenty of room for guests and little wanderers, like Rory Schroeder."

"Do you not like our apartment in Manhattan?" Dr. Braun asked.

"Oh yes, Papa, it is a beautiful place, but you know how

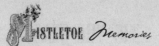

I feel about the city." Annaliese angled toward Stephan. "We live in an impressive building, in the Dutch style, in fact. But our apartment is rather supercilious for my taste. I prefer a more homelike atmosphere."

"I know your taste is not the same as your mutter," her father said.

"I fear, Papa, we have allowed our home to become somewhat of a museum to her memory," Annaliese said.

"You may decorate *die* apartment any way you desire, mein liebchen."

"There is only so much that can be done with ten-foot arched windows, Papa. And the ornate marble fireplaces." Annaliese tapped Stephan's sleeve. "Do you know that our ceilings are fourteen feet in height?"

"That sounds like Bonaparte's mansion," Stephan said. "I take it you would not be comfortable there, either."

"Not at all. Too much pretense." Annaliese curved her shoulder and grinned. "Although I would not mind visiting Point Breeze someday, just to take it in. It must be grand. I do not see why Mr. Bonaparte would ever need to resort when he owns such a place."

"One thousand acres," Stephan said.

"He should have moved here and bought all of Schooley's Mountain," she said. "I would have."

"Would you settle for a little piece of it, Annaliese?" Dr. Braun called from the back.

Annaliese spun around. "I would!"

"Then, Stephan, you may stop up ahead, as I asked you to earlier," the doctor said.

Stephan snapped the reins and they continued up the

steep dirt road. He turned the carriage onto a cleared path and parked in front of a large, newly shingled house.

Annaliese looked curiously from her father to Stephan and back again. "Papa, what are we doing here? Does anyone live here yet? I have seen the house being built but did not realize it was yet finished."

"It is not finished," Stephan said, before jumping down from the carriage and securing it. He took a rope and tied the horses to a black gum tree.

Dr. Braun stepped down, onto the soggy leaves littering the drive. "Annaliese, the ground is too *vet*. You shall have to remain in the carriage." He winked at Stephan and turned back to his daughter. "You will have to keep the docktors company."

"Papa! Don't be ridiculous!" Annaliese protested from her perch, readying to get down.

Stephan chuckled and eyed Annaliese's father. "If I may?"

Dr. Braun nodded.

Stephan swooped Annaliese into his arms and carried her up the front steps of the house. He leaned down for the door handle, released the latch, and gently kicked the door open.

"Oh!" Annaliese sighed.

Papa cleared his throat behind them and Stephan set her down on the unfinished oak flooring.

Annaliese spun around, facing her father. "Papa, it is beautiful! Who owns it?"

"Why, you do, liebchen," Dr. Braun said, taking her hands in his. "Do you like it?"

"Oh, yes, yes. Am I dreaming?" she asked.

"The previous owner decided to move to the shore and

took the builder with him. So I have bought it for you. . .if you agree to spare a room for your dear alt vater in his retirement. I have asked Stephan if he might finish the interior so we can move here by Christmas."

Annaliese's eyes glistened as she looked from her father to Stephan. He placed his hand over the missive from Bonaparte and knew at once he must decline the generous offer. He might not be able to give Annaliese his heart, but he at least could give her a home.

❧

The fresh scent of new wood and plaster filled Annaliese's senses as she wandered from room to room in the fine, two-story house. She could hardly believe that this charming dwelling would soon be her home. She made her way from the dining room back to the double parlor where Papa and Stephan engaged in conversation about the house. "In time for Christmas, you said, Papa?"

"Ja, I have an interested buyer for our apartment in Manhattan. His stipulation is that his family be allowed to move in by Christmastime," her father said. "So what do you think? Shall I agree to his terms?"

"A home for Christmas? Yes!" Annaliese twirled around and nearly bumped into Stephan.

The corners of his eyes crinkled as he gazed at her. "You are pleased with your new home, ja?"

"I am. And have you agreed to finish it for us?" she asked.

Stephan grinned. "I try to finish what I start."

Annaliese looked up at him, narrowing her eyes. "What do you mean?"

Stephan leaned his palm against the door frame. "I

worked on the house this summer, during my hours off from Heath House."

"No wonder I hardly saw you around the resort."

"Stephan, you are a very industrious man," Dr. Braun said. "Now we shall have to find you a place to stay once Heath House locks up for the winter."

Annaliese tilted her head. "Perhaps the Hendricks would allow you to stay with them."

"Well, if it would be all right with you, Dr. Braun, I could reside here while I work on the house. Perhaps Mr. Marsh would allow me to borrow a cot."

"You will freeze," Annaliese protested.

"The fireplaces are in working order," Stephan said. "As long as you don't mind me christening them."

Papa walked over to the hearth. "You would need to light them anyway so you have some warmth while you work. It sounds like a fine solution to me."

"Then it is settled. You have yourself a home." Annaliese joined Papa near the fireplace.

"Until Christmas," Stephan said.

"Und vat will you do after that?" Papa asked him.

Stephan shrugged. "I have not yet decided."

Annaliese ran her hand over the frame surrounding the opening of the fireplace. She thought of the request Stephan received from Joseph Bonaparte, the good Bonaparte, as Americans called him. Would he accept the invitation of permanent employment in Bordentown? That was so far away, in southern New Jersey. She might never see him again.

Stephan walked toward her. "What type of mantel do you envision, Annaliese?"

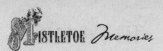

The deep timbre of his voice brought her out of her contemplations. "Oh. . .I do like the look of carved wood. Nothing overly ornate though."

"No beasts or dragons?" he asked.

"Heavens, no!" She giggled.

Stephan angled his jaw. "Cherubs, perhaps?"

"Can you really carve all those things?" she asked.

"Woodwork is my specialty," Stephan said. "May I suggest some dentil molding with some botanical carvings, and fluted columns on each side? A medium stain of oak, possibly?"

Papa chuckled. "Ha! You know my daughter quite *vell*."

Annaliese beamed. "Your suggestions sound perfect to me." She floated toward the large bay window at the front of the house. "Could the window and door trim match?"

"Ja. And the balustrade and railing for the stairway as well." Stephan smiled broadly. He seemed to take joy in his work, and in pleasing her. Or was that her imagination?

Annaliese looked up the stairwell. "Is it safe to go upstairs? I would like to see the bed chambers."

Stephan gazed upward, past the hard oak treads. "It is safe. But the walls remain unplastered. There are only the partitions there now."

"I would like to look around," Annaliese said. "Which room will be mine?"

"Any one of your choosing, dear," Papa said as he opened the front door. "Stephan, you go up with her. I vill check on the docktors. We do not want them running off again."

Annaliese climbed the first tread and looked back at her father. "Hippocrates and Galen will need to become accustomed to this location as their new home." She clamped down on her lower lip, widening her eyes. "I did not notice a barn. Is there a stable for them?"

Stephan joined her at the bottom of the stairs. "There is a shed behind the house, ample enough for a temporary shelter for the horses and the carriage. But I can build a barn, come spring."

Annaliese noticed the muscle in his jaw twitched. Perhaps Stephan's statement was premature, unless he had hopes of returning to Heath House next year. Or was something else on his mind? On any account, she must discourage it. This talented man had a great future in store for him, and she was certain that it did not include a spinster like herself.

CHAPTER 6

Bracing his elbow on his knee, Stephan leaned over and swung his hammer into the warped frame of lattice on the rear of the spring house. The enclosure guarded the reservoir of healing waters that streamed into the upper-level basin and the lower-level bathhouse for those who wished to take the cure. With November nigh upon them, he busied himself with end-of-season tasks, including the maintenance of the mineral springs. He climbed up on top of the low roof, with the aid of some nearby boulders, and went to work securing several loosened shingles. He tossed a small fallen branch onto the ground.

"Hey, what are you doing up there? You almost hit me!"

Stephan peered over the edge and saw young Rory Schroeder standing with his arms crossed over his chest and a scowl on his face. Stephan wiped the perspiration from his brow with the back of his hand. He hadn't counted on seeing the boy quite so soon. "Sorry, son." Stephan groaned inside. Why had he called him that?

"Mr. Yost! It's you! Are you all right? You don't look so well," Rory called up to him. "Here, let me come up and help." He bounded up the huge rocks before Stephan could protest.

Stephan grabbed Rory by the shoulders as the lad steadied his footing on the low-pitched roof. "How did you do that so fast, boy?"

"I always climb up here," Rory said. "Let me show you where I sit." He planted himself down, back against the wall of the upper part of the building.

Stephan lowered himself down beside him, knees bent and boots holding him secure. He looked at Rory. The boy sat leaning forward, with his arms crossed over his knees. "What do you see out there?" Stephan asked.

"It is not so much what I see, but what sees me." Rory angled his head, looking up at Stephan. "It's the water coming down the mountain in that trough. They call it healing waters."

"That they do," Stephan said. "You are a deep thinker for a kid."

Rory stared at the water coming down the hill. "That's what Uncle Rolof says. He does not like to listen to my prattle."

"How is your uncle?" Stephan asked.

"He is feeling better, but he was mighty sick." Rory looked at Stephan. "Do you know him? I told him that you drove us to the mill the other day to help, and he said you had a familiar-sounding name."

"I reckon there are many Yosts in this region. I hear there are many in Pennsylvania and New York as well," Stephan said.

"Are they all relatives of yours?" the lad asked.

Stephan chuckled. "Nee, I have no relatives in America." *Except one.*

"Nee? What does that mean? Wait, let me guess." Rory scrunched his face, looking up. "Hmm. . .it means 'no.' Am I right?"

Stephan smiled and nodded his head. "You are right. Now

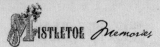

you know a word in Dutch."

Rory scratched his head. "How do you say 'yes'?"

"Ja." Stephan's gaze settled on the boy's blond hair, so much like his, and large brown eyes, like his mother's.

"That is German," said Rory.

Stephan nodded. "It is. But it is the same in Dutch."

"Dutch. . . Is that where you are from?"

"I am from Holland. Dutch is the language spoken there."

Rory tossed a little twig off the roof. "I would like to go to Holland someday. And Germany."

"It is very far from here," Stephan said. "It took me six weeks by ship over the Atlantic Ocean."

Rory's eyes widened. "I have never seen the ocean before. Are there sea monsters?"

Stephan laughed and pointed to the stream of water. "About as many as there are swimming down that trough. But I will tell you this. Do you know who Napoleon Bonaparte is?"

"He was that evil emperor from France. We learned about him in school," Rory said.

Stephan cocked his head. Of course the boy went to school. Stephan had noticed a few log school buildings in the area. So why did it surprise him? Rory was a very bright boy. His boy.

Stephan pulled in a deep breath. "Napoleon's brother, Joseph, the good Bonaparte, as Americans call him, lives in southern New Jersey. I used to work at his estate, and I helped build his new mansion."

"He does? You did?" Rory's eyes got even bigger.

Stephan nodded. "Ja, the Bonapartes are no longer allowed

in France. The story goes that Joseph Bonaparte was out hunting in the Pine Barrens one winter day when he came across tracks in the snow that looked like a two-footed donkey. He followed them and heard a great hissing sound and a fearsome creature suddenly appeared. It had the head of a horse and legs like a bird, and great wings." Stephan held out his arms. "Then suddenly it flew away."

Rory stared at Stephan with his mouth open. "Is that one of those tales made up by Miss Braun's friend? The one who wrote about Rip Van Winkle?"

Stephan laughed. "Nee, that creature is called the New Jersey Devil. But that account might have been made up by Mr. Bonaparte."

Rory narrowed his eyes. "You don't think that creature knows its way to Schooley's Mountain, do you?"

"If there were such a creature, I do not think he could find his way here. He most likely has a distaste for the mineral water. Too much iron in it," Stephan said.

Rory frowned. "It would probably make him too heavy to fly."

"Ja," Stephan said with a nod.

"I like the water. But Uncle Rolof will not allow me to go to the cataract down the road by myself. He says it is too dangerous for me. So that is why I come here. I like the sound of the water flowing down the wooden pipe."

Stephan placed his hand to his ear to make a show of listening. "Mmm-hmm. It does sound nice." The pair sat in silence for a little while, looking out at the stream coming down the mountain.

Rory stared straight ahead. "Reverend Hendricks says if

we believe in Jesus Christ, that His Spirit is like streams of living water flowing in us."

Stephan slowly turned toward Rory, though the lad remained focused on the water flow. What caused a boy his age to contemplate such profound thoughts?

"Do you believe that, Mr. Yost?"

Stephan slid his hand back over his hair, his mouth taut. "Ja, Rory. I do." But why did that "living water" inside him feel so stagnant at times? "Is that all the water makes you think of, Rory?"

"I think about my mutter. I did not know her. But she knew me. . .for a few minutes after I was born. My grandparents told me that she loved me and I will see her in heaven. It is the gift of Jesus."

A well of emotion surged through Stephan. He clenched his fists and turned his head away from Rory. He blew out some shallow breaths, hoping the boy would not hear him. Then he stood.

"I have a bit of spare time. How about we take a walk down to that cataract, if you think your uncle would not mind, since an adult would be accompanying you."

Rory jumped to his feet and climbed over the edge of the roof onto the boulders. He bounced around on the ground. "Schnell, Mr. Yost, schnell!"

Stephan put his tools aside, and he and Rory tromped down Schooley's Mountain Road toward the waterfall, partway to Hackettstown. The day was yet mild for that final week of October and the trees were a vivid display of red, orange, and yellow. Rory skipped ahead every once in a while, whistling "Yankee Doodle" while he waited on the fence posts that lined the turnpike for Stephan to catch up. At least the whistling could do no harm this time.

Rory hopped off the fence and came bounding back toward Stephan, up the middle of the dirt road, twirling around like a top. Suddenly, the ground vibrated beneath Stephan's steps, and the clopping of horse's hooves and wagon wheels thundered from behind him. Stephan spun around. A stagecoach and six-horse hitch rumbled full speed down the mountain. He turned back with a shout. "Rory!"

Rory tripped and fell on the road and started to get up, but when he saw the stage nearing, he froze. Stephan bolted toward him and swept him out of the road, the two of them rolling toward the fence.

The stage whirred by in a blur of red and black. Stephan's heart thumped wildly within his chest, and gravel dug into the skin on the back of his hands. He looked down at Rory, cradled in his grip, his eyes closed, his face deathly white. *Oh, God, nee!*

ᴈ

Stephan patted Rory's ashen face. "Wake up, son. Wake up!" The boy's eyes fluttered open and Stephan sighed with great relief.

Rory looked about. "Why are we on the ground?" He sat up abruptly. As realization dawned, his glassy eyes widened. "We were almost run over."

"You are safe now." Stephan looked at Rory with concern, scanning his small body. "Are you all right?"

Rory pushed to his feet and stood. "Ja, I think so." He shrugged and wiped the dirt from his sleeve.

Stephan rose, and as he did, he noticed that the stagecoach

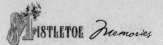

had come to a stop and the team of horses stood, restless. A man dressed in striped trousers and a tall beaver hat tromped up the hill and called out, "Everyone all right here?"

"We are fine." Stephan nodded, brushing the dirt from his bruised hands.

The man narrowed his eyes at Rory and then glowered at Stephan. "Keep your son out of the road! What kind of father are you?"

Stephan clenched his teeth, glaring at the arrogant man. He stepped forward, shielding Rory from the stranger.

The man swatted his gloved hand into the air dismissively and turned around, heading back to the coach. Stephan and Rory stared at him as he stalked away, his dark coattails flapping as he went. The stagecoach pulled away, stirring up dust in its wake. Stephan released a swoosh of air through his teeth. He glanced down at Rory, shaking his head, and the side of his mouth curved.

Rory grinned at Stephan. "That man thought I was your son."

Stephan slid his palm over his chin. "Ja."

&

Annaliese sat on a rock overlooking the cataract. Water cascaded over and between boulders and mossy rocks from the steep embankment leading up the side of the mountain. The tranquil setting was what she needed as a retreat from her busy days, but this day she shared it with her assignment from Mr. Marsh to write an advertisement for *The Fashionable Tour*. She sat on a dry rock, basking in the sun of the early autumn afternoon, the sound of the rippling water soothing her. She laid her writing notebook and graphite pencil down beside her. The pencil rolled down the rock and plopped into the stream below. She released a deep sigh as it floated away, disappearing behind some rocks. Her gaze landed on a scattering of brightly colored leaves floating upon the waters pooled within a small gorge. As the water flowed into the pool, two leaves spun around in a magical dance, and she imagined that one of them was she and the other Stephan.

Plop. An acorn dropped from a branch above and splashed into the water between the two leaves, sending them in opposite directions. Is that how it really was with her and Stephan? Annaliese's attention traveled over the tiers of waterfalls trailing from the mountain, and she thought how pretty it would be to see this place in winter, when the waterfall froze in place. With a new home on Schooley's Mountain by Christmastime, she would be able to come and see the curious sight—the flow of water frozen in time. Was that how her life had become? She was hidden away, year after year, in the shelter of this serene dwelling, her life neither retreating nor moving forward. Yet, she was indeed growing older, as was Papa. Was it selfish for her to think that perhaps someday she might have a family of her own? She'd resisted the idea for so long that time had seemed to stand still. But like Rip Van Winkle, would she awaken someday to find that life had passed her by?

Annaliese stood and stretched her arms toward the tree tops, the colorful canopy of splendor overhead. God's glorious creation, His banner of love. *Lord, please help me to be open to Your will, and not seek my own way.*

She placed her small notebook inside her redingote pocket and began her descent down the rocky slope—laden

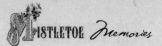

with leaves, fallen trees, ferns, and other woodland plants.

"Hello!" a voice called from the ridge above.

Annaliese turned back, shielding her eyes from the sun, her abrupt movement causing her to nearly lose her footing.

The man shuffled his way down to help her. With his feet planted at an angle on the slope, he extended his hand to her.

She took hold of his grasp, found firm footing, and let out a little breath. "Thank you, sir. 'Tis slippery."

The man tipped his tall Parisian hat and smiled. "Harlan Beatey, at your service."

Annaliese glanced about and spied Galen where she had tied him to a tree at the bottom of the hill. 'Twas awkward to be alone with an unknown man in the woods, or anywhere for that matter, although it occurred to her how safe she had felt with Stephan when she had first met him. "Annaliese Braun."

"It is a pleasure to make your acquaintance, Miss Braun," the man said. "It is miss?"

"Yes," she said uncomfortably, her eyes scanning him from his fuzzy reddish sideburns to his peculiar, new-fashioned striped trousers.

The man glanced down at a compass in his hand and grimaced. He pulled a paper from his pocket and unfolded it, holding it in his other hand. "I can't understand this thing. The needle spins contrary to my reckoning of this map."

"You are lost then? Perhaps I can be of assistance," Annaliese said.

The man's eyebrows made a subtle dip as his gaze roamed her form. "Perhaps you can."

CHAPTER 7

Galen." Stephan glided his palm over the withers of the gelding and looked at Rory. "This is the Brauns' horse."

"What is he doing here?" Rory stroked the horse's neck and answered his own question. "Maybe Dr. Braun is taking a hike at the cataract. He sure has a strange-looking saddle."

"That is a sidesaddle for a lady," Stephan said. "I think it is more likely that Miss Braun is the one visiting the cataract."

Rory jaunted ahead and turned back to him. "Let's go find her!"

Stephan strode forward, calling, "Be careful on that hill." He glanced upward, chuckling. How had he managed to care so deeply for two people within a few days' time?

"Look, there she is! Miss Braun!" Rory shouted.

Stephan and Rory stood on the side of the mountain, almost to the ridge, and beheld Annaliese being scooped into a man's arms, her arm wrapping around his neck. As they came closer, Stephan stared into her eyes. "Annaliese. Forgive us, we did not mean to intrude." He put his hand on Rory's shoulder. "Come, Rory, let us go back."

"Wait!" Annaliese cried.

Stephan turned back. "Is everything all right here?"

"I assure you—" the man began.

"I was addressing the lady." Stephan glared at him.

Rory tugged on Stephan's sleeve. "That is the man from

the stagecoach," he whispered. Sure enough, it was the same arrogant fellow in his striped pantaloons.

As Rory took a step closer, Annaliese cried, "Be careful, there is a snake!"

Stephan tugged Rory back by the collar.

"There it goes!" Rory pointed with a stick as the snake slithered away.

"*Er schuilt een adder in het gras.*" Stephan locked eyes with the stranger, the Dutch proverb ringing true. His gaze darted around the mulched hill looking for the serpent, but, God forgive him, the one that concerned him the most was the one clutching Annaliese.

"You may put me down now, Mr. Beatey." Annaliese pointed to the large rock near Stephan and Rory. "On that rock, please."

The corner of Stephan's mouth curved in satisfaction. Annaliese preferred his protection over this dandy who was vastly overdressed for an outing in the woods of New Jersey. Stephan took her hand and helped her steady herself beside him.

Annaliese glanced up at him. "Mr. Beatey was trying to save me from the snake."

"How do you know that *he* is not the snake?" Stephan said in a low growl.

"Thank you for your assistance, Mr. Beatey. I would like you to meet my friends, Stephan Yost and Rory Schroeder."

The man tipped his fancy hat. "I believe we have met already."

Annaliese looked from Mr. Beatey to Stephan, raising her eyebrows.

"There it is!" Beatey shouted. He started snapping at the ground with his shiny black walking stick.

The snake slithered toward them. Rory picked it up with a stick and held it up in midair. "It is only a queen snake." He laughed as he looked up at Stephan and then flung it into the woods.

"Not a rattlesnake, eh?" Beatey said. "Well, I am not familiar with these parts."

"Mr. Beatey is lost," Annaliese announced. "His compass misguided him."

"*Een slecht werksman beschuldigt altijd zijn getuig,*" Stephan muttered under his breath.

"What does that mean, Mr. Yost?" Rory asked.

A bad craftsman blames his tools. But he wouldn't tell Rory that. He needed to temper the green-eyed monster that was rearing its ugly head. "A Dutch proverb, 'tis all."

Stephan addressed the strange gentleman. "Tell me, Mr. Beatey, what is your intended destination?"

Beatey held out his map. "I was scouting out this iron mine. The one that is circled."

Stephan surveyed the map. "And you found your way here to the cataract? The mine is on the other side of this ridge, about a half mile down."

"May I see your compass, Mr. Beatey?" Annaliese asked.

Beatey placed the round brass instrument in her palm. She took a few steps around the area.

"Is it broken?" Beatey asked.

"It works perfectly well," Annaliese said. "Come see."

The group came near and hovered over the compass.

"Blasted! It is broken," Beatey growled.

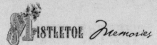

Annaliese looked up at him. "Sir, there is a child present."

"And a lady," Stephan said.

Beatey frowned. "Do pardon. Now, what is the issue with that worthless instrument?"

Annaliese turned the compass around in her hand. "Do you see no matter which direction that I turn, it continues to seek a westerly bearing? The magnetism from the iron in these rocks is attracting the needle."

"Do you mean to say that I found iron?" Beatey gloated.

Annaliese smiled at the man. "No sir. The iron has found you."

"There is iron all throughout this region, Mr. Beatey," Stephan said. "But the iron you are looking for is that way." He pointed over the mound of boulders.

"That is where my interest lies. I am hoping to acquire that mine to add to my holdings at the Van Syckle Mining Company."

"You have no surveyor?" Stephan asked.

"I fired him today, the incapable dolt. The map looked simple enough. . . ." Beatey tapped on the ground with his cane. "What say you, Mr. Yost, would you care to show me the way? I shall pay you for your services."

"It really is not necessary. You can find the way easy enough. It is at the bottom of this ridge," Stephan said. "If you leave your compass in your pocket and simply follow the map, you will have no trouble at all. There is a trail down there, back out to the main road near the stage stop. I suspect that is how you came in."

"Do you mean to tell me that I already passed it by?" Beatey asked.

Stephan shrugged. "More than likely."

"I have never seen one of the mines before," Rory said.

"There now, Mr. Yost. Wouldn't you like to show your son that iron mine?" Beatey asked.

Annaliese looked from Rory to Stephan. She placed her hand over her mouth to cover a giggle. "He does have the looks of you," she said. "It must be his blond hair and that little cleft in his chin."

"So, Mr. Yost, Stephan, is it? You said it is not far from here. It could not possibly take much of your time. Unless, of course, Miss Braun would like to take a stroll with me."

"I really should get back to my work at the springhouse," Stephan said.

Annaliese's mouth opened, and she looked at Stephan, pleading with her eyes.

Stephan took a deep breath. "Very well."

The troupe made its way down the shallow descent of the mountain. Beatey endeavored to charm Annaliese with his attentions to her, taking advantage of every opportunity to hold his hand out to her, help her over a log, or take her by the elbow. Did she enjoy his attentiveness to her? Did she find a man in striped pantaloons and a fine cutaway frock coat appealing?

"I don't think she likes him," Rory whispered to Stephan.

"What makes you say that?" Stephan whispered back.

"She kept rolling her eyes when he looked away." Rory snickered.

"Ja?" Stephan asked, elbowing the boy.

"Ja." Rory elbowed Stephan back and laughed.

"What is so funny up there?" Annaliese called.

Rory turned around. "Nothing. Mr. Yost is just teaching me how to speak Dutch."

"I thought folks were mostly German in this area," Beatey said.

"Most of the early settlers and their descendants are," Annaliese said. "But Stephan is not from around here, though he now works up at the Heath House resort."

"A laborer?" Beatey asked, sniveling out the words as though it were a disease.

"He is a talented carpenter," Annaliese said.

"I see," Beatey said. "And you, Miss Braun?"

"My father is the resort's physician."

"Do you reside here year round?" the iron baron asked her.

"Not yet," she said, glancing at Stephan with a smile.

The terrain became rocky and Beatey took Annaliese's arm and wrapped it around his elbow. "I am staying at The Belmont. I understand this summer was their first season. They expect the resort will far exceed the spa at Saratoga with all the amenities they have installed—the bowling alleys, tennis courts, the fine cuisine."

"I do prefer the more rustic atmosphere of Heath House," Annaliese said. "It, too, has a great many amenities and has rivaled Saratoga Springs for years. Isn't that right, Stephan?"

"I have not been to a finer resort," Stephan said.

Beatey chortled under his breath, "You?"

I think the New Jersey Devil is in our midst, Stephan thought to himself.

"Folks love coming to the mountain," Annaliese said. "We have the purest chalybeate springs in the country, according to tests that have been done by esteemed scientists."

"Perhaps if my mining interest works out, I may move to Schooley's Mountain. I understand there is some fine property up by Budd's Pond."

Stephan groaned inwardly.

Beatey projected his voice, purposefully, Stephan thought. "Miss Braun, a fine lady like you must enjoy some of the finer things of society. The Belmont is holding their end-of-the-season ball tomorrow night, and I would be most grateful if you would accompany me."

Stephan's ears perked up, and coming to the bottom of the hill, he swiftly turned to wait for the pair. . .and to observe Annaliese's answer.

"Why, Mr. Beatey, that sounds delightful."

&

"Yet unfortunately, I must decline." Annaliese's heart pattered within her chest. Whether it was due to the exertion of coming down the ridge or from the sudden influx of admiration by this unwelcome stranger, she did not know. Oh, she tried to be courteous, but nothing about the pompous iron baron appealed to her in the slightest.

"That is a pity. May I ask why?" Mr. Beatey scratched his wiry ginger sideburns.

"I am otherwise engaged," Annaliese said, casting her eyes to the ground. "You see, Heath House will be holding its own celebration of the season's end. It is an annual tradition."

"Surely you could miss it this once," Mr. Beatey said.

"I am responsible for planning and preparing for the party. So I must be present," Annaliese said. "Thank you, however, for your invitation."

Mr. Beatey looked at Stephan. "Are you going to be

enjoying that party with Miss Braun?"

Stephan stood on the incline, leaning his weight on one boot. He looked steadily at her with his perfect green eyes and hiked his chin subtly. "If she would like me to."

A flurry of butterflies danced in Annaliese's belly. Was that a challenge? Did Stephan want her to clarify her preference of suitors right here and now? She pressed her palm against her woolen redingote and pulled in a deep breath. "All of the Heath House employees will be there. I hope you will attend." Annaliese could feel the warmth rising in her cheeks, despite the chilled air that was quickly descending upon them.

Stephan nodded and issued a satisfying grin toward Mr. Beatey.

Annaliese had the distinct feeling that Stephan had just staked his own claim. She cupped the side of her face with her gloved hand and glanced down. When she looked up again, she caught Stephan looking at her with the hint of a smile in his eyes.

"Perhaps another time, then, Miss Braun." Mr. Beatey looked at Stephan and shrugged. "Or perhaps not."

"Come," Stephan said, motioning for the group to follow. "The mine should be right over there." He looked up. "The cold is setting in and the sky is looking rather bleak. I hope we are not expecting an early snow."

Rory looked up. "Snow!" Then he looked down and held out his foot. "It's a good thing I have my new boots."

Annaliese looked at the lad with the slightly oversized boots, his corduroy breeches, and tiny waistcoat. "Yes, it is, Rory. But you aren't wearing a jacket today." *He really needs a mother's touch.*

"All right, let's get on with it. I'd like to take a look at the mine while there's daylight yet." Mr. Beatey marched forward, digging his cane into the hard ground.

Rory ran ahead, jumping over a log. "Is that it? That cave?"

"It sure is," Stephan called to Rory. "Go easy. And don't go inside until we get there."

In a moment they were all assembled around the dark opening of the mine. The large hole, as tall and wide as the men's height, had no supporting frames. It appeared as a simple hole carved out of the rocky slope. Annaliese walked over the broken rock surrounding the area and peered in. A bat flew out and she gasped.

Rory climbed up on the hill over the top of the mine, his arms stretched high into the air. "Look at me, I'm King of the Mountain!"

"Do be careful, Rory," Annaliese said.

Mr. Beatey proceeded to inspect the area. He took out his compass. "The needle is going berserk again. I guess we are in the right spot."

Rory pointed and called to them, "Hey, look! Your horse!"

Annaliese spun around and saw Galen, his reins dangling on the ground. "Oh no! He must have been frightened and come loose. How did he find his way up here?"

Stephan came to her side. "He must have followed your voice. Let's see if we can surround him." He looked at Mr. Beatey. "Would you help us circle her horse so he doesn't run off again?"

Mr. Beatey grumbled beneath his breath and tossed down a mining tool that he had found. As it hit the ground, it pinged when it landed against a rock. Galen startled, and his

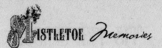

head perked up, but he did not run.

The three adults crept forward, encircling Galen. Mr. Beatey made an overzealous attempt and Galen trotted several yards away.

Stephan eyed Mr. Beatey and mouthed, "Slo—ow."

They continued their pursuit, arms held out, closing in on Galen. Annaliese rubbed her finger and thumb together, making some clicking sounds with her tongue as she tried to get Galen to focus on her. She slid her hand into the pocket of her long coat and thankfully discovered a small piece of carrot. She held it out in the palm of her hand and inched closer to him. Finally, she was near enough to grab his reins, but Galen jerked his head and the leather straps slipped through her fingers.

Then Stephan appeared on the bay's other side and gained a firm hold on his halter. He instantly began stroking the horse's neck to calm him.

Annaliese gathered Galen's dangling reins and gave him the promised carrot. "Oh, my naughty boy." She looked at Stephan and smiled relief.

"Are you talking about him, or me?" He cast her a sly grin.

She whispered, "Both."

Annaliese and Stephan walked back toward the mine. Mr. Beatey was far ahead of them, having wasted no time in getting back to his mission.

The iron baron called out as they came near, "The boy is gone!"

Annaliese caught her breath. "Perhaps he is hiding somewhere."

"Do you have the horse?" Stephan asked, his face tense with panic.

"Yes, go!" Annaliese held Galen with a secure grip, and Stephan sprinted ahead. She tied Galen to a low branch and followed him to the mouth of the cave.

Mr. Beatey turned around. "The boy is inside the mine. I can hear him calling for help. The cave floor slopes down and he must have fallen into a crevice."

Annaliese's hand flew to her mouth and she felt as though she would be sick. *Oh, Lord, please save him!*

Stephan came out from the dark entrance and wiped at his face, leaving a smear of moisture and dirt behind.

Annaliese rushed up to him. "Oh, Stephan, it is dangerous in there!"

"It does not matter. I must save my son!" His words froze in the air between them.

"*Your* son?" Her mouth went dry as she attempted to process this revelation.

Stephan pushed his hair back from his tense brow and nodded.

Annaliese couldn't speak. She, too, felt as if she had been sucked into that dark hole.

CHAPTER 8

Stephan swallowed hard. The pained look on Annaliese's face pierced through him. "I will explain later."

"There is no need, Stephan." Annaliese shook her head, her eyes filled with concern. "What happened to Rory?"

Stephan clenched his jaw and took a deep breath. "Rory is caught in a deep cavity of rock. The opening was covered with boards, but he fell through, and the boards are wedged on top of him. He says he is uninjured."

"Please, tell me what I can do to help." Her eyes darted up, and she looked at him with alarm. "It is beginning to snow."

Stephan glanced about. Indeed, large flakes began their descent like a bad omen. Beatey had slipped past them into the mine and now came out again, rubbing his arms. "It is like an icehouse in there," he said.

"Ja, I saw icicles hanging as the mine goes deeper," Stephan said.

"I could find no tools in there." At least the man had the sense in all of this to be industrious.

"Maybe we'll find something out here," Stephan said. What a time for him to be without his tools. He could go back and get them at the springhouse, but time was running out. The snow was falling and it would be dark before long. The three of them began a frantic search, kicking through the leaves on the ground, looking behind rocks and logs, the moss and peat.

"Over here," Beatey shouted.

Stephan rushed to where an old crate jutted out from a dense tangle of vines, strangling the thick trunks of nearby trees. He tore the slats from the top of the box with his bare hands. Out of the corner of his eye he saw Annaliese wince.

"Mining tools!" she gasped when he succeeded in opening the box.

Beatey reached inside and pulled out the broken end of an auger. "I don't know what good this will do."

"Bring it anyway," Stephan said, retrieving a crowbar.

"Look! A shovel." Annaliese pointed to the ground where the rusted spade stuck out from beneath a mass of dead leaves.

Stephan uncovered the shovel and then groaned, discovering the handle broken off midway. "At least it is still useable." He pivoted around and dashed toward the mine, the others following.

Annaliese looked around at the light flakes of snow floating down from the sky. "I'm going to give Rory my coat."

Stephan caught her by the sleeve as she stepped ahead of him. "Nee!"

She spun around.

"It is far too dangerous. Do not go in there, Annaliese." He couldn't bear it if anything happened to her as well.

Annaliese nodded.

"Pray," Stephan said.

"I am."

At the entrance of the mine Stephan turned to Beatey. "Ready, Mr. Beatey?"

"Yes. And call me Harlan. Now let's go get the child."

Stephan nodded, but his heart stung. His child. *His* child.

"Please be careful," Annaliese said, looking at Stephan with a wealth of emotion in her crystal blue eyes. She offered him a faint smile, bolstering his hope. Could she really care for him, even though he was such a wretched soul?

Once the men had shuffled down the slanted floor of the mine, Stephan knelt over the opening that Rory had fallen through and called inside. "Rory, can you hear me?"

The lad's mumbled words echoed upward. "*Ja! Erhalten sie mich bitte heraus!*"

"What did he say?" Harlan asked.

Stephan knew not what Rory said, but he knew how to answer. "Do not be afraid. I am coming for you. God will help us."

"Are you sure about that?" Harlan asked, handing Stephan the auger.

"I am," Stephan said, ripping up the worn boards. "Give me the crowbar." With a strong grip on the end of the crowbar, he pried at a wide plank lodged between the dirt and rock walls. With a grunt, he fell backward as the plank released.

Beatey reached and pulled the board up. "It's a good thing that did not fall down and land on the boy."

"Ja," Stephan said. *Lord, please protect Rory. Give me strength and wisdom.* He glanced up at Harlan in the dim light. "We need to widen the opening so he can get back up. Those rocks tumbled in when he fell through."

Harlan squatted down, clearing the boards away. "Does he have enough air down there?"

"I hope, but I do not know how long it will last." Stephan drove the shovel into the pit. He grunted as it lodged in a crevice. "It's stuck. Let me have the crowbar again."

"Good God," Harlan said.

Stephan prodded against the shovel with the long iron tool. "That's who I am counting on." The shovel loosened, but the force slammed both shovel and crowbar against the hard rock lining the cavernous space. Stephan pulled with all of his might, but the tools would not budge and clung to the rock, too far from his reach to get better leverage.

Stephan stood and rubbed his sore hands, which were burning from the friction.

Harlan looked at him with surprise. "Are you giving up?"

Stephan stared at him and then grabbed the auger head and strode over to the wall of the cave. He placed the metal piece against the rock and it clung to it, like a magnet.

Harlan tried to pull it loose, without success. "It is magnetized."

"I am afraid so," Stephan said, wiping the perspiration from his brow. "That is what makes iron mining around here very difficult. I've heard some say that the force is that of a hundred pounds when trying to separate their tools." Stephan leaned back over the hole. "Hang on, Rory. . .Rory?"

"Hello!" Rory shouted back.

"I will return soon, Rory," Stephan hollered down. A burst of air sprang from his lungs at hearing the boy's raspy voice. Had Rory been crying? Was the air growing thin? Were there toxic vapors down there that would harm him?

Stephan dug his heels into the gravel as he ran to the entrance of the mine, Harlan following. The bright white almost blinded him as he took in the dusting of snow covering the landscape. He looked around for Annaliese, but she was gone—as was her horse.

Stephan's chest tightened as he anxiously scanned the forest. Then he caught sight of Annaliese through the trees in her long purple coat, riding away on Galen.

"It looks like she found some rope," Harlan said, picking up a coil of rope from atop a boulder. "And there is a note." He handed the paper to Stephan.

Stephan read the note aloud. "Gone for help. Found some rope in Galen's satchel."

Harlan looked up at the white-gray sky, briskly rubbing his hands together. "I wonder how much daylight we have left."

Stephan blew warm air into his cupped hands. "We should build a fire. Can you do that?"

"Yes. I have a tinderbox for my pipe in my coat," Harlan said.

"Build it near the mouth of the mine," Stephan said, "and then bring me some light."

"How do you expect me to do that?" Beatey asked.

Stephan took off his neck cloth and gave it to Harlan. "Tie this around the top of a thick branch and rub some sap on it so it will burn slowly."

Harlan looked at the neck cloth in his hand. "What will you be doing?"

"If I can use your cane, I'll continue digging to widen the pit. Then we can lower the rope down and pull Rory up."

"He's your lad?"

"Ja, but I only learned of it recently." Stephan took a deep breath. "I cannot lose him now."

Harlan tossed him the cane. "You already had one close

call with him today. I apologize for that. I pushed the driver of my stage because I was anxious to find the mine in the daylight."

"I appreciate your help now," Stephan said, and hurried inside the mine.

Before long, Stephan had cleared the hole, with the help of the iron baron's wooden cane. It proved to be the perfect tool for the task. The hard silver cap on the bottom of the walking stick was not attracted to the magnetized iron embedded in the rock.

The dark space brightened as Harlan appeared carrying the primitive torch. He jammed it into a crevice. Stephan took the rope and knotted the end into a loop.

"Are we ready to do this?" Harlan asked.

"That we are." Stephan tied the other end of the rope around his waist and lay down on the ground in front of the hole. "I'm trusting you to hold onto me to keep me from falling in."

Harlan held Stephan by the legs. "No worries, my friend. Now get that boy of yours."

Stephan called into the dark pit, "Rory, I'm going to bring you up!"

"I'm ready!"

Stephan lowered the rope, and he felt Rory tug on it when it reached him. "Put this rope over your head and beneath your arms, and I will pull you up. But you help me by climbing, the way you do at the spring house."

Stephan secured the rope around his wrists and, hand over fist, hauled Rory out to safety.

Rory threw his arms around Stephan, and Stephan held

him tightly, never wanting to let the boy go. "You were very brave, son. Very brave."

"You said God would help us, and I heard some water trickling down there, so I knew I would be all right."

Harlan put his coat around Rory. "That is the best sermon I have heard in a long time."

Stephan chuckled as they stood. "Mr. Beatey has been a great help." He extended his hand toward Harlan. "Thank you."

"It is the least I could do since I almost ran this boy down today." Harlan ruffled Rory's hair. "You are awfully cold, Rory. Let's go out by the fire to get warm."

They made their way out of the mine and warmed themselves by the small fire.

"Ah, the snow has stopped," Stephan said.

Rory looked up at him. "I did not know it was snowing at all."

At the sound of voices, they looked up to see Annaliese, Dr. Braun, Mr. Marsh, and Mr. Schroeder coming up the hill toward them, carrying lanterns and blankets.

Annaliese's gaze met Stephan's from across the firelight. "I met up with them at the springhouse looking for Rory."

Rory ran toward his uncle. "Onkel Rolof!"

"Mein *junge!*" Mr. Schroeder embraced Rory.

Annaliese wrapped a blanket around Rory's shoulders, "Oh, Rory, I am so glad you are all right." She then gave Harlan a blanket, thanking him for his help.

When she met Stephan and handed him a quilt, it took all the restraint he had to keep from taking her in his arms. Instead, he reached beneath the quilt and clutched her hand, whispering, "Thank you." The slight pressure of her fingers against the back of his hand was a soothing balm for his labor.

"Glad to see you are all right," Mr. Marsh interrupted, handing Stephan a bottle of mineral water and his gloves. "I found these with your tools at the springhouse, thought you might need them."

"Thank you." Stephan placed the gloves on his cold hands, though he hesitated at letting go of Annaliese.

"Are you well, nephew? I told you never to come here," Mr. Schroeder said, looking directly at Stephan.

"You told me not to come alone. I was with mein vater," Rory said, to the astonishment of all.

Mr. Schroeder faced the boy, holding onto his shoulders. "You mean your heavenly Father."

"God was with me, but I mean Mr. Yost, Onkel. He is my father. I heard him say so."

Stephan stiffened as everyone faced him. Rory couldn't have heard him from inside the mine.

Rory's uncle glared at Stephan. "Is this true?"

Stephan walked over to Rory, squatted down in front of him, and looked into his large brown eyes. "Rory, I *am* your father. But I only discovered the fact a few days ago. Had I known—" Stephan swallowed the lump in his throat.

"At the cemetery?" Rory bit his lip.

"Ja, how did you know that?" Stephan asked.

Rory gave him a worried look. "I go to my mother's grave sometimes on my way to school. I saw you there and heard you talking to Reverend Hendricks. . . . I did not mean to spy." His eyes became moist pools.

"You heard me say that I was your father?"

"Ja. I was hiding behind the stone church."

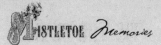
Stephan swallowed hard. "I need to tell your uncle something that you did not hear me say." Stephan stood and faced the man who had helped raise his son. "I came to Schooley's Mountain with my cousin in 1809. I fell in love with a beautiful girl named Luisa and we were secretly wed. She feared telling her parents because we were so young, and rightly so. It was an impetuous decision, so I left the resort but regret that I did not know that she was to have a child. Our child." He glanced at Rory, pained at the years he had missed in his son's life.

"Stephan, is that why you came back to Schooley's Mountain?" Dr. Braun asked.

"I came back to find Luisa. To apologize for leaving her to live with the secret of our marriage. I was so wrong." Stephan shook his head and tears streamed from his eyes as he bared his soul in the presence of all.

"If only we'd known. Luisa went to her grave with that secret." Mr. Schroeder shook his head. "She must have loved you very much."

"I have sought the Lord's forgiveness and I now ask the same of you, Mr. Schroeder." Stephan gave Rory a light touch on his shoulder. "And you, son."

"You are whiter!" Rory exclaimed.

"Whiter?"

"Look, it is snowing again, and you have flakes on your shoulders. God has forgiven you and you are whiter than snow!"

Stephan could not help but chuckle at Rory's proclamation, and the others joined in—Annaliese laughing and crying at the same time. No one could deny the truth of what Rory had said, not even himself.

Mr. Schroeder looked at Rory seriously. "Do you want Mr. Yost to be your father, Rory?"

Rory stepped toward Stephan. "Ja! Er ist mein vater. How do you say that in Dutch?"

Stephan pulled Rory into his arms. "I will tell you once we get out of this snow. You go on to the horses with your uncle Rolof and the others, while I put out the fire."

"I can take care of that if you wish," Harlan said.

"Thank you, but I have another matter to tend to as well." Stephan looked at Annaliese, and Harlan grinned. She whispered something to Dr. Braun and he looked back at Stephan, hesitating before he nodded to her.

The others departed, heading toward the trail where their horses and Mr. Schroeder's wagon waited. He would have to make haste. Annaliese came to him, and he pulled her into his embrace.

"Stephan," she said softly. Her beautiful eyes glistened as she stood by the firelight with the snow gently drifting around them.

He placed a finger to his lips. "Annaliese, I have a confession for you. You must allow me to tell you here and now."

She looked at him with concern. "There is nothing that you can say that will change my good opinion of you, Stephan."

"I am unworthy, but I must confess that I have loved you since our first kiss," he said, his voice raspy.

She pressed her mittened hand against the collar of her coat, and a blush crept over her face, though her eyes remained fixed on his.

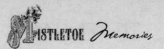

Stephan touched her cheek. "I have learned that life hastens by—this early snow may melt by the morrow. I do not want to waste another moment of my life."

"Nor do I," Annaliese whispered.

Stephan wrapped the quilt around her shoulders. "I. . .I love you, Annaliese. I need you, and Rory needs a mother. I want to spend this, and every, season with you."

"Oh, Stephan. There is a time to love, and I love you now. . .and have from the time we met."

"I haven't much to offer but my heart, and a home for you by Christmas. Would you be my Christmas bride?"

EPILOGUE

Annaliese twirled around in the parlor of her new home on Schooley's Mountain Road. "I can hardly believe it is true. A home for Christmas!"

"I did promise you, my love," Stephan said, taking hold of her hand.

"That you did, and I never doubted you for a moment." Annaliese slid her hand along the shelf of the magnificent mantel that Stephan had carved, and faced him. "You did a remarkable job. I am so proud of your fine workmanship and for hiring a crew to complete the house in time. Everyone has been so nice to help us move in, and that includes your uncle Rolof," she said, looking down at Rory.

"I helped, too," Rory said, skipping toward the staircase. "I sanded the railing."

"Ja, and you did a fine job at that." Stephan nodded.

"We worked on it together, father and son," Rory said.

Annaliese walked toward the tabletop Christmas tree sitting in front of the large bay window. She admired the garlands, berries, glass balls, and candles with which they had decorated the tree. She toyed with the tiny pair of Dutch shoes that Stephan had carved and hung by a piece of twine. "'Tis our first Christmas tree together."

"Ja, a tradition that both the Germans and the Dutch share," Stephan said.

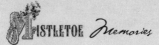
" 'I feel the influence of the season beaming into my soul from the happy looks of those around me,'" Annaliese recited. "That is from our friend Washington Irving's *Sketches of Old Christmas* that he sent to us."

Stephan gazed over her high-waisted evergreen gown with gold netting. "Have I told you this afternoon how enchanting you look—and how enchanting you are?"

She tugged on one of her long, white kid gloves. "Thank you. I am pleased to be escorted to the Christmas party at the Marshes' by my handsome men, dressed in your fine suits and Wellington boots." She walked toward Rory and straightened his cravat and kissed him on the nose.

"Before we attend the party, we have something to tell you, Rory," she said.

"Once we are married you will live here in this house with your new family—Annaliese, Dr. Braun, and I," Stephan said. "But you may visit Uncle Rolof anytime you wish."

Rory beamed. "That is the best Christmas gift ever!"

Annaliese grinned. "Now, please put your coat and scarf on and tell Dr. Braun that it is time for us to leave."

"We will meet you at the carriage, son." Stephan took Annaliese's red cape, trimmed in white fur, wrapped it around her shoulders, and donned his own overcoat. "Come." Stephan opened the door and led her to the front porch. "Reverend Hendricks has agreed to marry us here in your new home on Christmas Eve day, if you will have me. That way you will be my bride by Christmas."

"You mean *our* new home," Annaliese said, smiling. "The timing is perfect. We can be presented to the congregation the following Sunday, on New Year's Eve."

"What is so important about that?" Stephan asked.

"That means I will not have to enter a new year as a spinster!" she said, hugging him.

Stephan chuckled. "*I hou van je*—I love you."

"And I love you—*Ich liebe dich*." Annaliese glanced overhead to the small gable above the porch steps and beheld a ball of mistletoe hanging from a red ribbon. She tilted her chin at Stephan. "Where did that come from?"

"Here on Schooley's Mountain, of course. Do you remember that first day we met, when Rory caught us kissing?"

"Yes, he pointed over our heads and there was mistletoe hanging from that branch."

Stephan nodded.

"Truly? You went out there in this weather to get mistletoe?"

"It is not just any mistletoe." Stephan grinned. "It is our mistletoe. And you do know what that means?"

She glanced up with her finger on her chin.

"The docktors are harnessed and ready to take us to the party," Stephan said. "You wouldn't want me to whistle, would you?"

"Oh no. I shall have to keep you from doing that. Unless *I* whistle first." Annaliese pursed her lips. Stephan lowered his mouth to hers, claiming her lips like a man who intended to become her husband.

When they pulled away and slowly exhaled, the clouds from their warm breaths mingled in the cold air. "We share the same air, and our hearts become one," Stephan said.

Annaliese gazed up at him. "Ever since you told me that you loved me on that ridge six weeks ago, I have felt as though

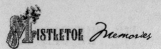

I am living in a dreamland."

Rory popped out from behind a holly bush.

"Papa, is she your liebchen?"

When they both answered "Ja," Rory leapt up the steps and threw his arms around his new mama and papa.

MERCY MILD

Gina Welborn

DEDICATION

For my precious girls—Jerah, Rhyinn, and Niley.
You are my Polly and Irena, and I hope you
see in them little glimpses of yourselves.

*Let us therefore come boldly unto the throne of grace,
that we may obtain mercy, and find grace to help in time of need.*
HEBREWS 4:16 KJV

CHAPTER 1

T he home of eccentric Essie Hasenclever was *not* an option for the child.

As the stagecoach rocked and rolled up the Washington Turnpike, Deputy Sheriff Ezekiel Norcross winked at the three boys on the opposite bench, earning a smile in return. He then tapped the nose of little Irena next to him. She glanced away from the badge on his lapel long enough to exchange a grin.

On the other side of Irena, Polly Reid drummed her boot on the coach floor. Her troubled gaze focused on the gold streaks in the sky created by the setting sun. The nine-year-old urchin's shoulder-length blond ringlets hung loose under a dark blue glengarry with a red torrie on top and pink ribbons added to the red ones hanging down the back. Instead of being steeply angled atop her head like a Scotsman would wear it, the boat-like "bonnet" rested level on her head and low enough to reach her eyebrows. How it came in her possession, Polly wouldn't say. Nor did she have even a hint of a Scottish burr.

The coach hit a bump in the road, and the children bounced on their seats. The boys laughed, and Irena giggled.

Polly uttered an elongated "ugh."

"How much further, Mr. Norcross?" she asked for the eighth time—and he was counting—since they passed Chester, five miles back.

"All the way up the mountain ridge," he answered, even though in a quarter mile they'd be at their journey's end.

Polly groaned. Her foot-tapping resumed.

Zeke smiled yet didn't tell her he was only teasing.

Unlike the other children whom he'd had to coax responses from, Polly had jabbered freely during the three-hour ride to the orphans' new parents and new life. Until now. The closer they came to their destination the more agitated she'd grown. Her lips pursed tight, hands clenched together and twisting.

Not that he faulted her.

Despite his external calm, his stomach was doing its own inner handwringing. No matter how persistent Essie Hasenclever was—and he fully expected the aged woman to be—in offering to care for Polly, he refused to allow it to happen. His duty as a Morris County deputy, and as a man of God, demanded he protect all under his wings.

Especially widows and orphans.

The court had charged him to escort these orphans to the potluck dinner at the German Valley Inn. Not to claim them for himself. Since the war ended, he'd dreamed of coming home to a passel of children. The boys as towheaded as he. The girls with dark brunette locks like their beautiful mother. Lately, every time he saw Marianne Plum, he'd think the reasons he had for not courting the reserved widow weren't worthwhile reasons at all.

He gave his head a shake.

No sense fantasizing about a life he could never have.

"Stop!" Polly stood and banged on the ceiling. She leaned out the window and yelled to the driver, "Sir, I must attend to the necessary. If you don't stop immediately, I will—"

"Whoa!" came from the driver amid the rattling and squeaks as the carriage slowed.

Before it came to a complete stop, Polly yanked open a door, scrambled down the steps, then darted into the woods.

James deRoses and the Adams twins looked beseechingly at Zeke.

"Do you three need *necessary attending* also?"

They nodded vigorously.

Zeke opened the door on his side of the carriage. "Get on with your business." As they scrambled out, he looked down at little Irena Barimore. "And you, sweetheart?"

She nodded.

Holding her close, he climbed out and walked to the side of the forested road to where Polly had disappeared. If she'd been able to wait a few minutes longer, they'd have been at the Inn just around the curve in the road.

"Polly," he yelled, "I need you to finish up and come help Irena."

"Might be a minute!"

"Better hurry. Bobcats live in these woods, and I can't shoot what I don't see."

"Really?"

"Really."

"Deputy Norcross?" the driver called out. "I am already behind schedule. Folks are waiting to be picked up at the Inn, and the Heath House will pay extra for this delivery if I get

it there before seven."

Zeke removed his watch from the pocket of his red plaid vest, the metal warm against his palm. Nearly a quarter to six. They needed to hurry before the valley was consumed by darkness. His black wool suit suited him well during the day, but once the sun set. . . He wasn't any more dressed for freezing temperatures than the children were.

"Go on," he ordered, sliding his watch back in his pocket. "Leave the children's luggage in the Inn's coatroom."

The driver tipped his hat. With a flick of his wrists, the horses resumed their path to the last stage stop before heading up Schooley's Mountain.

Zeke patiently waited for the children to return. Instead of a ten-foot walk off the stage and into the Inn, now they'd have a hundred-yard one. Could be worse, he reasoned, with the temperature in the forties (or lower), instead of the pleasant upper fifties and no wind. He presumed all the children in the Highlands of New Jersey were praying for a white Christmas three days from now. While he'd known Polly Reid all of three hours, he *knew* she would soon start praying for snow, too, if she hadn't begun already.

"Sorry about that," Polly said, grinning broadly as her boots crunched the fallen leaves. "Ma says sharing your need to attend the necessary isn't polite, and I tried not to, but I figured it's better to spew your words than things that are not proper to mention."

Proper or not, she had him there.

She took Irena from Zeke, who pressed his lips together to keep from laughing.

"I'll take Irena," Polly said. "We will be back shortly."

Then they were gone, into the woods.

≈

The violin quartet played. The people in the hall chatted. And Marianne Plum stopped shifting the order of the food on the serving table to look to the open double-door entrance to the Inn's dining hall. She fanned her neck with both hands.

He was going to be late.

True, the clock had yet to strike six, the time the potluck was to begin, and no one else seemed bothered that the guests of honor had yet to arrive. But she knew Ezekiel. He was either early or late, never on time, and never consistently one or the other.

Marianne placed her palm on the bodice of her blue silk gown. Her heart raced, and she felt out of breath and a bit damp, which was either from the heat from the bodies filling the hall or in expectation of Ezekiel's arrival. Likely the heat. After all, she and Ezekiel had spoken just a week ago when she had been in the General Store buying mineral water, and he had stopped in for a bottle, too. There had been no way he could have known she was there. Yet, they were there. Together. Unplanned.

Warmth swept underneath her skin.

"Stage!" someone yelled.

She turned to her friend, Ruth Schroeder, who was standing next to her and holding an apple pie that smelled more of cinnamon than apples.

"Oh dear," Ruth muttered. "Why am I so nervous?"

"You are to meet the child you and Lemuel are adopting." Marianne took the pie from Ruth and gave her a sympathetic grin. "Your life is about to change. Go wait with Lemuel."

"Should I?"

"Yes."

Ruth's gaze focused longingly where her husband stood at the dining hall's entrance, where Ezekiel and the orphans would soon appear. Yet she didn't move.

Surprised at her friend's uncharacteristic hesitancy, Marianne walked to the end of the serving table. She placed the pie on the table then noticed the trembling of her own hands. *She* wasn't adopting a child. Her life wasn't about to change, so she had no cause to be nervous or expectant or out of breath from anticipation. Yet she was.

And the curiosity of it all sent her fleeing into the kitchen for serving spoons.

꒰

As the rocks crunched under his polished-to-a-shine low boots, Zeke glanced over his shoulder. The orphans trailed him like ducklings around the curve of the desolate Washington Turnpike. At the back of the line, Polly looked at him with a crooked smile and a hop to her step. While the hem of her pink calico gown hung uneven midcalf, her white socks were as soiled as Irena's bonnet, and the red cashmere shawl wrapped around her twice clearly was one made for a woman not a child, Polly still bore an aplomb he found captivating.

"Mr. Norcross," she prompted, "how much further?"

Ahead was their destination—the German Valley Inn, a white-framed three-story building with steam rising from chimneys and music from a violin quartet filtering from the open windows. A dozen or so rocking chairs sat unoccupied on the wraparound porch. When he'd been a child, the black shutters that framed the windows reminded him of eyes warning, *God is watching*.

Which was why he had never misbehaved near the German Valley Inn, but once he'd made it up the mountain. . .

Every summer of his childhood, his family had left their home in Camden and come to Schooley's Mountain for the "magical" spring waters. After earning a degree from Rutgers, he'd journeyed out West and ended up scouting. Then came the war, and more traveling. For the past couple of years, he had been living in the county seat of Morristown, and yet Schooley's Mountain, with its businesses and homes nestled between the trees, would always be the place he considered home.

Tipping his bowler hat back an inch, Zeke schooled his grin, turned in a circle, and looked around as if he were a new arrival to the area, even though he'd been born on the second floor of Belmont Hall.

"Uh, children, where was it we were headed?" he asked, pretending to be lost.

A small hand gripped his fingers. He looked down at little Irena Barimore chewing on the end of one of her chestnut braids and smiling up at him with all the trust a four-year-old could give. An impressive feat, considering she appeared ready to fall asleep at any moment.

His chest tightened.

If he were her adoptive father, for Christmas he would give her a doll and paints and a new white bonnet.

He felt another grip on his other hand.

"Yes?" he said, looking from Irena to Polly.

"You don't remember?"

He gave Polly his best panicked look. "You still have the map, right?"

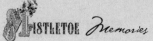

As he expected, Polly eyed him as if he were trying to sell her an elixir to cure all ills. "Sir, you never gave me a map. You have to know where we are going. Don't you live here?"

"I think I live in Morristown."

"You aren't sure?"

"I am getting old," he answered with a shrug. "They say your memory is the first to go." Considering how often he awoke at night from dreams of the war, he rather wished his memory would start to go.

Polly's nose scrunched. "How old are you?"

"Thirty-seven come spring."

Her blue eyes widened. "That *is* old."

Restraining his chuckle, he released her hand then scooped little Irena up in his arms. "Do *you* remember where I am supposed to take you?"

Irena placed the tip of her finger in the cleft of his chin. Her gray-green eyes looked at him adoringly. "I go home with you," she said in that soft-spoken voice of hers that sounded like a loud whisper.

He placed a kiss on her nose. "I would take you home with me, sweetheart, but God has a new family prepared for you. Let's go meet them."

They hadn't traversed another ten yards when Zeke heard a timid question.

"What if they hate us?"

CHAPTER 2

Zeke wasn't sure which Adams twin had spoken, so he stopped and turned to face the children. Any other time he would have continued jesting, but with the six-year-old twins and seven-year-old James deRoses looking as exhausted as Irena, he knew he needed to allay their fears.

"Remember in the stage what I read to you? The information about your new families?" While he hadn't shared who was going to which parents, he'd at least given names.

James nodded.

The twins looked ready to cry.

Polly stepped between them and gripped their hands. "Sir, what if our new parents aren't good people?"

Zeke knew almost everyone in Morris County. Those he considered good people and those he wouldn't give even a snake to. Under orders of the orphans' court, he'd investigated all the adoption applicants. But a crazy feeling told him that if he couldn't convince Polly of the goodness of their new parents, she'd grab the twins and run.

"I know them. Will you trust my judgment?"

"People lie," one twin said.

"People die," the other added.

James nodded again.

Still clutching Irena, who was now gently snoring, Zeke

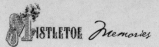

knelt in front of the children. He touched the top of James's black hair. "Mr. deRoses, who is the Father of the fatherless?"

James whispered, "God."

"That is right." Zeke moved his hand to the top button of the boy's frayed tweed coat, over a heart that he could feel beating against his palm. "Who will never leave or forsake you?"

"God," the twins and Polly answered in unison.

"Correct. God has never left me, so I know He will never leave you."

Polly and the twins smiled.

James didn't. "How do you know?"

"Because I am fatherless, too."

James stepped forward, wrapping his arms around Zeke. Immediately Polly and the twins followed suit.

"I trust you," one of the children whispered. Which one didn't matter.

Zeke closed his eyes, aware of the intense ache in his chest. He no longer grieved for his father or stepfather, or how he'd been unable to earn their approval in their lifetimes. God had healed those wounds. Yet in the last three hours, a crucible of emotions had seized him. He felt ripped asunder. On the tip of his tongue was the promise that he would take these orphans home with him, that he would be their father, that he would never leave or forsake them.

But they also needed a mother, and he had no wife.

Unless he could have Marianne Plum, he would do without a wife. But even if he had her, he would still have to do without the only other thing he desperately wanted this side of eternity—children. Marianne simply didn't want any.

The irony of it all.

With tightness in his voice, Zeke said, "Let's get on inside."

He led them up the Inn's front steps, past delighted-to-see-them townsfolk milling about the foyer, to the lavatory where they cleaned up, then to the spacious dining hall brimming with a violin quartet and more people than he'd ever seen in one place since the last Independence Day celebration. He guessed upward of two hundred, all applauding their arrival. A row of chairs circled the white wood-paneled room—added seating needed for those unable to find a seat at one of the round cloth-draped tables. A cloud of smoke floated in the far corner of the room where several prestigious men in the county, including Judge Fancer, the man whom he needed to speak to about Polly, stood enjoying their cigars near two open windows.

While those around him took turns welcoming the children, Zeke's gaze sought for and found the lovely brunette near the serving table. He knew her well enough to know that she was making sure the silverware in the bowls and on the platters was in a uniform pattern. Every so often she would adjust one. Her brow furrowed enough to deepen a worry line in her forehead.

Her head tilted, her lips pursed ever so gently as, he knew, she counted the number of serving pieces on the table. As many as were out would be the exact number returned. Marianne would ensure it. No one valued order like Marianne Plum. He loved her for it. He loved her. And that mole near the upper right side of her mouth—

He couldn't breathe.

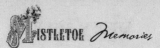

He wanted. . . . Well, he wanted her to resume wearing that atrocious black crepe mourning veil so he'd feel less tempted to kiss her.

A year after her husband's death, Marianne had discarded her widow's weeds. Tonight, she wore a light blue gown. She could afford new dresses, yet she seemed content with the older ones. Content with her lot in life. That was the only reason Zeke could figure why none of the bachelors in the township had tried courting her after her year of mourning ended. It was partly why he hadn't.

No one else could possibly know what Henry Plum had shared with Zeke about his wife.

Zeke felt his cheek twitch.

Henry Archibald Plum.

Not the only enlistee in Company K of the 7th New Jersey who'd died during the war, but the only one he'd grown close enough to during their three years of soldiering together to consider a brother. As always, on Marianne's bodice, pinned over her heart, was a silver locket holding a strand of Henry's hair.

Marianne abruptly looked up from the table of food, her brown-eyed gaze meeting his unwavering one. A faint smile played across her lips, as if to say, *Good to see you are well.*

His heart leapt in his chest.

Zeke did his best to match her smile with an unaffected yet charming one that said *likewise*.

"I hear your heart breathing," Irena whispered.

"Sweetheart, that's my lungs taking in air."

She tilted her head to look at him. Her nose touched his cheek, nuzzling him. "Your lungs sound happy."

Polly laughed and turned away from the person who'd been shaking her hand. "That's because he's looking at—"

"Evening, Norcross."

Zeke looked to the shorter yet brawnier man standing on his right, near the dining hall's entrance. Last time Lemuel Schroeder hugged him, Zeke had felt his spine pop in three places. His father, Rory, was just as exuberant with his welcomes.

"Evening," he answered with a nod. "You just arrive?"

When Lemuel grinned, the tips of his cheeks raised his spectacles. "Been standing here this whole time, but you never noticed." His knowing gaze momentarily shifted in the direction of Marianne.

Zeke uttered a quick prayer of thanks that he wasn't one to blush.

Lemuel stepped close to Zeke and whispered, "Ruth fears our child won't like her. Would you say something to ease her nerves?"

Zeke gave a slight nod, more to confirm he heard what Lemuel had said than to agree. Ruth needed words of comfort from her husband, not him. But knowing Ruth Schroeder as he did, the lovely redhead wouldn't stop helping Marianne in the kitchen long enough for anyone to offer encouragement.

Lemuel turned his attention upon the children. "Who do we have here?"

Polly stepped forward, smiling. "Sir, I'm Miss Polly Reid." She exuberantly shook Lemuel's hand then introduced the other children. With a raised brow, she remarked, "Your name sounds familiar."

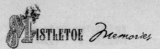

"I have the honor of becoming the father to one of you. Or two of you."

The Adams twins looked at each other and shared front-tooth-missing grins.

Zeke held back confessing that they were going to Lemuel and his new bride. Some Christmas gifts ought to be surprises.

Lemuel looked back to Zeke. "We were told there were four orphans. Who gets the fifth one?"

Zeke didn't have to glance at Polly to know she had tensed up. "Christmas came early this year, and someone has been very good."

"Deputy Norcross!" Mrs. Cottrell barked above the noise in the dining hall. The woman whose black gown emphasized the abundant gray in her hair pushed through the crowd with one hand, holding onto her husband's arm with the other. "It is about time you arrived!"

By the bitter edge in her words, Zeke knew she hadn't yet forgiven him for not choosing her to be an adoptive mother. Eliminating her hadn't been his choice, or Judge Fancer's. It had been her husband's. Zeke would go to his grave withholding that information from Mrs. Cottrell.

Everyone looked his way, and the hall quickly quieted.

Across the room, Marianne pointed their way, spoke to pale-faced Ruth Schroeder, then gave her friend a nudge forward. Ruth started working her way through the crowd.

"Children," he whispered, feeling the warmth of the room, "stay close to me now."

Mrs. Cottrell and her husband came to a halt in front of him.

"You poor, *poor* children," Mrs. Cottrell said, her scowl deepening the frown lines on her face. "I cannot believe he allowed the stage to desert you a mile back down the turnpike."

"We only had to walk around the curve," Polly clarified.

"Child, that is no way to speak to your—"

"Lavina," her husband warned.

Mrs. Cottrell fell silent. She clenched her hands together in front of her.

"Norcross, nice to see you." George Cottrell shook Zeke's hand.

While the reverend and his wife were in their early forties, only Cottrell looked it. Zeke suspected their son's death at Gettysburg had changed Mrs. Cottrell for the worse.

As soon as Cottrell released Zeke's hand, Polly secured it in hers. Zeke gave her fingers a reassuring squeeze.

To Cottrell, he said, "Sir, the children and I are ready to begin whenever you are."

Reverend Cottrell nodded. He withdrew a paper from the inner pocket of his coat. Zeke presumed it was the telegram he himself had sent moments before meeting the children at the rail station, asking the reverend to begin praying for each child by name.

Polly was not on the list.

Before Zeke could ask Cottrell to add Polly's name to the paper, Ruth stopped next to her husband.

"Say hello," Lemuel whispered.

Her mouth opened, yet she said nothing.

Mrs. Cottrell stepped forward and gripped Polly's shawl. "Dearie, let me take this."

"All right," Polly said, "but I'll keep my hat."

Mrs. Cottrell gasped. "Certainly not! That appalling thing—"

"Looks pretty on you," finished Lemuel.

Before Polly could give Mrs. Cottrell her shawl, Zeke took it from her. He handed the soft cashmere to Ruth then gave her his bowler hat and Irena's bonnet. "Would you put these in the coatroom for us?"

"I should—" Her gaze shifted to Mrs. Cottrell then the children then back to Zeke.

"All is well." He hoped she understood his implied *trust me.*

"Darling, I'll come with you," Lemuel offered.

"No, Lemuel, please stay with the children." In a voice Zeke barely heard, Ruth added, "I know you want to."

Zeke grabbed Lemuel's arm. "Corporal, I order you to escort Mrs. Schroeder to the coatroom and stay there as long as necessary to ensure the children's belongings are safe and secure from enemy hands." *Go ease her nerves.* He waited until understanding dawned in Lemuel's eyes then released his hold.

Lemuel clicked his heels together and saluted. "As you command, sir!"

Once the Schroeders left the dining hall, the ever-watchful Widow Decker claimed the spot next to Zeke that Lemuel had vacated. His mother's gray-blond hair had an additional streak of white at the temple, something new since he had seen her on Thanksgiving Day. Like Marianne, she wore a light blue gown, which, he knew, she'd debated returning home and changing upon seeing what Marianne was wearing. The two women were more alike than either would admit.

When his mother didn't speak, Zeke focused on Reverend Cottrell who, in that booming seminary voice of his, was explaining the first order of business to the crowd.

"Following the explanation of events for the evening, Justice of the Peace Rorick will pray for the meal. According to Mrs. Plum, the food is ready."

While Cottrell rambled about seating (the lack of it, to be precise), Mother leaned close, her shoulder against the sleeve of Zeke's frock coat. "It is a wretched day when a woman turns fifty-five and the only visitor she receives is her reticent neighbor."

"My apologies," he whispered back. "Sheriff Briant had me delivering warrants last week."

Irena touched the older woman's cheek. "Pretty."

"Thank you, sweetie," Mother softly cooed in a voice he knew was sincere. She adored children as much as he did. Her bejeweled hand cupped Irena's jaw. "You are as enchanting as spring's first flower. What I would give to have a granddaughter like you." Without looking away from Irena, she as-charmingly cooed to Zeke, "Did you not explain to Briant what day it was?"

"He did not need me to tell him it was Friday."

She gave him a look of mild disdain, yet she cradled Irena's hand in hers.

Zeke restrained his smile. "I'm confident your neighbor's actions were intended to be gracious."

"Gracious? She gave me pickled radishes and her blue-ribbon preserves."

"You must have felt like a prizewinner." He felt no remorse over how his comment increased the irritation in her

expression. It'd take a miracle to convince his mother of the lack of vileness in Marianne Plum.

"I abhor radishes, and blueberries give me hives." Her eyes narrowed to slits. "Ezekiel, I will have you know that woman wishes ill upon me."

"Would you have me arrest her? Cart her off to Morristown?" A tempting thought.

"I would have you—"

"Shhh," came from Mrs. Cottrell.

Zeke looked away from his mother to the good reverend.

"And please remember," Cottrell was saying, "to collect your dishes after the meal because. . ."

Zeke's attention faded from the man speaking and back to his mother. One of these days he'd bring about reconciliation between Widows Decker and Plum. To say anything would first require he have a heart-to-heart with his mother, something easy to avoid now that their relationship was the best it had been in years. He couldn't lose that. He had hurt her enough during his misbehaving childhood and the almost decade he'd spent out West when he never sent word of where he was or what he was doing.

Reverend Cottrell cleared his throat and moved on to the next order of business.

"Eating will commence following the announcements and the opening prayer." He momentarily glanced at the dining hall entrance. "Since the Schroeders haven't returned, let's go ahead and have the two other adopting couples go to the front of the line. Mr. Schroeder, you get on up there, too."

The crowd parted for the Kains, Sharpensteins, and a reluctant Rory Schroeder, who everyone in the hall knew preferred to let others go before him.

"Once the adoptive parents have their food and are seated, Deputy Norcross will introduce Irena Barimore, James deRoses, and William and Phillip Adams to their new parents. The ladies from the German Valley Missions Society will distribute gifts that have been contributed in support of the adoptive families. Thank you to those who donated. If you wish to send potluck leftovers home with adoptive families, let Mrs. Plum know." Cottrell looked around the room. "Benediction will be offered by the honorable Judge Fancer. Finally, don't forget the Christmas Day dedication of our war memorial! Sergeant Ezekiel Norcross of Company K of the 7th New Jersey Volunteer Infantry will be speaking."

While the crowd broke out into applause, Zeke froze. Internally, he winced at the reminder of the speech he had been drafted into giving. The very same speech he kept waking in night sweats about. He could think of at least a handful of veterans more deserving of the honor.

Justice of the Peace Rorick waited until the applause died down before offering the prayer.

Unlike Polly, James, and the twins, who closed their eyes and bowed their heads, Irena stared straight at Zeke. She placed her hands on his bristled cheeks then nuzzled her nose against his. She smiled, he smiled, and she rested her head on his shoulder and fingered his badge.

Zeke looked across the room to where Marianne stood.

Like him, her head wasn't bowed in prayer.

Unlike him. . .she wasn't smiling.

CHAPTER 3

"Amen" resounded throughout the hall, and people began moving to the serving tables. Yet Zeke kept his attention on Marianne. He tried not to make presumptions on why—*or delight in the fact that*—she was watching him.

He gave her a look hoping to imply *what is it?*

She shook her head and turned her attention to the table of food.

They had a connection. He felt it. She had to have felt it, too, so why did she retreat every time he made the smallest step in pursuit?

Polly tugged on Zeke's hand. "Sir, can we go eat?"

"Not yet."

He wanted to take them to supper as much as he wanted to chase after Marianne to see what plagued her, but he needed to inform Judge Fancer of Polly's arrival.

Looking around the hall to find the judge, Zeke noticed Essie Hasenclever limp over next to Mrs. Cottrell. The at-least-three-score woman spoke to Mrs. Cottrell, yet her greedy gaze was upon the children. If he placed Miss Hasenclever in a fairytale, she would never be on the side of the beautiful, tragic princess. He wouldn't say she was evil. Neither would he say she was of the soundest mind. She was merely wealthy enough to be allowed to go her way.

Zeke turned to his mother. "Would you see that the

children's plates are filled?"

"I would think *you* would want—" Her confused gaze shifted in the direction of his. "Certainly!" She scooped Irena out of his arms and into hers, then, smiling, she offered an outstretched hand to the Adams twins. "Shall we?"

The four older children looked to Zeke.

"Stay together," he ordered. "This nice lady will help you put more vegetables on your plate than you will eat in a year."

"But what about you?" Polly asked, still clinging to Zeke's hand.

"I do not eat vegetables. Ever," he said matter-of-factly. "Too vegetable-y."

"Children, ignore him," his mother chided, yet her blue eyes twinkled with amusement.

Zeke motioned them toward the serving tables. "I'll introduce you to your new parents in a few minutes."

"But—" Polly broke off. She then drew in a breath and pointed at Reverend Cottrell. "Mr. Norcross, that man didn't pray for me like he did for Irena, James, and the twins. He mentioned three sets of adopting parents, and you said the twins would stay together." She patted her chest. "I'm number five. No one was expecting me, were they?"

Zeke's throat tightened. How was he to answer her? Even he hadn't known she was coming, and he was under the jurisdiction of the orphans' court. Until he found the distant cousins of hers that supposedly lived over in Pleasant Grove, he had been ordered not to say anything to her.

"I told you, Christmas has come early for someone who's been very good."

Her eyes watered up. "I am not a present, sir. I'm a person."

"I know, sweetheart. You will have a home *and* a family. I promise."

"But I don't have a family to go home with tonight."

"What is this?!" Mrs. Cottrell stepped forward, her face flushed.

Essie Hasenclever followed step and practically yelled, "That orphan said she has no home to go to tonight."

The two women placed their hands on the twins' shoulders. The boys tried to jerk free, but Mrs. Cottrell and Miss Hasenclever held firm. The twins immediately began crying.

In a heartbeat, Polly moved from Zeke's side, frantically slapping at the women's hands. "Let them go! I said *I* have no home. They do!" Polly freed the boys then shoved them behind her back. They huddled together in front of Sarah Howe Norcross Decker, who had a look in her eyes Zeke hadn't seen since he'd been unfairly (albeit logically) blamed for using the billiards sticks at Heath House as javelins on the front lawn.

With Irena clinging to her neck, his mother, Polly, and James formed a protective circle around the twins. According to their records, the boys had been at the Soldiers' Orphanage in Richmond for two years, Irena a year, and Polly five months.

Reverend Cottrell ended his conversation with the men next to him and turned toward Zeke. "Norcross, what is this commotion about?" His question came as the noise in the room decreased.

"We have an extra orphan," Mrs. Cottrell announced for all to hear.

"An extra orphan?"

Recognizing the gravelly voice, Zeke stayed silent and waited for Judge Fancer to push through the crowd. Fancer stopped next to Mrs. Decker and the children.

Removing the cigar from his mouth, Fancer's gaze settled on Zeke. "Well?"

"We have an extra orphan," Mrs. Cottrell repeated before Zeke could speak. "She needs a home. I will take her."

"No, I will," Essie Hasenclever offered. "My house has more room than yours."

Judge Fancer twisted his fingers around his cigar. "Norcross, I knew of four orphans coming to this county. Why am I learning about a fifth only now?"

From his inner coat pocket, Zeke removed the papers he had been given on each child, as well as the ones on the adoptive parents Judge Fancer had chosen for them upon Zeke's recommendations. Among the papers was a letter from the orphanage's director detailing everything he had told Zeke on the train platform while the children and the director's wife had eaten their lunch inside the rail station.

He unfolded the letter and handed it to Judge Fancer. "Your honor, what you need to know is right here."

He waited as the judge read about how an orphan's investigator for the Commonwealth of Virginia discovered that Polly's mother had cousins in Washington, DC. The man traced their travels after the war to the Highlands of New Jersey. He then contacted the Morris County Sheriff's Department about a Victor and Eliza Ralston living in the county. Recent tax records placed them in Pleasant Grove. The orphanage's director had asked Zeke not to inform Polly of the existence of her cousins perchance they could not be found. Sheriff Briant had agreed.

Yet the director had apparently assumed the cousins would be found, because at the last minute he had added Polly to the train. If the cousins weren't found and no suitable couple came forth to adopt the child, she was to be placed in a state orphanage.

Feeling a hand on his back, Zeke turned his head to see Ruth standing beside him, a renewed confidence in her expression. Lemuel gave Zeke a nod. He acknowledged them both with a tip of his chin.

Judge Fancer scratched his bearded cheek. His gaze shifted to the children, still huddled in front of Zeke's mother.

Zeke looked around the dining hall. He couldn't see the Sharpensteins from Springfield who were to adopt Irena, but James's soon-to-be parents, the Kains from Hackettstown, were holding their food-filled plates at the end of the serving table, near where Marianne stood. All three sets of adoptive parents would graciously offer to care for Polly—*that* he knew with confidence. As long as Miss Essie Havenclever wasn't chosen, Zeke would be content with whoever was given temporary care.

"Deputy," Judge Fancer said, folding the letter, "how long will it take you to resolve this situation?"

"Two days, sir."

Fancer offered the letter back to Zeke. "What we need is someone to provide Miss Reid a home for the duration of your task."

"I will take her," Essie Hasenclever offered again.

And ensure she spends the next two days scrubbing every inch of your home. Zeke replaced the letter along with the others inside his coat pocket. Until the judge asked for his advice, the law—and his duty as an officer of the court—required he remain impartial.

"Your honor," began Mrs. Cottrell, "I would like—" Her husband wrapped his hand around hers, drawing her attention. He shook his head.

"Your honor," Reverend Cottrell said, "presuming the child will be going to a set of parents in the next two days, would it not be wise to place her in the care of an individual?" He paused. "Someone who would not pin hopes on a permanent relationship. Someone who would have the financial wherewithal to support the child until Deputy Norcross finds a permanent home for her."

"I said I'd take the extra orphan," Essie Hasenclever bellowed. "I've made it sixty-three years without becoming attached to a child. Doubt I will start now."

A few murmurs rose in the crowd.

Although Mrs. Cottrell clearly looked ready to argue a case in her own favor, she stayed silent. Likely because of the continued hold her husband had on her hand.

Judge Fancer nodded at Zeke. "Your thoughts?"

Zeke didn't have to look at his mother to know she'd already grown attached to the children. The home of eccentric Essie Hasenclever was not an option either. Only one person could fit the wise and practical parameters Reverend Cottrell had set *and* be a caregiver that Judge Fancer, not to mention Zeke, would approve.

Only one.

And Zeke was in love with her.

The problem was, Marianne fled *from* children quicker than he fled *to* them. Even though she baked sweets and mended clothing for the orphanages in German Valley, Chester, and Pleasant Grove, she always had her housekeeper's husband make the deliveries.

She will never allow Polly in her home.

Polly would be good for her, he argued, silencing his inner doubts.

Despite—or more aptly, because of—all the unexpected, magnificent, and insanely frustrating emotions he bore for Marianne, Zeke kept his attention focused on the judge.

"Your honor, I recommend the widow Mrs. Henry Plum to be temporary caregiver."

CHAPTER 4

The attention of those in the dining hall shifted from Deputy Norcross to her—a literal (action if not sound) *whoosh* of heads turning. Marianne's heartbeat increased. She clasped her hands in front of her to keep anyone from noticing them shaking. The moment the discussion turned to providing the child a temporary home, she should have grabbed her shawl and made for the buggies.

Her chest felt like a giant was standing on her.

Take a child into her home?

Her home?

To care—no, to provide care for it?

No. It did not matter if it was for two hours or two days; absolutely she would not do it. Anyone who truly knew her would know that was her answer. Children were messy. Children disrupted the order in a home. Children were needy, noisy, and nuisances.

She shook her head. No.

Yet everyone in the dining hall still looked at her in expectation of a response, as if they hadn't noticed her reaction. Or maybe they had and they couldn't believe she'd say no.

Oh, that rather vexed her.

For twelve years she had lived on Schooley's Mountain. Twelve! The worst bit, of all the people in the community who knew her best—the only one who knew of her past—Ezekiel

117

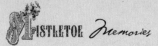

Norcross should have known better than to recommend her as a temporary caregiver.

"Mrs. Plum," Miss Hasenclever grumbled, "we all know your dislike of children. Tell them you will not take the orphan so we can be about our business finding someone proper and loving like myself to care for her. Instead of someone cold and heartless like you."

Marianne placed a cordial smile on her face, despite the frustration building inside. Agree to care for the child being thrust upon her, or decline the request, the easier decision of the two. Judge Fancer, of course, would insist she give reason for her refusal, whereupon she would have to admit she had no good reason, which would make her look selfish.

She could not share the truthful reason without exposing how inadequate she was to be a mother. The truth kept Ezekiel from seeing her as something more than a friend.

The truth can set you free.

No, Lord, it would change how they all feel about me.

To save her good name, she had to take the child. Had not Ezekiel confirmed it would be but for two days? For a night or two, she could feign mothering skills. After all, she wasn't being asked to offer love to the child. Her heart wasn't capable of that, anyway.

She drew in a steadying breath.

"I will do it," she said loud enough for all to hear.

"You will?" her neighbor, Widow Decker, said, staring wide-eyed. The little girl she held shifted in her arms to look at Marianne, her head tilting, a smile growing.

The three boys and the older girl smiled as if they accepted Marianne, too. Why that made her feel strangely pleased wasn't something she had time to ponder.

"Certainly I will, Mrs. Decker, presuming Judge Fancer accepts Deputy Norcross's recommendation." Marianne didn't look at her neighbor's son out of fear he would see the hurt—no, anger—she felt toward him at the moment. She'd hoped he cared for her.

If he did care for her, he would not have trapped her in this situation.

Judge Fancer turned to face Marianne, blocking her view of Ezekiel. "Mrs. Plum, are you sure you can do this?"

"Why wouldn't she be?" Ruth Schroeder asked, as a faithful friend would.

Many heads nodded in support of Ruth's question.

Essie Hasenclever shook her head yet stayed silent.

Mrs. Decker, for all her criticisms of Marianne, surprisingly stayed silent, too.

"Then by order of the court," Judge Fancer said, "I appoint Mrs. Henry Plum, widow, as temporary guardian to Miss Polly Reid until Deputy Ezekiel Norcross secures permanent guardianship in accordance with the dictates of the Soldiers' Orphanage of Richmond, Virginia."

A round of applause followed his announcement.

Before Marianne knew it, enjoyment of the evening resumed. She made herself a plate of food. The tables were all filled, as were the chairs about the dining hall. Determined not to speak to Ezekiel, she found a chair in the kitchen and awaited the introductions of the parents to the children. *Oh, dear Lord, what have I done?*

&

Later that evening, when the dining hall was nearly empty—save for Marianne, the newly expanded Schroeders, and

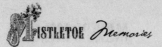

Polly Reid, Ruth swept the floor while Marianne washed the tables, likely more times than they needed it. Once the hall was clean, they would all leave for home.

She and Polly would leave for home.

Together.

The two of them. Alone.

True, her housekeepers, Jacob and Charlotte Graff, lived at the Plum house, too, so she and the child wouldn't be completely alone, but the thought did little to ease the tension growing in Marianne's stomach. She'd barely eaten a bite. How could she, knowing what fate awaited her? Two days with a child to care for. She should have said no. She really should have.

Ruth nudged Marianne's shoulder with the end of the broom handle. "She is watching you."

Marianne stopped wiping the table. Polly Reid sat at a table next to Lemuel, who held a sleeping twin. His other newly adopted son sat with Lemuel's father, Rory, talking a mile a minute despite the lateness of the hour. Polly's blue eyes were fixed on Marianne. There had been times throughout the evening when Marianne had felt someone watching her. The first time was Ezekiel right after he arrived with the orphans. Later, during the meal and the distribution of gifts for the orphans and adopting parents, she'd turned to see him staring at her. But he looked away both times.

Hopefully, a response in shame over the quandary he had put her in.

She had noticed the orphan girl staring, too; only at those times, Marianne had been the one to look away. They hadn't spoken a word to each other after their initial introduction, when the other children had met their new parents. Holding the little girl's hand while Reverend Cottrell prayed for a blessing on the children had felt. . .peculiar.

Had there ever been a time when she'd held her own mother's hand? Her memory held no reminders. Her heart held no hope that there had been a time.

With her father, the last time she had held his hand had been the day—

Marianne's fingers tightened around the wet cloth, and she blinked to clear the tears from her eyes. She wasn't going to cry. The past was past. No sense reminiscing.

"I imagine the child is wondering who the strange woman is who has been assigned to care for her," she finally answered then corrected, "to provide care for her."

Ruth stopped sweeping and did her own staring at Marianne. Neither of them had been asked to clean the dining hall. Yet Marianne didn't feel right leaving the room dirty. Besides, she enjoyed cleaning and putting things back in proper order, and Ruth enjoyed helping. What brought them together as friends was their desire to *see a need, meet a need*. That, and the fact that both of their husbands had left for war and later died during the same battle.

Ruth placed her hand on Marianne's arm, stilling her from moving to another table to clean. "Marianne, we need to talk."

"About?"

"I saw you shake your head when Ezekiel first suggested you," she whispered, even though her husband's and new son's laughter echoed about the room. "Why did you change your mind?"

"My reasons are complicated."

"Because of Deputy Norcross?"

How was she to answer? So many of her life's choices in the last year had been influenced by Ezekiel Norcross. He was constantly on her mind, from sunrise to sunset, to the point of distraction. She could still remember the tingle from his hand pressing against the small of her back as they'd climbed the church stairs to attend the Schroeders' wedding. Had that been eight months ago? It felt like yesterday.

She felt her cheeks warming.

"Perhaps," she murmured.

Ruth turned Marianne so that their backs were to the table with the men and the children. "Do you have feelings for him?"

"Perhaps," she muttered again, because she had no inclination to lie. Yet the depth of her feelings scared her too much to admit.

"Does he know how you feel?"

"He has given no indication."

"Men are slow-witted when it comes to deducing a woman's romantic feelings," Ruth said matter-of-factly. "Do you think he feels the same for you?"

Marianne stared absently at the damp cloth she held. "Sometimes I believe he does. Mostly I am unsure."

"You could ask him."

"That would not be proper."

"I know." Ruth sighed. "And there is his mother."

This time Marianne sighed. Despite her attempts to make peace with Mrs. Decker, the woman refused to forgive whatever it was Marianne had done to offend her. And she wouldn't tell Marianne what her offense was, which added to the tension between them. If Ezekiel attempted courtship, his mother would demand he choose between them.

Yet, even if his mother were not a conflict, Marianne had watched as he'd doted on the orphans, and how they'd doted on him. One thing she knew for certain about Ezekiel Norcross: he wanted to be a father. He'd make a wonderful one, too. And she had no yearning to be a mother, and...well, that put an end to any possibility.

"Wife," Lemuel called out, "our boys would like to see their new home."

Ruth nodded. To Marianne, she said, "We have room in the wagon for you and Polly."

"Jacob left the buggy for me."

Ruth took a step.

Marianne didn't follow.

"Are you coming?" Ruth asked over her shoulder.

"Oh, Ruth, I can't." Fear weighted her legs to the wooden floor. Feeling the blue eyes of the child still staring at her, Marianne wrapped her fingers around her friend's hand. She pulled Ruth to her. "I have made a grave mistake."

"In agreeing to take Polly?"

"I have no idea how to be a mother."

Ruth smiled softly, giving Marianne's hand a little squeeze. "Oh, Marianne, I know exactly what you feel, because I felt that way earlier until Lemuel reassured me. Do what your mother did and all will be well. You turned out just fine."

Marianne nodded because doing so was the expected response. She released Ruth's hand and started to the serving table to collect her empty dishes. She could be a caregiver. She

could do all things through Christ. Yet Ruth's advice brought no abatement to the tension and fear taking root inside. Do what her mother did?

No child should have to endure what her mother had done.

CHAPTER 5

I like cats." The child swung the basket holding two empty pie tins as they walked down the hallway to the Inn's coatroom. "I've always wanted one for a pet. Do you like cats, Mrs. Plum?"

Moonlight streaming through the heavily curtained hallway windows left shadows on the walls. The wind caused the trees to move and sway and shift, like a person moving. Watching. Waiting.

Marianne swallowed at the tightness in her throat. The Inn had guests. Even though it was midnight, they weren't alone in the building. The shadows weren't anything but trees.

Still, her pulse raced. Why hadn't she left with the Schroeders?

Desperate to distract her mind, Marianne focused on the child's strangely comforting cap, with the fuzzy red ball on the top and pink and red ribbons streaming down the back. Someone in the serving line had mentioned the girl being highly possessive of it. Called it Mr. Toodles, like it was a pet. In all her thirty-two years, Marianne had never had a pet, and none of her neighbors ever had pets either. Even Mrs. Decker.

Marianne nervously fiddled with the silky blue fringe on the hem of her bodice. That she was fearful was ridiculous. No one was in the hall with them; her mind was merely

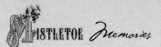

playing tricks. Not to mention, she was the adult. She was the one who was supposed to be fearless and brave. Not someone listening for squeaks, bumps, and screams in the night, like she'd done every day of her childhood.

"Mrs. Plum?" the child prompted. "I asked if you liked cats."

"Yes," she blurted, despite having no idea if she truly liked felines or not.

She knew without a doubt that she disliked the darkness. And shadows. And hearing her heart pound between her ears. Her mouth was dry. Why was it so dry? Had they missed the turn to the coatroom? They should be almost to the front door. *Fear not,* she chided herself. *Be calm for the child's sake.* The silence only enhanced her non-calmness. She needed to fill it. Talk about something, anything.

What did one talk about with children?

"Do, uhh, do you like dogs?"

"I love dogs!" The child stopped and blocked Marianne's path. "Do you have a dog? Please say you do. Please, please!"

"No dog." Then feeling a curious rush of sympathy, she added, "I'm sorry, I wish I had one for you to play with. I have never had any kind of pet."

"Really?"

"Really."

The child's sudden smile filled her face. She grabbed Marianne's hand, and they resumed walking. "I used to have a rabbit named Arthur and a hog named Randy, but we had to butcher Randy after. . .well, the war and all. Ma made me eat him, and that made me cry, but he tasted good. I wished he hadn't, because he was my friend. Do you have a rabbit or a hog?"

"She has a goat," a voice whispered.

Marianne bit back her scream before it could leave her mouth.

"Mr. Norcross!" The child dropped the basket and ran to Ezekiel leaning against the Inn's front door.

He caught her up in a hug, yet his bowler hat amazingly stayed perched atop his head. "Surprised to see me, Pollywog?"

"Nope." She wrapped her arms and legs around him. "I knew you wouldn't leave without saying good-bye."

He held her as if she weighed nothing. "You are right in that."

Breathing slowly, Marianne covered her heart and waited until the rapid pounding under her fingers abated to a natural rhythm. She had never been more relieved to see Ezekiel. She scooped up the discarded pie basket and, as she walked to them, noticed a red shawl atop a carpetbag on the floor.

"Evening, Deputy," she said, in her best attempt not to sound pleased upon seeing him.

"Mrs. Plum," Ezekiel answered in a tone that said he was *delighted* to see her.

Which vexed her even more. The man conscripted her into agreeing to be caregiver to an orphan, almost scared the wits from her, and now was gazing upon her as if she were his everything. If she were less of a lady, she would slap him.

After she kissed him. But they had an audience, and no proper Christian woman kissed a man in public. Nor would Marianne allow passion to dictate her actions.

Ezekiel shifted the child until she was on his back. "Hold on, sweetheart." He then grabbed the shawl and frayed carpetbag from the floor. "Ladies, shall we go?"

"Go where?" the child asked, her arms around his neck.

He opened the door. "Home."

"Home?" Marianne repeated as her heart flipped in joy at the thought he actually meant *their* home.

"I had thought of a moonlight ride to New York City, but since you insist upon home, ma'am, then home it is."

She stepped across the threshold. "You mentioned home first."

"Did I?"

Marianne refused to let his faux innocence charm her. "You needn't have come. Jacob left me the buggy."

"About that. . ." Ezekiel followed her outside then closed the door. "I sent him on home with it." He hurried down the steps to Mrs. Decker's covered buggy at the bottom.

On the tip of her tongue was the question, *Why?* Yet there, in the tenderness of his gaze, was the answer, and her heart flipped. Because he knew how her mother used to leave her tied to the porch at night. He knew her fears of the dark.

The child slid off his back and onto the middle of the bench. Taking the red shawl from him, she wrapped it around her shoulders. "You're funny, Mr. Norcross."

"You're funny, too, Miss Reid." Ezekiel placed the carpet-bag at her feet. He then rested an arm on the side of the buggy and looked to Marianne again. "Are you coming? The walk home is all up mountain."

Marianne started down the stairs then halted three steps from the bottom. Could the tenderness in his eyes have meant something more?

"Why are you here?"

He looked at her with eyes as blue and frank as his

mother's. "Same reason you are—for Polly."

She shook her head. "No, here. Right now. At midnight."

"Ahh, at midnight." He shrugged absently. "The spell."

"The spell?"

When he said no more, Marianne gave him a look. Truly, he was a vexing man. *That*, and charming, joyful, and noble, but his virtues notwithstanding, she was still rather peeved at his actions this evening and his cryptic answer just now. The spell? What was that supposed to mean? His head tilted to the side, and he peered at her as if the answer was obvious and he wondered why she couldn't see it. But she couldn't see it! What was it he knew and she didn't? Even the child was smiling as if she knew.

"What spell?" she demanded.

Ezekiel walked forward. He stepped onto the first stair, to where their eyes were level. "My lady, your coach turned back into a pumpkin. I brought a buggy so you would not have to walk up home in your glass slippers."

"Into a pumpkin?"

"That often happens"—he winked—"at midnight."

Ezekiel Norcross, with his even features and cleft chin, was undoubtedly a handsome man. Even with the day's growth of blond bristles on his face that she ached to touch. Even when he wasn't taking things seriously. Even when he was oblivious to how much she loved him.

How much she *loved* him?

She nervously dropped her gaze to the top brass button on Ezekiel's red plaid waistcoat. Henry had wanted her to find love again. In the letter she'd found packed in his belongings, he had insisted on it. *Be brave, darling,* he had written five

times throughout the letter. Maybe she should be a little less proper, a little braver, and take the initiative. If she descended one step, she would be close enough to kiss Ezekiel.

Could she do it?

Needing to know if Ezekiel was feeling as she was, she looked up from his vest. His gaze was on her mouth. Then he looked up and whispered something. Her heart was pounding so loudly that she didn't hear what he had said.

"What happens," she whispered back, "at midnight?"

His foot moved to the step between them. He leaned forward a fraction. "The prince chases after the woman he loves."

Marianne parted her lips. She wanted him. She wanted a kiss. She most desperately wanted to be the beauty he would pursue. And by the look in his eyes, she believed he wanted that, too, even with what he knew about her.

She eased her shoe to the edge of the step.

"He's pretending you're Cinderella," the child called out, breaking the magical spell Ezekiel had woven around them.

Ezekiel drew back.

Marianne blinked. Who was Cinderella? Fearful they would realize her ignorance, she released a nervous giggle then, lifting the front of her skirt, stepped around Ezekiel and hurried into the buggy. She set the pie basket at her feet.

As cheerfully as she could, she patted the child's leg. "Widows like Cinderella shouldn't be wearing glass slippers at night."

Polly Reid looked at her strangely. "You don't know who Cinderella is, do you?"

Marianne lifted her lips in what she hoped looked like an *of course I do* smile.

Ezekiel settled in the buggy on the other side of the child. "Everyone knows who Cinderella is," he said in his usual lighthearted manner. He flicked the reins, and the horse and buggy started up the mountain.

"Mrs. Plum doesn't know."

Marianne kept her gaze on the road as he turned his head to look at her.

"You don't?"

She maintained her easy smile because that was all the answer she was going to give. Yet in her peripheral view, she could see his eyes were wide with shock.

"Marianne, have you ever read *The Renowned Tales of Mother Goose*?"

She sighed. If she didn't answer, he would nag her until she did. "No."

She could have explained more—like how her parents had never read to her or how she never attended school or even how she hadn't learned to read or write until her husband had taught her after they'd married. Besides the Bible, the only books she'd read on her own were *Gulliver's Travels*, *The Scarlet Letter*, and *Oliver Twist*, and only then after Henry had left for war. Not that there weren't other books in her husband's library. Reading was something they had done together. When she buried him, she had buried her interest in journeying to a literary world.

She could have explained that to them. Clearly Henry hadn't shared everything about her past with Ezekiel. Some inexplicable part of her wanted to be open and vulnerable with the staring-intently-at-her pair, but she let her "no" be the end of it.

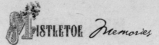

She could not have them think less of her.

"Ma used to read it to me," the girl said, with sadness in her tone. The buggy hit a bump in the road, and she bounced on the bench. "The only book we were allowed to read in the orphanage was the Bible. After I arrived, they took all the books I had brought with me. Even *Mother Goose*. It wasn't fair. So when they tried to take my father's glengarry—I screamed and fought until they gave up." Her lips pinched together.

Marianne listened to the *clip-clop* of the horse's hooves on the hard road. Someone who'd had a good mother would speak encouraging words during a moment like this.

Do what your mother did.

Never. Never that.

Suddenly, the girl—Polly—reached over and took Marianne's hand in hers. Marianne flinched, but Polly squeezed her hand.

Hold tight, Marianne remembered her father saying the last day they'd been together. She fought the tears in her eyes. It wasn't fair. None of it! Children should grow up happy and blessed, in a house full of love with parents, where they could read *Mother Goose* and *Gulliver's Travels*, not to escape life, but for the sense of adventure.

Even with the upbringing she had, Marianne knew that. Somehow in the two days she had with Polly, she was going to help her remember that life doesn't have to continue to be how it has been. Life can change.

I can change. I can be fun like Ezekiel. I can love others as freely and easily as he does.

She wrapped her other hand around Polly's and held it snugly in her lap.

They continued in an easy silence to Marianne's home.

Once they arrived, even though she didn't ask him, Ezekiel saw that they were safe and secure inside the house. Marianne and Polly waited at the front window and watched him drive the buggy to Mrs. Decker's.

With Ezekiel out of sight, Marianne turned to Polly. "I know it's too late to still be up, but would you like—"

"Yes!"

"You don't even know what I am offering."

"Will I be with you?"

"Yes."

"I'm not tired. Really." The sleepiness in her eyes belied her energetic tone.

Marianne looked to the grandfather clock. The hour was late, but what could staying up a little longer hurt? Polly could sleep until noon. In fact, they both could.

Content with her decision, Marianne grabbed a crystal lamp and led Polly to the library. Together they searched the shelves, laughing at the obscure titles, until Marianne challenged Polly to find a book written by a woman. By the time the grandfather clock struck one, Polly found *The Wide, Wide World* by Elizabeth Wetherell. Having read the book with Henry, Marianne agreed it would make a fine choice.

She took Polly upstairs to the bedroom wallpapered with tiny yellow flowers. She tucked Polly in bed, sat next to her, and they took turns reading until Polly fell asleep.

Smiling, Marianne placed the book on the bedside table. She carried the lamp to her bedroom. She *could* be a temporary caregiver.

It didn't seem that difficult at all.

CHAPTER 6

G ood morning, Mrs. Plum."
     Marianne opened her eyes. By the amount of
sunlight streaming into the room, she must have slept later
than her usual sunrise waking. Polly, in a green-and-red plaid
dress, set a wooden tray on the side of the bed. Instead of
pink ribbons, today her cap had green ribbons pinned to the
red ones hanging in back. In a room with white and ivory
curtains, bedding, and window-coverings, Polly's colorful
attire made her stand out.

"Good morning, Polly." Marianne pulled to a sitting
position, her dark hair hanging in a loose braid over her
shoulder. She smiled. "You look lovely and festive. Did you
sleep well?"

"Absolutely! I made you breakfast all by myself." Polly
placed the tray on Marianne's lap. "Mrs. Graff said you
wouldn't mind."

"She spoke truthfully."

"I used to cook for Ma before she. . ." She shrugged,
an action Marianne had realized last night was her way of
answering when she became emotional.

"Polly, while you are with me, I want you to feel at home,
all right?"

She nodded.

"Now what do we have here?" Marianne said, turning her
attention to the breakfast tray.

On a dinner plate of Marianne's best china sat three toasted biscuits next to a glob of strawberry preserves, pats of butter, and five slices of bacon—all looking as delicious as they smelled. And more than she could eat. Next to a goblet of goat's milk, the aroma of the steaming black coffee in the teacup chased away what little tiredness she felt.

"This looks wonderful. Thank you."

Polly grinned broadly. "I'm glad you're pleased."

"Have you eaten?"

"Ma says a hostess should see that her company is served first."

"You are *my* company." The adoration in Polly's blue eyes warmed Marianne's heart. She patted the spot next to her. "Come enjoy this bounty with me."

"Really?"

"Really."

In a flash, Polly was snuggled under the covers and next to Marianne, who immediately handed her a napkin to catch her crumbs.

As they ate, they talked about *The Wide, Wide World* and what Polly thought might happen next.

Marianne eased the breakfast plate closer for Polly to reach her second biscuit. "Many in the township donated items to the adopting families, but since you were unexpected, I thought we could go shopping. Would you enjoy that?"

Polly nodded vigorously. "Mrs. Plum, do you like Christmas?"

"Why do you ask?"

"You don't have any decorations."

Marianne sipped the last of her coffee as she pondered

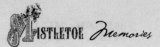

what to answer. The lack of decorations wasn't a result of any disfavor toward Christmas. When Henry had been alive, he relished all festivities. The twelve days of Christmas could have been twenty-four for him, and they had been the year before the war began. He always said the grander a holiday party the better. A ball held at the Belmont? They were there, at every one, because he wished it. At the Heath House? They were there, too. She pretended to have fun, for Henry's sake. Most of the time, she had felt as alone in a room of four hundred as she did in a room of two. Until after the war.

What began as gratitude toward Ezekiel for becoming her husband's closest friend changed this last year into something more than she'd ever thought possible. There at the Schroeders' wedding, sitting next to him, she'd realized she no longer felt alone. Polly didn't need to know that, though.

What had they been talking about? Oh yes, decorations.

"After my husband died, I had no cause to adorn the house for the season."

"Did you love him?"

She cradled the empty teacup in her hands. What she'd felt for Henry had been a gentle, steadfast, committed love, and he had loved her, too. With more passion than she deserved. Henry had rescued and redeemed her from the life set before her because of her parents.

She released a heart-heavy breath. "Henry Plum was a good man, Polly. Yes, I loved him, but not as much as he deserved, and my regret haunts me. If he were alive, I would make it up to him."

Polly nibbled on the biscuit. "Where did you first meet Mr. Plum?"

"In Central Park." Seeing a blank look on Polly's face, Marianne clarified, "New York City. It was windy, and my bonnet was loose because I had sold my hair so Father and I would have money to pay our rent. Henry caught my hat in the breeze, and then he rescued me. Love makes a man do peculiar things." She blinked away her tears. "Alas, that is more than you needed to know."

"My ma said she had to give me up because she loved me." Polly put the half-eaten biscuit back on the plate. "But I know she really didn't want me anymore."

On the tip of Marianne's tongue was the insistence that Polly's mother *had* wanted her. But was it fair or kind to say something she didn't know was truthful or not?

"Polly, if your mother knew she could not provide for your well-being, then giving you to a family who could *is* loving of her. She wants the best for you." Marianne wanted to add that all mothers desire the best for their children, but she knew that wasn't true.

"Ma's dead."

"Oh. I am sorry."

Polly shrugged. She sniffed then wiped her nose with the back of her hand instead of the napkin on the breakfast tray.

Marianne cringed yet kept herself from correcting Polly. Her task was to be Polly's temporary caregiver. For today and tomorrow. The child's future mother would teach her manners. The child's future mother would also remind her every day that she was wanted.

Hoping for that, Marianne slid off the bed, attended to her toiletries, then hurried into her dressing room to find a suitable day dress. She had a grand day planned. No sense

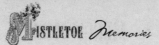

dawdling in bed feeling morose over the past.

To fit the anticipation she felt for the day's events, she chose a purple and white horizontal-striped taffeta gown. Upon seeing the silky fabric at the New York City modiste's shop, Henry had ordered a day dress made out of it, even though he had already ordered seven other day dresses and three ballgowns. Henry did everything extravagantly.

Making money had been a joy to him, as had spending it on those he loved.

Without him to spend the returns on his investments, in the last four years since his death, the fortune he had made off his inheritance had doubled. Once a quarter, Marianne traveled to New York City to discuss her financial situation with Henry's older brother and listen to her in-laws beg her to move back. Not only had God blessed her with a godly husband, but his family's continued acceptance and generosity meant a great deal. They would say extravagance on an orphan was fitting.

After all, it was Christmastime.

"Mrs. Plum," Polly said as Marianne exited the dressing room, "if you were my mother, I would make breakfast for you every day."

"That would be—" Marianne stopped buttoning the side of her gloves.

Polly stood beside the opened door to the hallway, breakfast tray in hand. Yet where she had been sitting, biscuit and bacon crumbs spotted the white sheets. The grease from the bacon alone— Marianne pinched her lips together to stay calm, yet, unable to stop herself, she could feel her eyes widen in mortification and her heart pounding.

Child, you will clean up this mess immediately!

Her mother's voice. . .in her head. . .had to make it stop.

I am not her, I am not *her. I have been made new in Jesus. I am redeemed and righteous and changed.*

Marianne took several deep breaths then, as unaffected as possible, continued on the path to the door. Accidents happened. The sheets could be washed. All would be well.

"Now wasn't that a delightful breakfast?" she said, following Polly into the hall. "Tell me, what is your favorite color?"

As they made small talk, they walked to the kitchen to return the tray. Charlotte would say they should have left the tray in the bedroom for her to collect, but Marianne hated adding an additional task to the younger woman's daily list. Sadly, with the bedding being as it was. . .

Marianne sighed.

"Is something wrong?" Polly asked.

"No, no." She opened the door to the kitchen and allowed Polly to enter first. "I was merely thinking of something I needed to ask my housekeeper to—" Her mouth dropped open in a most unladylike manner. "Oh, my dear child," she said with measured calmness, "what have you done to my kitchen?"

೭

Zeke checked the mare's saddle one last time before leading her out of the carriage house. Thankfully the above-seasonal warmth was continuing, but knowing how much cooler the temperature was on the mountain, he elected to wear the gray frock coat he had left at his mother's when he'd last stayed with her at Thanksgiving. He should have been on the road

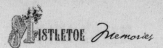

already to Pleasant Grove. He would have left earlier, if he'd been able to fall asleep upon climbing in bed. Thoughts of Marianne had kept him up half the night.

He'd almost kissed her.

She would have kissed him if Polly hadn't interrupted.

He knew it. Felt it, and had no idea what to do about it.

A ride across the mountain would help him sort this out. Zeke grabbed the saddle horn and prepared to mount. That is, until he heard a door slam shut. He looked to see Polly racing across the yard separating the two houses. Marianne stood on her back steps wearing a purple and white dress he hadn't seen before. It only accentuated her beauty.

"Polly, please come back here," Marianne called out in a composed-yet-firm manner.

Polly kept running until she reached the back steps of the Decker House. Instead of knocking on the back door, she sat on the bottom step. Marianne didn't follow, likely because she didn't want to risk a confrontation with her neighbor. Not that Zeke blamed her. When his mother was convinced she was right, *nothing* could change her mind.

She turned and walked back inside her house. Unlike Polly, she didn't slam the door.

Zeke checked his pocket watch. He could spare time talking to the pair.

After tying the mare to a hitching post, he jogged over to where Polly sat with her knees drawn up to her chest and her arms around her legs. Her glengarry had slid down near her eyes. Zeke sat next to her, setting his bowler on the top step. In a dandified manner, he stretched out his legs before him then crossed one booted foot over the other. He rested his elbows on the step behind him.

"Rough morning?"

With her gaze focused on the ground in front of her, Polly nodded.

He gave her back a gentle pat. "Care to talk about it?"

"Mrs. Plum is angry."

Zeke blinked twice in shock. Anger wasn't an emotion he could ever remember seeing in Marianne Plum. But in Polly's perspective, Marianne was angry, so saying otherwise wouldn't help the situation.

"What happened?" he asked instead.

Still not looking at him, Polly shrugged.

"Did you do something that upset Mrs. Plum?"

Polly shrugged again.

Zeke took that shrug as a yes. He tugged on the back of her glengarry until the front tip was back in the middle of her forehead. "Do you think she had a right to be upset?"

Polly nodded. As she looked to the side, her eyelids blinked rapidly against the growing tears. "I want her to love me." A tear slid down her cheek.

Zeke cradled her against him. He knew the feeling. "We can't make people love us, but we can do and say things to show them how much we care. Then we put our hope in that one day they will receive our love, and return it. Does that make sense?"

Polly nodded. "Mrs. Plum read me a book and tucked me in bed and said she would take me shopping." She sniffed then wiped her nose with the long sleeve of a different calico dress than she had on yesterday. "Why can't she be my mother?"

When Reverend Cottrell mentioned choosing a temporary

caregiver who would not become emotionally involved, they should have taken into consideration Polly attaching to the caregiver. He should have seen it. He should have cautioned Polly last night.

Zeke didn't enjoy saying the words, but he had to. "Sweetheart, God has a new mother for you, and I hope to talk to her today. I need you to let go of that desire you have"—he tapped her chest—"in here of Mrs. Plum being your mother. A temporary caregiver is all she agreed to be."

Polly didn't respond.

He continued to hold her as, he hoped, she thought about what he said.

Several minutes later, she pointed and asked, "What's that?"

Zeke looked to the lean-to glass building. After he'd graduated from Rutgers, he and his mother celebrated with their first summer holiday at Schooley's Mountain since his father's death four years earlier. Before they got to Heath House, his mother had noticed a lush garden beside a glasshouse built against a lengthy brick wall. She'd insisted on investigating. Mr. Theodore Decker, widower, had spent the rest of the afternoon explaining to the enchanted woman how he borrowed the technology from a greenhouse in Massachusetts to create a one-hundred-foot-long wall with flues built into it where warm air could pass through from a wood stove.

"That is my mother's greatest treasure, her greenhouse. On the side is the door, if you would like to go in and look at her plants."

Polly perked up. "Really?"

"Really."

She took off running, the ribbons of her glengarry flapping in the wind.

Zeke stood. He brushed off the back of his black trousers then grabbed his hat, plopped it on his head, and gave the brim a smooth swipe. With a smug grin, he walked to the Plum house. He had successfully fixed one-half of the relationship.

Now to fix the other.

CHAPTER 7

While she hadn't responded to the chaos in her kitchen in the best manner, things could have been worse. The mess only seemed as messy as it did because the room was small.

Marianne piled the last of the dirty utensils and cookware on the worktable in the middle of the kitchen and tried to retain a smidgeon of optimism. How Polly managed to coat the stove, dry sink, worktable, and mantel above the hearth with flour, well, she wasn't sure she wanted to know. Or why Polly had to rearrange the formerly alphabetized and neatly stacked canned goods in the pantry. And the bacon grease—At least it had stayed in the cast-iron skillet.

She could clean the mess herself. Or have Charlotte do it, since she had repeatedly volunteered. Sending her housekeeper upstairs to attend to her usual duties and to clean the crumbs Polly had left on the bed seemed the wiser course of action.

Maybe she ought to go over to her neighbor's and bring Polly home.

No. For all her orneriness to Marianne, Mrs. Decker had a soft spot for children. She would cheer Polly up and help her see the situation from an adult's perspective. Then Polly would return home. That's when Marianne would have a gentle talk with her about tidying up after oneself, and then they would clean the kitchen together so they could go shopping.

She rested against the edge of the dry sink and released a stream of breath between her lips, the action relaxing the tension in her shoulders. Yes, she could still make this work.

She wasn't the worst caregiver.

Even though she didn't like the crumbs on the bed or the disorder brought to her kitchen, she had not responded to Polly like her mother had to her—with screams and condemnation. And Ezekiel wasn't anything like her father. After three years of being his friend, she could trust him to help her, like she had trusted Henry.

How could she convince him to let go of whatever was holding him back from pursuing her? How could she tell Ezekiel she needed his strength? His joy? Him. They could have a wonderful life together even without the children he yearned to have. Because if being a father was that important to Ezekiel, he would have already married, right?

Surely a life with her alone would be enough for him.

Be brave, darling.

Had Henry told her that because he didn't think she had it in her? Or because he did, and he wanted her to see what he saw?

Staring absently at the flour-sprinkled wooden floor, Marianne ran the tip of her thumb along her bottom lip. Could she be brave?

The back door to her kitchen opened. She looked up.

Ezekiel walked inside wearing a gray frock coat over a cranberry- and floral-striped waistcoat that would look garish on any other man. On him it emphasized how, without a doubt, he was a prime specimen of the male sort. Then again, much could be said for how he confidently yet humbly wore

the badge on his lapel and the holstered pistol at his hip.

As he closed the door behind him, his gaze moved across the kitchen. He nodded in a most approving manner. "Disorder to your order. No wonder Polly thinks you are angry."

"Oh, I am not angry."

"I never thought you were."

With a coy smile, she raised her brows. "Yet you seem rather pleased at the mess made to my kitchen."

"Woman, you seem rather pleased that I am pleased," he said in what she took as his attempt to sound accusatory but came out—dare she presume—as flirtatious.

Maybe that's what she needed to be to convince him she desired to be more than friends. And even if he refused her, at least she took a risk.

I can change, Lord. I want to be free to love even if love brings disappointment. I am weary of being alone.

Marianne grabbed an unused towel off the dry sink. The kitchen being the size it was meant that in five steps she was standing in front of him. "Deputy, since you insist on cleaning this disorder," she said, hearing a smile in her words, "then please do."

"I never offered to clean anything."

"You are so kind to insist." She placed the towel in his hand and wrapped his fingers around it. "I accept."

His nose scrunched up; the right corner of his mouth lifted. He looked so charming and kissable that her heart skipped a beat, and in an act of self-preservation, she pressed her lips together to hold back the brimming laughter. What was it about him that brought out merriment in her?

Somehow around him, she felt her burdens lifted.

She felt free to rest and to have fun.

Around Henry she'd felt like she needed to meet his needs. She had to be the ideal wife to keep his favor. Not that he'd *ever* demanded that of her. Henry was too gracious and sincere for that. Why couldn't she have accepted his love without feeling like she had to do something to prove she was worthy of it?

Her heartbeat increased. She had to speak, had to be more than flirtatious, had to be vulnerable and confesss her darkest secrets. Now. While she felt brave and free. While she had nothing to lose but her pride.

"Ezekiel," she whispered, "I need you."

"To clean the kitchen?"

"In my life."

He gazed at her and didn't speak, didn't move, didn't even acknowledge he had heard her confession.

Marianne didn't look away. "I am not cold or heartless."

"I never said you were."

"My mother did. Essie Hassenclever did. Even your mother thinks I am."

"They are wrong," he said in a firm tone that would allow no argument from her. "In many things."

"When I was twelve, my mother ran off with another man. I never attended school. Henry taught me to read and write, and the day after my wedding, I put my father in an asylum."

"Your father's illness made him violent, Henry was an honorable man, and your mother was—wasn't a good person."

Knowing that did not lessen the shame she felt. Her

decision to put Father in the asylum, like her mother's in deserting them, had been selfish. Someday she would atone for what she did. But that was not what she wished to discuss.

"Ezekiel Norcross," she said, gathering her remaining courage, "I love you with a passion that I never thought I was capable of experiencing. Even if you do not return my feelings, I praise God for falling in love with you because doing so showed me that being reserved does not make me cold or heartless."

"Even if I don't—?"

Before Marianne could be shocked or offended by the oath he uttered, he had wrapped the towel behind her back, and holding both ends, he pulled her to him.

Then he kissed her with an intensity she had never experienced before.

But soon reality captivated her thoughts, and Marianne forced herself to draw back. "About children—"

He groaned.

Marianne understood. A discussion was not what she wanted either at this moment.

"Later," he whispered. "I've waited too long. . ." and then found her lips again.

"But I. . .don't," she said between kisses, "and. . .you. . .do."

"Shh." He pulled her even closer, until she could feel his heart beating against hers. His lips slid from her mouth to her cheek and then back to her lips, kissing her as if she were his everything—his all.

And then, abruptly, he let her go.

"I have parents," he said, breathing hard, "to find. . .for Polly."

He looked as dazed as she felt.

"By order of the court," he muttered.

"Yes, you should go," she said, wishing her voice were a bit steadier.

He handed her the towel. "I will return."

"But about your mother—"

"Later."

Before she could form a reply, his lips were against hers again, kissing and whispering words she was too distracted to comprehend.

And then he was gone.

If it weren't for the tingle on her lips or the lingering woodsy scent of his cologne, she wouldn't have known he had been in her kitchen.

Breathless, Marianne absently walked to a stool near the unlit hearth. She sat, intending to patiently wait for Polly to return so they could have a day of adventure. Her heart had never felt so full. Even though Ezekiel had not specifically said he loved her or asked her to marry him or agreed to her desire not to have children, her smile grew.

This was truly the best time of the year.

She wouldn't even mind a little snow. After all, it was Christmas.

Christmas!

With a gasp, Marianne stood. She couldn't let Polly leave without experiencing an extravagant Henry Plum–style Christmas.

❧

While Jacob took the wagon in search of a tree, mistletoe, and other greenery to liven up the mantels and tables throughout

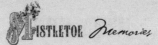

the house, Marianne enlisted Charlotte to help bring down the Christmas decorations from the attic. This had not been a simple task, because of the old trunks and hatboxes the former owners had left. They unpacked stockings, colored paper and crystal bells, cards from previous Christmases, gold-plated and tin Saint Nicholas figurines, pinecones surprisingly still holding a cinnamon scent, ornaments and feathers, three hand-carved nativities, and yards and yards of red ribbon.

"Mrs. Plum!"

Hearing Polly calling out, Marianne said, "We are in the front parlor."

Polly came running down the hall and into the room, her cheeks rosy, her smile broad, her hands behind her back. She stopped abruptly. Her eyes widened. "What happened in here?"

"What does it look like?"

"Like you spit Christmas all over the room."

Marianne couldn't help but laugh. "I suppose we did."

Charlotte closed the last emptied trunk with a thud. "Ma'am, would you like me to make a list of food supplies we need?"

"Please."

The petite housekeeper stepped to the secretary and withdrew a sheet of stationery and a pencil. "If you don't mind, I will work in the kitchen."

Marianne nodded. Like her, Charlotte married at age nineteen. Six weeks later, President Lincoln made his second call for enlisted men. After the war ended, Jacob returned alive yet no longer able to give his bride a child. The Graffs adored children. The young couple loved delivering clothes and food to the boarding school and to the orphanages in Chester and Pleasant Grove. Judge Fancer would have chosen them as an adoptive family. . .if they'd had their own home and the financial means.

Instead of faulting Charlotte for her brisk action and tone, Marianne ached for her. Life had dealt the Graffs an unfair lot.

After Charlotte left the room, Polly whispered, "Did I do something wrong?"

"No."

Polly stepped around the settee then wove around the trunks to reach Marianne. "I am sorry about the mess I made in the kitchen. Here." She offered a bouquet of pink camellias.

Marianne paused. Only one person had flora growing abundantly in December, and fanatical was the gentlest word that could be used to describe how the woman viewed her plants.

Even though she knew—and dreaded—the answer, she asked, "Where did you find such beautiful flowers?"

"Mrs. Decker has a greenhouse. It's warm and smells like heaven." The wonderment in Polly's tone matched that in her eyes.

"Did you have permission?"

"Yes."

Marianne realized she'd been holding her breath. Pleased that Polly hadn't trespassed, she went to the kitchen and found a vase. She took the list Charlotte had compiled. Until Jacob arrived with the tree and the greenery, decorating would have to wait. Shopping for toys, clothes, and a Christmas feast could not.

But first, Polly had to clean the kitchen.

By sunset the house was bedecked in evergreen and mistletoe. To Marianne's delight, Jacob had also brought a bushel of pinecones and cuttings of bayberry, inkberry, and ivy, and the house smelled like Schooley's Mountain. Minus the fauna.

The only thing left to finish decorating was the tree.

With the twigs of holly berries now inserted and ribbon and strings of popcorn wrapped around the branches, Marianne and Polly wedged in old Christmas cards and dried sugared fruit wherever there was space. Later Marianne would place the gifts under the tree, including a hatbox for Polly's precious last memento of her father and the gifts Polly had chosen for Ezekiel. She glanced at Polly, who was so like Ezekiel, with her blue eyes and sandy-blond hair. Not to mention their affinity for keeping a hat on their heads.

Perhaps she could convince Judge Fancer to allow her to keep Polly for the remainder of the week. That way they could celebrate Christmas Day together, instead of Polly leaving tomorrow on Christmas Eve. Ezekiel would certainly spend part of the holiday with them, too. They could be Polly's temporary family.

"Mrs. Plum, look!" Polly raised to her nose a card with a gilded picture of Saint Nicholas's face. In a deep voice, she said, "Young lady, have you been good this year?"

Marianne curtsied. "Every day, sir."

"Every day!" Polly groaned. "All this goodness is too much! I am sure to run out of gifts." With the hand not holding up the card, she reached up and patted Marianne's shoulder. "I insist you no longer be good on Fridays. Can you do that for me?"

"I shall try my best."

"No, child. Try your worst."

Chuckling, Marianne lowered the card covering Polly's face. "You would *not* make a good Saint Nicholas."

Polly merely smiled. And Marianne smiled, too. The girl could be Ezekiel's child for all her natural ability to make Marianne feel happy.

Joyful.

Like every day was Christmas.

"Mrs. Plum, can I put the angel on top?"

Marianne glanced from the seven-foot tree to the folding ladder next to it. Polly had already stood on the ladder to decorate the top half of the tree. Putting the angel on would certainly be safer for the child to do instead of Marianne in heels and a full crinoline. Or they could wait for Ezekiel to arrive. She looked to the grandfather clock near the front door of the house. Almost six o'clock. Why wasn't he back yet?

With a smile to keep the worry out of her eyes, she turned to Polly. "Yes, but I will have to hold the ladder."

Polly squealed, handed Marianne the Saint Nicholas card, and then ran to the settee where she had placed the angel earlier.

At the pounding of her door knocker, Marianne's heart flipped against her ribs. Ezekiel! She laid the last three Christmas cards on a step near the ladder's middle. Then, brushing the pine needles off the front of her striped dress, she walked to the door.

She opened it, letting in a crisp breeze.

Mrs. Decker stood on the front steps, looking as irritated as when Marianne had given her pickled radishes and blueberry preserves for her birthday last week.

"Isn't this a pleasant surprise," Marianne said graciously. "Do come—"

"Polly, stop!" Mrs. Decker yelled, pushing Marianne to the side as she rushed past.

"But I can do it."

Marianne turned in time to see Polly's foot slip on the Christmas cards, causing her knee to jam into the step above and her chest to lunge forward. The ladder wobbled. Polly scrambled to hold on to the rails. Her grip on the angel loosened, and it fell to the wooden floor, the porcelain head shattering upon impact. Polly screamed. Mrs. Decker screamed. The ladder continued to wobble until Polly's weight sent it—and Polly—careening into the tree. Within seconds all three lay on the ground, the ladder in a bed of pine, Polly on the Persian rug.

Marianne ran to her and knelt, her hands shaking and pulse racing. *What do I do?*

Polly drew in a sudden gasp of air, the breath having been knocked from her lungs.

With a confidence and calmness Marianne admired, Mrs. Decker examined Polly's legs, muttering "everything is all right" as she worked. Yet she never muttered to Marianne that everything was all right. Why would she? Polly's fall was Marianne's fault. If she hadn't turned her attention away from Polly. . . If she hadn't left the Christmas cards on the ladder's step. . . If she hadn't already given Polly leave to climb the ladder. . .

Marianne awkwardly patted Polly's shoulder. "There, there."

Polly continued to lay motionless, her gaze on Marianne, her eyes filling with tears. "I'm sorry."

"Polly, where does it hurt?" Mrs. Decker asked.

She grimaced. "Nowhere."

Mrs. Decker helped Polly stand. "Now does anything hurt?"

"No." Polly's gaze shifted to the downed tree. "I should clean up—"

"Nonsense," Marianne interjected. She forced a smile. "Mrs. Decker, would you be so kind to take Polly to your house?"

"Of course."

"But I want to stay with you!"

"I appreciate that, Polly." Unable to stand the condemnation on Mrs. Decker's face, Marianne focused on Polly. She kept her voice emotionless despite the wellspring in her heart. "However, Mrs. Decker will know what to look for if you have injuries we cannot see. Deputy Norcross will be bringing news of your new family. That you are at his mother's home will spare him the walk here. I fear the weather is turning for the worse."

Polly's chin trembled. "But—"

"I insist."

After a shake of her head, Mrs. Decker wrapped her arm over Polly's shoulder. "Let's go, sweetheart. I have chicken and dumplings on the stove." She nudged her to the front door and outside. "Ezekiel will be delighted to see you. He will have wonderful news about your new parents and how..."

Marianne stood in the parlor listening to Mrs. Decker's

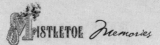

words until she couldn't hear them anymore.

Charlotte crossed the foyer and closed the front door. "Why did you send Polly away?"

Looking away from her housekeeper, Marianne eyed the crushed tree and ruined decorations strewn about the parlor floor. All their hard work in tatters. She hadn't wanted an extravagant Christmas for herself. She'd wanted it for Polly. She enjoyed giving. She enjoyed saying yes at the mercantile to anything Polly liked. She enjoyed making Polly feel loved and cherished and wanted.

Why *did* she send Polly away?

Marianne placed a hand on her chest, right where her heart beat strongest and hurt the deepest. Where existed a truth she could no longer ignore. How was it possible in such little time to have developed an attachment so rich, so beautiful, and so unmerited?

"Because she knows how to take care of a child."

Zeke exited the home of a lawyer he knew who lived on Schooley's Mountain and resumed riding south to Marianne's house. Despite the setting sun and dropping temperature, he saw no need to push the mare hard. He needed the travel time to sort out what he'd been advised, and then after the sorting, he needed to decide what to say to Judge Fancer tomorrow in Morristown. Tonight he needed to prepare his report.

In the eyes of the court, the best place for a child was with family.

Zeke, though, wasn't the court.

How much you going to pay me to take her? Victor Ralston had said upon learning his dead wife's cousin had given up her child to the Soldiers' Orphanage in Richmond before dying of consumption.

The question still grated on Zeke's every nerve. How much would he *pay* him?

"Nothing," he grumbled, even though no one was on the tree-lined road to hear. Polly came with no more than the clothes on her back and what little there was in her carpetbag.

To his shock, the lack of financial inducement failed to hinder Mr. Ralston from agreeing to take Polly. *A Christmas blessing,* Ralston eventually claimed she was. His three sons and the babe his wife had died birthing "could use a new ma." With Ralston's job at the granite quarry being what it was, Polly would be in charge of all the cooking, cleaning, and child-raising, leaving her no time to attend school. Not that a girl needed schooling anyway, according to Ralston.

"I will not put Polly in a home like that. I can't."

Ask Marianne.

That's what his legal advice had come down to—a marriage proposal.

Judge Fancer had already granted Marianne temporary custody. If she and Zeke married, they could petition the orphans' court for the right to adopt her and then hope Fancer would be merciful and choose their home for Polly's emotional, spiritual, educational, and physical well-being.

A drop-in-temperature breeze blew against his face, yet he felt warm. Hopeful.

It could work.

He loved Marianne, and she loved him. She seemed to genuinely like Polly. Once she knew of the life awaiting Polly with the Ralstons, her compassionate heart would help her

move past not wanting to be a mother.

Proposing to Marianne had only been a matter of time, not a *"Should he?"* No sense spending weeks or months courting. They had known each other since the end of the war, had been friends the last year.

After kissing—

What they shared in her kitchen was going to haunt him until they wed.

Best marry her tonight.

Reverend Cottrell would be willing to officiate. The man had been encouraging Zeke since summer to find a wife and settle down.

He looked heavenward. "Lord, unless in the next five minutes You direct me otherwise, this is the best solution." With a broad grin, he kicked the mare into a run.

He couldn't think of anything he'd like better for Christmas.

୬

By the time Zeke reached the Plum house, he knew his plan would work.

Thus he rode up to the front door, dismounted, gave the lapels of his coat a tug, tipped his hat at a jaunty angle, then walked to the half-built covered porch and gave the front door a resounding knock. Come spring, he would add a paved walk. Maybe even replace a second-floor window with stained glass. Or add on a room in the back to enlarge the kitchen.

Before he could continue his architectural additions, Charlotte opened the door. She ushered him past the parlor. He took curious note of the downed yule-tree. They stopped at the dimly lit library. The Christmas-decorated room smelled of pine, cinnamon, and *home*. Marianne sat in a chair near the hearth, a diminishing fire inside. Although she held a book in her lap, she stared absently out the window.

Charlotte said nothing as she walked away.

He entered the library and knelt before Marianne, covering her hands with his. "Will you marry me?"

She met his gaze. "Why?"

Of all the answers he had imagined her saying (*Yes, Yes! Absolutely yes!* and—his least favorite—*What took you so long?*), *Why?* had never crossed his mind.

He kept his hands atop hers. "The cousins I investigated as a possible home for Polly are unacceptable to me. I won't allow her to be put back in an orphanage. What makes sense is you and me marrying and petitioning Judge Fancer to adopt Polly. She loves you. I know you will make a great mother."

"No."

Zeke stared at her, flummoxed. He had never claimed to understand the female mind, but what had he done wrong? He should have kissed her, wouldn't have minded, certainly wanted to, but after this morning, he knew better than to kiss her again before they were married.

"No?" he echoed.

"I knew a man once who proposed for the sake of rescuing a girl from an unacceptable-to-him situation. That is not the right reason to marry. Polly needs a mother and a father who both want to be parents. I do not. It would be selfish of me to ask you to settle for a life without children." She withdrew her hands from under his, placed her book on the floor, and stood.

Zeke stood, too. Still unsure how to process her refusal,

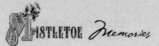

he followed her to the front door, asking, "Where's Polly?"

She gripped the door handle. "You will find acceptable parents for Polly. Be patient. Please tell Mrs. Decker that in the morning I will send over the gifts I purchased for Polly. Merry Christmas."

"Wait, why is Polly next door?"

"Because Mrs. Decker is a mother."

She opened the door and gave his arm a nudge to make him walk outside. Zeke stopped on the second step then turned to face her.

"I will see you tomorrow," he muttered, since that seemed most fitting.

She nodded and closed the door.

CHAPTER 8

The next morning as she stood at the kitchen's dry sink, staring out the window, Marianne watched the snowflakes fluttering to the ground. Outside, Ezekiel chased Polly on the acreage behind Mrs. Decker's house. She suspected the snow was delaying his trip back to Morristown to discuss Polly with Judge Fancer.

Despite the ache in her heart, she looked down at the crate of tropical orchid bulbs she'd ordered from England because Mrs. Decker loved orchids yet grew none due to the extravagant prices the bulbs fetched on the European market. This gift would be Marianne's last attempt to make peace with her neighbor. Once Christmas was over, she would accept her in-laws' request she move back to New York City.

"They are the only family I have."

At a sudden pounding, Marianne hurried from the kitchen to the foyer where Charlotte had already opened the door. White flakes blew across the wooden floor. The wind chilled the house.

A snow-covered Azariah Sharpenstein, the father chosen to adopt Irena Barimore, stood on the front step holding a crying child wrapped in a quilt. "Here," he said, giving the bundle to her housekeeper, "I need you to take Irena."

As Charlotte whispered soothing words to the child, Marianne stepped forward. "Why are you giving her to us?"

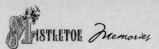

"The mess, the crying. . . Eunice can't—" His voice broke, and he rubbed his reddened eyes with the back of his gloved hands. "I love my wife and the child. Being a mother. . .it's . . . Irena is too much for Eunice. I have to choose. With you having the other orphan and all— Here. Give her to the judge."

Before she could question him more, he tossed a carpetbag into the foyer then pulled the door closed.

Charlotte drew the blanket off Irena's head.

Tears welled in Irena's gray-green eyes, but her crying stopped. She clung to Charlotte, who looked pleadingly at Marianne.

"You should take her," Charlotte said with a tremble in her voice, yet she clung to Irena.

Marianne gripped the box of orchids tighter. What was she to do with a four-year-old? The child needed a mother and a father and a home where she could feel cherished and wanted and loved, something the Graffs could give her if they had their own home.

And it all became clear.

Is this what I should do, Lord?

A sudden peace in her spirit chased away all doubts.

"Charlotte Graff, I am giving you and Jacob this house." Ignoring the confusion on her housekeeper's face, she continued, "You will provide a home for children like Irena." *And Polly.* "Henry would want me to spend his fortune wisely, and I can think of no better way. I will set up a trust—"

"No trust. Please," Charlotte begged as her chin trembled. "Jacob's pride suffers enough from living off your charity. We can make a go of this, given the chance."

Marianne wrapped her arms around the two. Once she heard her housekeeper's tearful "thank you," she claimed her woolen cloak.

Time to be brave and face down her neighbor.

❧

"So you think you can buy my affections?" Mrs. Decker's face held as much suspicion as her tone.

Marianne twisted the button on her cloak. Sitting down in the parlor would be more pleasant than having a conversation in the foyer, but at least her neighbor had invited her inside. Still, unsure what to answer, she looked into the parlor, where a yule-tree stood opposite the fire-filled hearth. She wouldn't mind curling up beside the fire with some eggnog and roasted chestnuts. Not that Henry had ever permitted roasting chestnuts in the stove. *What fun is that?* he'd say. *A man never misses a chance to build a fire and cook over it.* She suspected Ezekiel never roasted chestnuts in the stove either.

She turned back to her neighbor. "I am sorry for the things I have done to offend you. For the last twelve years, I have tried to cultivate a relationship with you because Henry believed God had provided us with a neighbor old enough to be my mother. He knew how I yearned to have one."

Her voice caught, and she fought against the pressure building in her chest.

"I thought maybe you would. . ." *love me*. Marianne wiped her eyes, humiliated at her outburst. "I am sorry. I should go." Turning away, she reached for the door.

"Stop." Mrs. Decker's voice softened. "Please."

Marianne looked into the older woman's blue eyes, so like her son's.

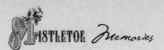

Mrs. Decker released a ragged breath. "Before you and Henry moved to Schooley's Mountain, my pickles won blue ribbons at the county fair. Then you arrived, and my pickles stopped winning. I have resented you and resisted your overtures of friendship because of your pickles."

"My pickles?" Marianne repeated with a nervous chuckle because the absurdity of it wasn't the easiest thing to comprehend. Her preserves had won more ribbons than her pickles.

"I daresay it must be the silliest reason for contention between two women." Blinking at her own brimming tears, Mrs. Decker pinched her lips together as if to stifle a laugh. Her shoulders shook, and she snorted. Her hand immediately covered her mouth, but then her gaze resettled on Marianne and the tension clearly building inside her burst.

Marianne felt her own lips twitch. Before she could hold onto any semblance of dignity, she was laughing alongside her neighbor.

And then she was in her arms, crying again and listening to Sarah Norcross Decker apologize for all the wounds her pride and jealousy had unfairly inflicted over the last twelve years. She led Marianne to the settee where they talked gardening, Christmas, Azariah Sharpenstein's return of Irena, and the reasons why Marianne was giving her home to the Graffs.

"Polly's fall was not your fault," Mrs. Decker said abruptly.

"How can you say that? You disapproved of my care."

"Disapproved?"

"You scowled at me."

"Oh, sweetheart." Mrs. Decker held Marianne's hand

between her own. "I was stunned that you were sending her away over a little accident. Polly told me all you have done for and with her. You would make—no, you *are* a wonderful mother."

Marianne flinched.

Unsure what to say in response, she stood. "It's almost noon. I should go." She pulled on her cloak.

Mrs. Decker walked with her to the front door. "I shall send Polly over after she has warmed up and had something to eat. She would like to spend a little more time with you before she goes to her new family."

She didn't know? "What did Ezekiel share with you about yesterday?"

"He said he met with the child's cousins and needed to prepare his recommendation to Judge Fancer. Why? Is there something else?"

"I cannot imagine Ezekiel withholding any pertinent information from you." Unless he had a reason.

Marianne gave Mrs. Decker a hug then hurried outside and ran back to her house. The snow had finally accumulated enough to blanket the grass since it had started falling early that morning. Although the sky was still white, who knew how much snow they would have—if any—by tomorrow. She wasn't too sure she wanted to go to the War Memorial Dedication. But she had to relinquish Polly and Irena to Judge Fancer's custody. She had to do her duty.

No matter how much her heart hurt.

❧

As his mother turned a bulb around, examining each side, she shared about how different orchids smelled like rose,

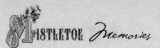

hyacinth, citrus, and even chocolate. Zeke couldn't imagine what she was looking for. Each of the dozen bulbs looked the same to him.

He paused in eating his stew long enough to ask, "Who are those from?"

Polly stopped eating as well.

"Marianne," Mother answered, "and I will not listen to you say one critical word about my friend's extravagant generosity."

Zeke felt his eyes widen. "When did she become your friend?"

She rested the bulb next to the others on the table then stared at him for what felt like forever. "Earlier. When she came over to share that she was gifting her home to the Graffs and returning to New York."

Zeke dropped his spoon next to his half-filled bowl. Schooley's Mountain wouldn't be home to him if Marianne wasn't here. He should leave. Travel to the frontier. Once he found parents for Polly, he would leave New Jersey. As long as Marianne believed her actions were for his benefit, she wouldn't change her mind about marrying him.

"Let's move to Colorado," he blurted, "like we discussed before you married Theodore Decker." He picked up his spoon, but his lost appetite caused him to drop it again. "I'll build you a greenhouse there."

"I'd like to move to Colorado," Polly offered.

Mother kissed the top of Polly's head. "My precious child." She then looked to Zeke, who couldn't tear his gaze away from the orchid bulbs. "Son, why mention moving now?"

He shrugged. "Change is good. You'd like the Rocky Mountains."

"Probably, but why move from this mountain where—" She gasped. "Oh, Ezekiel. I was so focused on my own feelings that I never noticed yours."

"For Mrs. Plum?" Polly grinned. "I did."

Zeke shifted on the wooden seat.

With a softening gaze, his mother stood and walked to his end of the table. She sat in the chair next to his. "How long have you been in love with Marianne?"

"Long enough." He reached out and took her hand in his, clinging tight. "Mother, I don't know what else to do to convince her to marry me."

She sighed. "Marianne will do what she thinks is best for others, even at a cost to herself."

"Mr. Norcross," Polly said, "what you need is a Christmas miracle."

"That's it!" Mother stood. "You two finish your soup. Ezekiel, if you've been good this year, and I think you have, I know exactly who to talk to."

❧

Since it was Christmas Day, Marianne decided it fitting to ride to the War Memorial Dedication in the fifty-year-old red barouche that came with the house when Henry'd purchased it.

With a spring in his step that she hadn't seen since his wedding day four years earlier, Jacob removed the barouche from its eight-year slumber then dusted and dressed it in mistletoe and ivy for the drive. Charlotte had even searched through the old trunks in the attic to find her husband a bottle-green velvet cutaway coat, tan breeches, and high boots that looked like they were last worn in the early 1800s.

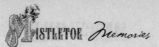
Looking ever the dandy with a black top hat, he sat in the front seat and drove the barouche down the center of the village for all to see.

Each wearing a dress in a shade of green, Marianne and Polly enjoyed the ride with Charlotte, Irena, and Mrs. Decker facing them backward in the carriage. They passed snow-dusted buildings draped in holly, red ribbons, and American flags.

By the time they arrived at the memorial site, the orchestra was playing and most of the two hundred wooden seats were filled. On the stage with other dignitaries, Ezekiel, in a black wool suit, wore an embroidered damask vest every bit as bold and green as Jacob Graff's coat. While his bowler hat was cocked to the side, he didn't look the least bit at ease.

Hand in hand, Marianne and Polly searched through the crowd and located three seats near the front, on the side of the podium where Ezekiel sat, seats he had promised to save for them. Yet when Marianne stepped back to allow Mrs. Decker to take her seat first, the older woman wasn't there. Instead, she stood on the steps to the left of the stage, talking to Judge Fancer, before he nodded and stepped back on the podium.

&

Zeke shifted in his chair for what had to be the twentieth time since the program started. How many war veterans in the audience deserved this honor more than him? All.

After Judge Fancer's introduction of him and as the crowd applauded, Zeke stepped to the podium. Whatever Fancer thought about the report on Polly's cousins that Zeke had given him upon arriving at the dedication, he had given no indication. Now he merely patted Zeke's back then walked off the stage and sat in the empty seat next to Marianne.

The judge leaned close, whispering in her ear. Marianne listened intently.

Then something he said caused her to immediately look to Zeke. Her beautiful face held no expression he could read.

She nodded, and Fancer patted her hand.

Now was not the time to wonder what the man had said, or asked of her.

Zeke focused on his notes, on words he could recite from memory. "On July 24, 1861, President Lincoln made his second call for three-years' men. Captain James M. Brown raised Company K of the 7th New Jersey, the first distinctively Morris County company."

Noticing the tremble in his voice, he breathed deep to still his nerves.

"In the first week," he read, "sixty-four men were enlisted, and the company soon had its full complement. We were together as a company at the First Presbyterian Church, Morristown, on the evening of October 1, when Captain Brown was presented with sword, sash, and pistol."

Zeke paused long enough to gauge the audience. Though most in the crowd remembered the events, they listened with rapt attention.

"Reverend David Irving presented each of us with a copy of the New Testament and Psalms, on behalf of the Morris County Bible Society." From his inner coat pocket, he withdrew the copy he had been given. He held it up. "This book never stopped a bullet, but it told me why I needed God's mercy, led me to His grace, and gave me new life."

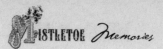

As the audience applauded and cheered, he rested the Bible on the podium. With little emotion, he listed the various engagements in which the 7th had taken part: Gettysburg, Manassas Gap, Bull Run, and Mine Run—before taking winter quarters in 1863 at Brandy Station, Virginia. By then, the New Jersey volunteer brigade was in the 2nd Army Corps. And by then, Henry Plum had become more than a brother to Zeke.

Somehow God used a man only three years older to mentor and father him. To show him that God was a warrior, mighty and terrible in battle, and that He intended for man to fight with Him. Henry had taught Zeke what things were worth fighting for.

Henry should be giving this speech.

Unable to continue speaking, Zeke looked up to see Silas Cutler standing in salute. During that winter at Brandy Station, Private Cutler's leg had been amputated the day after his seventeenth birthday. Gangrene.

Near the back of the audience, Jacob Graff stood.

Lemuel Schroeder stood.

One by one, men from Schooley's Mountain whom he'd served beside in Company K stood. *With him.* As if they could tell he was losing heart.

"On May 4, 1864," Zeke recited from memory, "we broke camp. By May 8 we concentrated around Spotsylvania Courthouse. After a day under heavy fire, at dawn on the twelfth of May, the 2nd Army Corps charged the enemy, capturing thirty cannons and Johnson's rebel division. In this battle—the severest of the war—the 7th New Jersey endured brutal losses in officers and men."

Sunlight glinted off the granite memorial in front of the stage. His enemy was no longer a man in gray. It was his own unworthiness to be alive when a godly warrior like Henry Plum should be standing in his place.

%

Marianne held onto Polly's hand, waiting anxiously for what Ezekiel would say next.

His gaze settled on her. "I'd been sent on a scouting mission and did not return until the battle was over. Good men died that day. Men better than I could ever be."

"Mrs. Plum," Polly whispered, "what does he mean by that?"

"I am not sure."

Ezekiel stepped to the side of the podium. "I am not the only man standing before you today who does not know why God was merciful and rescued us from an unacceptable-to-God situation. That day at Spotsylvania and the days after—"

Marianne did not hear the rest of his words because her own words came flooding back to her.

I knew a man once who proposed for the sake of rescuing a girl from an unacceptable-to-him situation.

God had been merciful and used Henry to rescue her from an unacceptable-to-God situation. Henry had then introduced her to Jesus. Without Henry—

Would she be who she was today?

"I have repeatedly asked," Ezekiel was saying, "would I be the man I am today were it not for Staff Sergeant Henry Plum? I choose to believe that God in His great mercy would have brought someone else into my life to teach me what it is to be a man of God, but I am thankful it was Henry."

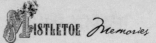

The light squeeze on her hand drew Marianne's attention away from Ezekiel's speech and onto Polly. According to Judge Fancer, Ezekiel's recommendation had been to place Polly in the Chester orphanage until a home—not with her cousins—could be found suitable for her educational, spiritual, emotional, and physical well-being. Yet because Judge Fancer had appointed Marianne as guardian to Polly until Ezekiel secured permanent guardianship, if she were to marry before he found a suitable family, then Judge Fancer, as he was granting custody of Irena to the Graffs, would be inclined to grant Marianne permanent custody of Polly. *If* she wanted to be a mother.

Her? She had no desire to be a mother.

She had *had* no desire.

Until Polly.

Overcome by the truth, Marianne made herself breathe. This was her opportunity to do for Polly what Henry had mercifully done for her. Yet, she had already turned down Ezekiel's proposal. How was she to go about accepting it?

Be brave, darling.

At that, all the passion, fear, and insecurity she had been fighting just. . .disappeared. She'd never been able to do enough to feel worthy of Henry's love because she had never been able to earn her parents' love. Her life's focus had been to give and to serve others to prove she was worthy of love, mercy, and forgiveness, but she could never do enough. God knew that.

That was why she needed His mercy new every day.

"Sweetheart," she whispered, drawing Polly's attention, "I would like to choose you to be my child, if that is all right with you."

Polly's gaze shifted to Judge Fancer, sitting on the other side of Marianne. "Really?"

"The court approves of Mrs. Plum," he answered. "She will, however, need a husband."

"Mr. Norcross loves her."

"Does he now?"

Marianne felt her cheeks warm at the amusement in the judge's tone.

"Yes sir. I heard him tell his mother yesterday."

"Then what she told me this morning must be true."

Marianne searched the crowd to spot Sarah Norcross Decker standing to the right of the stage, next to the Graffs and Irena.

"Mrs. Plum," Polly whispered, "you promised Saint Nicholas you wouldn't be good on Fridays, and today is Friday. I think that means you don't have to be proper like you always are either."

Not be proper? Could she?

Polly smiled. And Marianne smiled, too.

Today, after all, was Christmas, the perfect day for surprises.

❧

Zeke returned his well-worn Bible to his coat pocket. He'd never wanted his speech to be about him. The War Memorial was for the community, to honor those who lost their lives in service. God had reasons for keeping him alive and allowing Henry to die.

I trust Your purposes, Lord, and I will fight whenever You call me to battle, but. . .

Leaving the rest of the service to Reverend Cottrell, Zeke

grabbed his notes off the podium and walked across the stage, fully aware of the growing ache in his chest. He wanted more than another battle. He wanted more than protecting widows and orphans. Even if his mother didn't come with him, he was moving to Colorado.

He stepped onto the first stair.

"Deputy, where are you going?"

Startled out of his reverie, he looked to Marianne and Polly standing on the bottom step.

"Home," he offered with a cheeky grin, "before the clock strikes midnight."

He took a step down, and Marianne took one up.

"Fearing you will turn back into a pumpkin?" she asked, moving past him to the top step where their eyes were level. Before he could answer, she grabbed his lapel, keeping him from moving off the stairs. "I thought *at midnight* was the time the prince chased after the woman he loved."

"I. . ."

"Yes?"

The green-on-green print of her gown accentuated the brown of her hair, her eyes, and that kissable mole on the side of her mouth. He should speak. He should. Yet chasing after the woman he loved was the last thing on his mind when she was standing before him.

"I know," Marianne whispered.

"What?"

"I know why God kept you alive, Ezekiel. So that I could love you. So that you could love me. So that we could give a beautiful, clever, and funny little girl a home." She stepped closer to him. "If you will have me, know you gain an immediate child, too, and I know that's asking much—"

"Woman, *if* I will have—"

Zeke would have liked to have been the one who began the kiss, but he was man enough to admit Marianne pulled him against her and did the initiating, and that he gallantly held her close to keep them from toppling down the stairs. Like a true gentleman would.

Even though they were never in any danger of toppling.

Ignoring the whistles and applause, the sudden musical outburst from the orchestra, and Polly clinging to them, Zeke drew his lips from Marianne's to whisper, "Would you like to live in Colorado?"

Marianne released the front of his coat, wrapped her arms around his neck, and wove her fingers through his hair. "I will go wherever you take me."

Zeke raised a brow. "Even if my mother comes with us?"

"I would insist upon it."

"Really?"

Her grin took on a mischievous slant. "Really."

"Really!" Polly yelled.

Once again, Marianne began the kissing. Zeke didn't mind. His goal from the moment he arrived at Schooley's Mountain on Tuesday had been to find Polly a home. Not only did he do that, but three days later, he found a home for himself, too.

And he couldn't think of ever receiving a better Christmas gift.

MIDNIGHT CLEAR

Lisa Karon Richardson

CHAPTER 1

December 6, 1910

Olympia Paris crushed the cheap paper of the tax collector's letter in her fist. Trying to talk to him had been less than useless. And worse, she'd had to waste a dollar on the fare to Morristown for the privilege. A headache collected like a storm cloud behind her eyes. She had three weeks to come up with more money than she'd made in the last six months or they were going to lose the house.

Still clutching the letter, she all but flung herself from the slowly moving train as it pulled into the German Village station. How could she come up with that kind of money? She walked quickly, head down, not wanting to talk to any of her neighbors. She wasn't just going to lose the house; she'd lose the children, too. She wrapped her scarf more securely against the snow flurries trying to tickle her face and marched up the mountain to Mrs. Strauss's house.

She reached her destination huffing and puffing, but the exercise hadn't relieved her feelings one bit. She circled around to the back and gave a perfunctory knock before opening the kitchen door and walking in. Immediately, a warm cloud spiced with the scent of cinnamon, clove, and nutmeg engulfed her. A balm to her troubled heart.

Alice's earnest little face lifted from where she was playing with scraps of pie dough. "Limmy!" She broke into a grin and

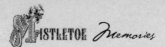

clambered from her seat, running for a hug.

Despite her inner fears, Olympia found a smile for the girl and scooped her up. "Have you been a good girl for Mrs. Strauss?"

Their good-natured neighbor dusted flour off her hands. "Of course she was. A regular angel."

"Good." Olympia kissed Alice's nose. "Are you helping?"

A big nod. "We're making punkin pies."

"Would you like to walk over to the school with me and wait for the boys?"

Alice pursed her lips. "Can I bring Lucy?"

"Of course. Go find her and she can come along." Olympia let Alice wriggle out of her grasp to look for her threadbare teddy bear.

Mrs. Strauss waited until Alice left the room then looked at Olympia with raised eyebrows. "Were you able to talk sense into old Arland Keckly?"

Olympia plopped into one of the chairs at the cozy kitchen table. "He said his hands are tied. Someone wrote to the state office and inquired about the back taxes owed. Since they haven't been paid, the state can auction the whole property off." Mechanically she accepted the cup of coffee Mrs. Strauss handed her. "And they have every reason to do just that. They have a buyer who can pay my back taxes, purchase the property, and presumably continue to pay the taxes going forward."

Mrs. Strauss sat beside her and put a commiserating hand on Olympia's arm. "How long do you have?"

Olympia sighed. "The auction is scheduled for December 26."

Mrs. Strauss pulled back, her mouth dropping open. "They'd throw children out of the only home they have on the day after Christmas? How much do you need? Maybe if we band together—"

"Two hundred fifty-six dollars and eighty-four cents."

The kind lady's hand flew to her mouth. "Oh my. I just don't—how can— That's outrageous."

Olympia let her head rest against her balled-up fists. "I don't know what to do." Hot prickles stung her eyes.

Alice re-entered the kitchen. She had Lucy, missing one of her button eyes again, hooked in one elbow. "Limmy, are you okay?" She raised a hand to touch Olympia's cheek.

"I'm fine." Olympia found another smile for the little girl. "Are you—" Her voice cracked and she cleared her throat and took in a deep breath. "Are you ready?"

"Wait." In seconds, Mrs. Strauss had wrapped up a freshly baked pumpkin pie in a napkin and handed it over. She squeezed Olympia's hand. "To go with your supper this evening. And don't fret, Olympia. The Lord hasn't gone anywhere."

Olympia nodded. "Thank you." She took Alice's hand and they set out.

"Father Christmas will come, won't he?"

Startled from her gloomy reverie, Olympia blinked. "I'm sorry, sweetheart, what did you say?"

Alice frowned up at her.

Olympia found a smile to display for the child and pulled her close for a one-armed hug. "I'm okay. Now what was that about Father Christmas?"

"Do you think he will come this year? Ellie Trout said

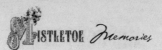

Father Christmas wasn't coming up the mountain this year. She said that 'cause Heath House closed, we're not gonna have Christmas."

Olympia's heartstrings twanged. "Of course we'll have Christmas. But I'll let you in on a secret. Sometimes the presents we get from Father Christmas are more valuable than toys and candy."

Alice's eyes lit up.

Olympia continued. "Things like love and hope and joy."

Alice slumped with the cynicism of the young. "I'd like a doll."

Olympia bit the inside of her cheek. She knew just how Alice felt. At the moment, all Olympia wanted was two hundred fifty-six dollars and eighty-four cents. Without a miracle, neither one of them was going to get what they wanted for Christmas.

ॐ

Theodore Carstairs let his hand glide over the glossy cherrywood banister as he descended the main staircase of Dorincourt House. The old place looked smaller than it had when he was a lad. In fact, the whole mountain looked smaller.

He'd been so confused then. Not sure whether to believe what the townsfolk said about him, or his own convictions. He'd been right to get out when he had. And now the good people of Schooley's Mountain were going to find out just how wrong they'd been about him.

He rubbed his hands together and stood in the doorway of the dining room. December wasn't the season for vacation travelers, but even so, the hotel dining room seemed underpopulated. He made for his table and sat, then spread a napkin over his lap. It was no wonder, really. The amenities and fixtures all smacked of the last century. Well-heeled travelers wanted up-to-date conveniences. While he was thinking of it, he should see the town council about allowing him to have the road up the mountain macadamized. That would make transporting guests smoother—he could even buy a modern autobus, rather than the old horse-drawn jitney Dorincourt used. He pulled a small notebook and a pencil from his pocket and began jotting down more ideas.

"Good evening, sir. We have two choices for dinner tonight. Filet of sole or beef medallions in a demi-glace with roasted potatoes and asparagus."

Theodore looked up and dropped his pencil. "Olympia?"

The black-clad waitress in starched white apron and cap blinked twice and then her eyes widened. "Teddy?" A huge, joyful grin lit up her features.

Teddy's stomach twisted. She was as beautiful as he'd always thought she would be. Olympia Paris was the one thoroughly good memory he had of his childhood. He stood hastily, snatching for the napkin he'd spread across his lap. He wanted to hug her close, but he couldn't presume on a childhood friendship. Who knew how she would feel about things. She could even be married. An unwelcome thought. He checked the impulsive gesture and instead extended his hand.

Realized it clutched a napkin.

Took the napkin in his other hand then made to shake her hand.

Apparently she had the power to turn him back into the

bumbling sixteen-year-old he'd been when he left.

She didn't seem to notice. She clasped his hand warmly. "Oh, Teddy, it's so good to see you. I want to hear all your news and how you are doing." A shadow seemed to pass over her features. "I can't believe you never wrote even once. I was so worried about you."

He opened his mouth. "I—" But his explanations stuck in his throat.

"It's no matter. I'm just so happy to see you safe and healthy. And so tall and handsome." She looked him up and down. "And so well dressed. You've done well for yourself, haven't you?"

Teddy pulled out a seat for her. "Won't you join me for dinner? We have a lot to catch up on."

The gesture seemed to draw her up short. She glanced around at the other diners, who were watching their reunion interestedly. "I couldn't. I'm working tonight."

Teddy's previous satisfaction with life evaporated. "I see."

"I do want to find out all about your exploits though. Perhaps you could come around for luncheon tomorrow?"

"I'd be delighted, but wh—"

A throat cleared pointedly at a nearby table, and Olympia glanced toward the diner. "I'm sorry, Teddy. I'll be back. Should I assume the beef medallions?"

He smiled. "You still know me."

She smiled back. "I'll return with your soup." She hurried to attend the old bat in dusty black who had been so officious.

As he resumed his seat, Teddy sent a glare in the crone's direction, but of course Olympia bent over the lady with gentle concern. She'd always been the kindest creature. His heart swelled until it felt like it might burst. He couldn't believe she had stayed in this old hole. And what was she doing waiting tables? She wasn't wearing a wedding ring, which could mean any number of things. Even knowing how thickheaded the fellows around here could be, he couldn't believe they had failed to realize what a prize she was.

He watched as she disappeared through the kitchen doors. Each time they swung open he strained to catch a glimpse of her. It seemed to take forever before she returned, though his pocket watch told him it had been only four minutes.

She carried a tray laden with offerings for her various tables. Starting with the biddy in black, she wended her way through them, attending carefully to every request.

He tried to plan what he would say next. It should be something warm and witty. But she was at his table before he had formulated anything.

"So what brought you back to Schooley's Mountain?" As she spoke she deftly switched the big tray from one hand to the other and reached for a steaming bowl of creamy tomato soup.

He grinned. Here was a perfect opening. If she'd stayed here all these years, she must like the place, so she would love his plan. "I'm planning to revitalize the whole town. I'm going to buy Graff House at the end of the month and build a brand-new resort on the property."

She froze, still holding the soup bowl in midair. "What?"

"The site of the old orphanage where we grew up."

She had grown alarmingly pale. He continued, less confidently. "I'm going to turn it into a hotel and save this town from ruin. Are you all right?"

"It was you. You demanded the auction of the orphanage?" Now her cheeks had gone cherry pink.

"One of my clerks actually. I had someone from my office in New York handle the details. Just this week in fact."

"How could you?" She upended the soup bowl directly into his lap.

Teddy yelped and jumped to his feet.

Olympia spun on her heel and marched from the room, her tray tucked tight against her chest like a shield.

The crone cackled.

Teddy dabbed ineffectually at his trousers. Olympia wasn't quite the angel of kindness he remembered. But why did she care about the old pile?

Mr. Harmon, the hotel manager, hurried out from the kitchen. "Mr. Carstairs, I'm so sorry. I don't know what came over the girl. Of course we will see that your suit is cleaned, and I'll have the girl sacked immediately."

"You will not. Not if you want to retain me as a guest."

"But, sir—"

"No."

"Is there something el—"

"As a matter of fact, there is. What can you tell me about Miss Paris?"

Ignoring his sodden lap and soaked seat, Teddy sat down again. He couldn't fathom why Olympia had reacted in such a way, but now that he'd seen her again, he wasn't about to let her go that easily. He was going to get to the bottom of this mystery.

CHAPTER 2

Olympia woke with a throbbing head and bleary eyes.

Grace poked her head in the door. "Are you all right? Are you coming down with something?"

"No, dear. Are the boys up and ready for school?"

"Not yet. Matt and Mark barricaded themselves in the necessary and said they're not going to school because it isn't any fun."

"I suppose that was Jonathan's idea?"

Grace nodded.

Olympia closed her eyes and rubbed the place between them. "I'm coming."

Grace closed the door softly behind her, but Olympia could hear her hollering. "Now you've done it. Olympia is coming and she's feeling poorly. She shouldn't have to get up to mess with the likes of you."

Olympia got up and wrapped her dressing gown around herself. She coaxed the boys from the bathroom, gave Jonathan a significant look, and then gathered the entire lot around the kitchen table.

Her gospels as she called them, Matt, Mark, Lucas, and Jonathan, sat on one side of the table. Grace, looking very nearly grown up in an old dress of Olympia's that had been cut down for her, sat opposite, flanked by little Alice.

Alice tugged at Olympia's sleeve. "Limmy, can we have pancakes?"

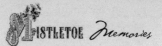

"I think we have time for that. But first I need to talk to you all."

Something about her tone must have gotten through to them, for the boys stopped pushing at one another and Grace stopped fussing with the bows in her neatly plaited hair. Freshly scrubbed faces looked up at her expectantly. God had brought each of these children to her. She fumbled for words. Then found she couldn't do it. Why set them fretting and stewing like she was? Better to let them retain their sense of security for as long as possible. Heaven knew, if there was ever a group of kids who needed some stability, it was this lot.

"What is it?" Trust Jonathan to ask the question. He was the kind to want to tear off a scab rather than let it fall off on its own.

"Money may be extra tight."

Jonathan snorted. "Nothing new about that."

"I made a mistake last night at the Dorincourt and I don't think I'll be able to pick up shifts there anymore to bring in a little extra." She hadn't waited around for Mr. Harmon to come fire her, just came straight home.

"Did you do something wrong?" Lucas asked.

"Yes."

"You got sacked?" Jonathan's eyes gleamed with new respect. "What did you do?"

"That is none of your concern." Olympia wasn't about to tell them the whole story. They would want to know why she would do such a thing. "Did you milk Gert this morning?"

Matt and Mark, sturdy six-year-old twins, chorused. "We did it."

Mark elaborated, "'Cause Jonathan said if we did, we

wouldn't have to go to school."

Jonathan nudged him with his elbow in a be-quiet gesture.

"I see. I'm afraid that you still must go to school." Olympia raised her hand to forestall any protests. "But since Jonathan was unable to keep his end of the bargain, he will be doing your chores for both of you this afternoon."

Jonathan slumped back against his chair. "That's not fair."

"Neither is tricking others into doing your work."

Disconsolately, he kicked the legs of his chair with his heels. Olympia ignored his pouting and turned her attention to making a batch of pancakes. Her head pounded as if she was coming down with a cold and her patience was wearing thin.

She plopped scoops of batter onto a hot skillet and waited for the surface to bubble. The children had cottoned onto her mood and were scrambling to complete their chores and get ready for school.

After breakfast, she kissed the tops of their heads as they piled out the door and headed for class, even Jonathan, though he tried to duck. Olympia wrapped her hair up in an old kerchief and set about her own chores, trailed by Alice. Wanting desperately not to think about anything, she attacked the old house, scrubbing the grates and tiles until they gleamed, sweeping the floors, and pulling down the curtains and setting them to soak. She even decided to pull up all the rugs and beat them out.

She lugged them out to the back porch and draped the first one over the railing. Then armed with a broom, she swung hard at the first rug. The magnificent *thwack* was the most satisfying sound she'd heard in weeks—maybe months. She

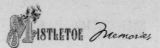

laughed out loud. Alice ran for a stick from the yard and together they beat the tar out of the helpless old rug until it released its last bit of dust and grit. They started on the next one and had a fine cloud of dirt going when behind them a throat cleared.

Olympia whirled.

Teddy stood on the porch, hat in hand.

She raised a hand to lower the kerchief she'd tied over her mouth. "What are you doing here?"

"You did invite me for lunch." The right corner of his mouth quirked up in a gesture she remembered well, and her heart gave a squeeze.

She refused to give way to nostalgia. He'd obviously changed from the boy she knew. "I would think that subsequent events made it clear the invitation had been rescinded."

"I didn't know you lived here, or that this old place was still an orphanage."

"And you didn't bother to find out."

He approached, and Alice scooted nearer to Olympia, one hand taking hold of her skirt. Teddy squatted before the little girl and narrowed his eyes. "You look like a bandit. Are you Jesse James?"

Alice tugged at the kerchief covering her mouth then thought better of removing it and said, "Yes. Hands up."

Teddy's brows went up along with his hands.

Alice stuck her hand out. "Now give me your money."

He laughed. "What would you do with my money?"

"Give it to Limmy so she doesn't cry."

Olympia inhaled sharply and put a hand on Alice's shoulder. "Sweetie, run inside."

Alice started to protest.

"No arguments. I need to talk to Mr. Carstairs."

Alice's eyes looked mutinous above her bandit's mask, but she obeyed, scuffing her feet the whole way, which she knew irritated Olympia.

Olympia caught the door before it could smack closed. It was also a convenient excuse to turn away from Teddy. When she turned back, her cheeks didn't burn as much as they had. "What precisely do you want from us, Mr. Carstairs? You'll not get our home before we are forced to give it up."

He leaned against the rail. "You were always afraid of change."

For that, Olympia didn't warn him that the rail was likely to give way and send him tumbling off the porch. "I am not afraid." Her jaw clenched so tightly it ached.

"Think how much easier you'd have it if you didn't have six kids holding you back. You were always smart. You could be anything you wanted. Go anywhere you wanted. I hear you make decent money from the short stories you sell to magazines, more than enough to support yourself, but not for a passel of kids and this old monstrosity." He patted the rail and it gave a little groan. He straightened hastily.

"And you should think of the kids. This sale will be a favor to them, too. They can go to an institution in one of the bigger towns nearby. Someplace they'd actually stand a chance of being adopted and getting families of their own. Why, without all the kids, I'd bet a lot of fellows would come courting." He waggled his eyebrows.

Olympia's vision blurred a little around the edges as fury consumed her. "How dare you!" Her voice was high and

squeaky from rage. "You get off this property and don't you ever speak to me again."

"Come on now, Olympia. You were never hotheaded. You know what I'm saying is right."

"Get out!" Olympia brandished the broom at him and he started back. She stepped forward.

"Olympia." He spread his hands wide.

She brandished the broom again.

"All right, I'm going. I know you're angry, but think about what I said."

If she thought about it any more she really would brain him with her broom. He retreated down the stairs and around the corner of the house. When she was sure he had gone she lowered the broom. She stared out over the land. Her land. By golly, she was going to find some way to pay her tax bill and keep Theodore Carstairs from splitting up her family and ever stepping foot on her property again.

❧

Teddy rubbed the back of his neck as he strolled down the lane. That could have gone better. What on earth had gotten into Olympia? She had always been the sweetest girl he knew, docile as a lamb. Not the kind of person to go around threatening people with brooms.

In retrospect, he supposed he should have approached her differently. She was sensible, and she knew the village needed jobs. Needed them desperately. Without them, it was in danger of drying up and disappearing. Then everyone would be forced to leave their homes. That's what he should have done—appealed to her sense of compassion. She'd always been a sucker for a sob story. How else would she have ended up trapped into minding Graff House?

She just couldn't see that she'd be better without that old millstone around her neck. When they were young she'd dreamed of traveling and seeing the world. Once she got a taste of freedom, she'd thank him.

A carriage approached and Teddy stepped absently to the side of the lane to allow it room to pass.

"Teddy Carstairs, I heard you were back in town, but I didn't believe it."

Teddy glanced over his shoulder to find Karl Krause, his least favorite person on the entire mountain, bearing down on him. Teddy nodded. "Karl."

"And looking so spiffy, too." Karl's plump sister, Heidi, simpered at him.

He touched his hat brim. "Afternoon, Heidi."

"I hear you're planning on evicting the orphans." Karl let his fancy tooled-leather reins hang loose in his hands as he leaned forward.

"Oh, Karl, don't give Teddy a hard time." Heidi flapped at her brother's arm. "We both know you'll be glad to see those little hooligans gone."

"You've got a point," he chuckled. "I just remember Teddy here calling me and Pop mercenary because we were going to make old Mrs. Graff pay a surcharge for delivering her groceries. I guess he knows a thing or two about the way the world works now."

Teddy's polite smile withered. He was nothing like the greedy Krauses—penny-pinching misers who didn't mind profiteering off the misery of their neighbors. "You two haven't changed a bit since I saw you last." He managed to

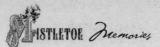

plaster a new smile in place so they wouldn't suspect he wasn't offering a compliment. "Miss Heidi, did—I guess it is still *Miss* Heidi?"

Her saccharine smile drooped slightly. "Yes."

"Ah." Teddy pretended not to notice. "Did you go on that tour of Europe I remember you talking about?"

She sniffed. "Not yet. I considered it gauche for an unmarried young lady. I am planning a European trip for my honeymoon tour."

"Honeymoon? You won't be Miss Heidi for much longer, I suppose. Who's the lucky fellow?"

She flushed to the roots of her hair. "Well there's no one specific as yet."

Teddy's infernal conscience got the better of him and he offered her an out. "The decision to marry shouldn't be entered into lightly."

"Precisely."

"When you do make your choice, I shall be able to instruct you on some of the finest sights in Europe that shouldn't be missed."

This proved too much for Karl. "Olympia doesn't seem to have taken too kindly to your scheme to take over the old Graff estate."

Teddy kept his expression fixed. He would not let Karl see him squirm. "She'll come around when she realizes the good that is going to come to the village."

Karl snorted like Teddy had displayed a hitherto unsuspected vein of naivete. "She won't come around. People think Olympia's so sweet, but she's as mule-headed as they come."

Heidi picked up on the theme. "And she's not all that

bright, either. She's had a couple of very good offers from nice, upstanding boys, and she wouldn't entertain any of them because they wouldn't let her keep all those squalid brats."

They were too vehement. Teddy figured that Karl had been one of those nice, upstanding boys.

Karl settled back. "It'll be good for her. She can move on, find a fellow, and settle down to raising kids of her own." He flicked the reins and the horses began to plod along. "Good seeing you, Teddy. Come to think of it, now that this auction is going to happen, I may bid. That's a valuable piece of property."

For an instant, Teddy's walking stick was more than a fashionable accessory, it was a necessity that kept him upright. What had he done?

CHAPTER 3

The next afternoon, Teddy tossed down his pen and growled as ink spattered. He couldn't concentrate on any of the pressing work that needed to be done. Hadn't been able to concentrate since seeing Olympia. Why had he ever thought coming "home" would be a good idea?

Because you wanted to show off. Mrs. Graff's voice sometimes invaded his thoughts if he wasn't careful.

"No," he said to the empty room, then caught himself. He pushed away from the desk. But where was he going to go? The room, the whole hotel, it all felt stifling. What he should do was go home to New York. Immediately. He could send Jeremiah back to deal with the details of the auction. There was no reason he had to be here in person.

Childish voices caught his attention. He went to the window and looked down. Nearly a dozen children stood in front of the inn. Some of the children shouted encouragement, others derision. The biggest girl seemed upset. They all stared at a fixed point somewhere to Teddy's left.

Teddy raised his window and stuck his head out, trying to get a glimpse of what had them all entranced. He caught sight of movement along the roof. He leaned out farther. Good grief. That was a young boy out there. A child of perhaps eight or nine scrabbling his way up the slippery shingles.

Teddy didn't stay to shut the window. He was out the

door and sprinting down the hall. He barreled down the stairs and through the main door, giving little heed to the yelps of the people he passed. He burst outside and jumped off the porch. The children were knotted together. Their shouting had turned to hushed awe.

Teddy looked up. The boy was wobbling his way along the highest gabled ridge. *Of all the silly*— Teddy bounded back up on the porch and grabbed the nearest post. Grunting, he levered himself up onto the flat porch overhang.

The boy's arms were outstretched as he tried to maintain his balance. His face had gone white and he was biting his lower lip. Teddy straightened. He would have called out to the kid, but he didn't want to startle him or break his concentration. Beneath his feet, Teddy could feel the vibration of the door as it slammed home.

"Here now. You children, what are you up to?"

The children paid the manager no mind, transfixed by the feats of the little boy on the gable ridge.

But the child on the roof heard and paused, his foot wobbling.

No.

The boy swayed from side to side, trying desperately to regain his equilibrium. He overcompensated and tumbled from his perch. No scream escaped, but Teddy could hear his sharp gasp.

His little body smacked into the slate and a groan escaped him. He slid feet first toward the edge.

Teddy readied himself, leaning out slightly over the edge of the porch. He'd only have one chance. The boy's momentum grew and as he pitched into space, Teddy snatched at him. His

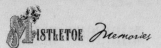

fingers closed over rough wool and he hung on, swinging the lad toward him with all his might. They went down together, Teddy clutching the lad protectively against his chest. Their impact shook the porch. Thank the Lord it was flat topped.

Teddy lay winded for a moment. When at last he came to himself he realized that a great number of people were clamoring below them. The little boy lay beside him, moaning and clutching his right arm.

Teddy struggled to a sitting position. "Are you okay, lad?"

The child sniffled. "My arm hurts."

"All right." Teddy crouched next to him. "What's your name?"

"Luke."

"Luke, we're going to get you to a doctor so he can see to that arm straightaway." Teddy looked over the edge of the porch roof. "I've got him." No one below seemed to hear. So he repeated himself louder.

The worried-looking girl peered up at him. "Is he all right?"

"A broken arm, I think, and some scrapes and bruises. But he'll live."

The girl breathed out and he saw some of the tension ease from her shoulders.

A ladder was produced and propped against the porch roof. Teddy scooped the boy up against his chest. "Hold on tight, Luke."

The boy wrapped his good arm around Teddy's neck. Gingerly, Teddy crawled to the ladder and backed onto it. He felt his way blindly, clinging precariously with one hand.

"Got him." Someone lifted Luke away and Teddy jumped

down the last few rungs.

It was good to be on solid ground again.

The spectators clustered around Luke. Wide-eyed, the children barraged the poor kid with questions.

Mr. Harmon, wringing his hands, approached Teddy. "Mr. Carstairs, I am so sorry. I don't know what the boy was th—"

Teddy waved him off. "I'm just glad he's okay. Has a doctor been sent fo—?" The sound of an altercation made him turn.

"You better pay up. He did it." Outrage crackled in the eyes of a scrappy kid with dark hair and a face splattered with freckles.

"He didn't get to the end, so he didn't do it." A blond boy in tweed knickerbockers and a good-quality woolen coat looked down a narrow nose at the other boy. He looked like a miniature lawyer who had just found a loophole.

With a howl of fury the smaller boy pounced.

"Hold it. Hold it." Teddy strode over and separated the combatants. "What's all this?"

"He's welching!"

"No I'm not! He didn't complete the bet."

"What bet might this be?"

Both boys clammed up and stared at their feet.

Teddy drew them aside and crossed his arms over his chest. "Can I assume it has something to do with why Luke was up on the roof?"

Nothing.

"Very well. What are your names?"

Silence once more.

Mr. Harmon approached. "Jonathan Paris, go at once to fetch the doctor. Arthur, I think you should go find your parents."

The befreckled lad nodded and ran down the drive while the blond boy hurried inside. Both of them looked relieved to be spared further interrogation

Paris? So he was Olympia's son? The thought landed like a lead weight in Teddy's stomach.

"I wanna go home." Luke was shrugging away from his inquisitors.

"Where is his home?" Teddy asked Mr. Harmon.

Harmon raised an eyebrow. "Luke is one of Olympia's orphans."

"Another one?"

Harmon waved a hand at the remaining children. "Most of these little urchins are hers."

Teddy blinked. This could be the perfect opportunity to get back into Olympia's good graces so that she would listen to him. "All right, kids, come on with me. Let's get Luke home." He knelt before the injured boy. "You want me to carry you?"

The little fellow nodded tearful assent and Teddy picked him up, careful not to jostle his arm more than necessary.

Two even smaller boys, who looked like mirror images of each other, trotted along behind them, and the older, worried-looking girl fell in step behind the twins, taking the hand of the smallest little girl of all.

Teddy shifted the child in his arms. "Boys, can you run on ahead and tell Miss Olympia we're coming."

The pair of bookends nodded eagerly and tore off down the lane, delighted to have an important task to do and delighted to have an excuse to run.

The older girl came up alongside him. "Thank you for

catching Luke, mister. And for taking care of him."

Teddy glanced over at her. "My pleasure. What's your name?"

"Grace Finley."

The smaller girl tugged on Grace's hand. "Don't talk to him. He's bad."

Teddy barely heard. He was reeling. "Grace? I used to know you. I was an orphan here, too. You came not long before I left. You were the tiniest thing. Only a year or so old. But as I recall, you were good-natured and very. . .practical. You'd always elect to play with a spoon and pot over a rattle."

Grace stared at him with burgeoning interest. "Did you know my parents?"

"Yes. Not well, I'm afraid. I was still rather young myself. But they were well loved in Schooley's Mountain."

The smaller girl tried to pull free of Grace's grasp. "He made Limmy cry. Don't talk to him."

"Alice, stop it." Grace tightened her grip.

Luke straightened, pulling his head away from Teddy's shoulder where it had rested. "You're the one? Why would you try to get rid of us if you were an orphan, too?" His eyes were glazed with physical pain, overlaid now by the pain of betrayal.

Teddy pulled his head back. "I'm not trying to get rid of you."

Luke shook his head. "Let me down." He started to squirm.

"You're liable to fall and make your arm worse."

Luke kicked and pushed away from Teddy with his good arm. "I want down!"

"Okay. But I'm still going to walk with you to make sure you get home." He bent to lower the lad to the ground. "Be careful. You might get dizzy."

"I'm not dizzy."

Teddy straightened to see Olympia tearing down the path, looking as if she'd like to horsewhip someone.

❧

Fear squeezed Olympia's chest and made her lungs forget how to work properly. She couldn't seem to catch her breath.

She rounded a corner in the lane and saw the children with Teddy Carstairs. Luke looked like he was struggling. She charged toward them. "What are you doing to that child?"

Grace intercepted her. "He's not doing anything but being kind. Luke is throwing a tantrum."

"Oh." Olympia would have preferred to be able to vent more spleen on Teddy, but she turned her attention to the children. "What were you thinking, Luke? You might have been killed."

Luke had been shivering and tear-streaked, but now he burst into sobs and Olympia instantly felt like a brute. She dropped to her knees in the road and opened her arms to him. "Baby, come here. Let's get you home and get that arm taken care of."

Luke practically leaped into her embrace and she hugged him close, stroking his fine hair. "It's going to be okay. All right. It's okay. We'll make it better." Still holding him close, she picked him up and turned toward home. He'd grown in the past few months and regaining her feet wasn't easy.

"I can carry him for you," Teddy said.

"That won't be necessary," Olympia said, but then she

stumbled, her foot catching on a rut, and Luke whimpered in pain. She couldn't let her pride get the better of what was good for him. "Perhaps it would be for the best."

Luke went to Teddy without protest, his little face taut with pain, tears streaming.

Olympia led the way. Teddy carried Luke up to the room he shared with Jonathan then turned to leave.

Olympia stopped him. "Thank you." The words hurt as much as chewing glass, but she got them out.

He nodded. "You're welcome." Then he slipped out the door.

Olympia's heart gave a painful squeeze, mourning the loss of their camaraderie. She opened her mouth to call him back, but then snapped it closed again. There was no time to think about might-have-beens. She focused on easing Luke out of his damp clothes and into a clean nightshirt. Then she dosed him with laudanum to ease his pain.

She'd just gotten him settled when Grace appeared with a steaming mug that smelled enticingly of sweet, rich, hot chocolate. "I thought it would be okay."

Olympia couldn't help calculating the cost of cocoa and sugar, but she smiled. "It was a good idea. Thank you, Grace."

She helped Luke sip from the mug. He smacked his lips at the treat, but his eyes were drooping. At last he eased back against his pillow, and Olympia handed the mug back to Grace and tucked him in.

"Now, young lady, what happened?"

Grace stared doggedly into the cooling dregs of chocolate. "We were trying to raise money by putting on a circus for the kids down at the hotel. Mark and Matt did that trick where

they walk on their hands, Jonathan did some card tricks, and I juggled apples."

She raised her eyes for a second to see how Olympia was taking this. "Then that boy, Arthur, said it wasn't a real circus unless someone walked a tightrope."

Olympia tamped down the sigh that threatened. "I suppose this was all Jonathan's idea?"

Grace shrugged as if the answer should be obvious. "So Jonathan said we didn't have any tightrope, and they ended up settling on the roof. Luke volunteered because he hadn't done an act yet. He was going to try to get Mrs. Strauss's cocker spaniel to jump through a hoop, but he wasn't sure it was going to work.

"So he climbed up, and about the time he got up there, Mr. Carstairs came tearing out of the hotel and started climbing up after him." Grace's words came faster as if she could see the end of the story in sight and just wanted to get there. "And it was a good thing, too, because Mr. Harmon stormed out and startled Luke and he started to fall and he would have gone right to the ground but Mr. Carstairs caught him first."

Olympia's throat tightened at the thought of what could have happened. She owed Teddy a debt of gratitude.

Now that she had confessed, Grace's burden seemed to have lifted. She leaned toward Olympia. "I do think Mr. Carstairs is most awfully dashing, don't you?"

The clatter of Dr. Newman's rattletrap old buggy spared Olympia from having to respond.

She cleared her throat. "Go greet Dr. Newman and bring him up, please."

Olympia retreated to her room, where she lifted the corner of her mattress and pulled out an oft-mended stocking. She unrolled it and pulled out the five dollars she had squirreled away over the year. She had hoped to use the money to buy the children Christmas presents.

She sat heavily on the bed and let her head fall into her hands. That wasn't going to happen now, and she was that much further from being able to pay the back taxes.

CHAPTER 4

Olympia hefted her basket from the tailgate of the wagon and lifted up the clean tea towel that covered the contents.

Ernie Lockland, the stationmaster, sniffed appreciatively. "That smells awful good, Miss Olympia."

She glanced at him as she reached to help the children with their baskets, and smiled. "Go ahead and have one, Ernie. We appreciate you letting us borrow a table and set up here."

"It's nothing." Reverently he picked up one of the delicate iced cookies she had revealed. "They sure are pretty. Did you make them all yourself?"

"The children and I did."

He couldn't restrain himself another moment and sank his teeth into the confection. "Mmm." Two more bites and the cookie had vanished. Ernie wiped his mouth, fastidious as a cat grooming his whiskers. "That's some of the best gingerbread I've ever had, and that's the truth."

"I was thinking I'd charge five cents apiece."

Ernie shook his head sagely. "Charge 'em ten cents. They're rich. They can afford it." He didn't wait for her response but stepped over to Luke's side to ask about his cast.

Olympia blew out a burst of air that ruffled her hair. She hoped this scheme worked. She'd spent the last of their cash on the ingredients for the cookies. But the passengers coming in on the train were always hungry. The staff at the inns complained about how grouchy the guests were until they got fed. Surely they wouldn't be able to pass up the opportunity to get a treat. Especially if they had children.

The train's whistle sounded long and shrill and she gestured to the children to hurry. By the time it chugged into the station they were ready and waiting, with cookies and teacakes arranged enticingly on plates. The passengers disembarked stiffly, and Olympia wished she had thought to make some sort of sign. Now that there were all these people, she wasn't sure she could play huckster.

She needn't have worried. Jonathan was a born horse trader. He wove his way among the passengers, pointing out the table of goodies. Within minutes a cluster of appreciative customers clamored around the table. Olympia's heart lifted. No one blinked at paying a dime per cookie. Next time she would bring coffee and cocoa to sell as well.

She handed half a dozen cookies to a woman who had tried one and come back for more. Hmm. A quick calculation in her head indicated that they could make over twenty dollars if they sold all their goodies. If she could bring home that much in one afternoon, there might be a real chance that they could raise the money they needed before it was too late. Of course, she would have to deduct the cost of supplies.

Deeply absorbed in her calculations and in passing out cookies, a man's suddenly raised voice shocked her.

"I said, I want my money back."

She turned to look, as did most of the other passengers.

"This is gingerbread and I don't like gingerbread. You should have told me what it was first."

"You could have asked. And if you didn't like it, why did you eat all but one little nibble?" Grace's chin jutted out pugnaciously and Olympia hurried to intervene. The last thing they needed was trouble.

"I'm sorry you didn't care for the cookie. Here's your money back."

Grace glared daggers at her and the man harrumphed and turned away. He seemed to have forgotten the umbrella under his arm, because as he turned, it swept along the table and sent two platters of cookies and teacakes crashing to the ground. The other passengers shrieked and jumped out of the way.

"You did that on purpose!" Grace and Jonathan shouted in chorus.

Olympia stared open-mouthed at the destruction but had the presence of mind to grab hold of Jonathan before he could dive over the table and tackle the fellow.

The erstwhile customer went wide-eyed then turned and hurried away.

Jonathan squirmed. "Lemme go. Someone needs to teach that guy a lesson."

"Fighting will only cause more trouble."

A sigh as big as the great state of New Jersey filled her. Could nothing work out well? She was so tired of the constant struggle to provide. Maybe Teddy was right.

No. She put an end to that line of thought. He was not right. The children needed to stay together, at least until families were found to adopt them. She refocused them on selling the rest of their wares then borrowed a broom and dustpan from Ernie. There would be no salvaging the plates.

She would be lucky now to make half what she had hoped. Although...that was still more than she might have cleared if she had only charged a nickel as she had originally intended.

"God," she whispered, "help me to trust You through all this. I know You love the children and want the best for them, too."

"Olympia, is this your gingerbread?"

Jumping at the sudden question, Olympia cracked the back of her head against the underside of the table where she had been reaching for a few final shards of crockery.

"Teddy, you always know just when to make an appearance." She withdrew from beneath the table, rubbing the back of her head.

"Sorry." He offered his hand. "I used to lie in my lodging house in New York of a night and dream of your gingerbread."

She accepted his hand and stood. While a large part of her still wanted to kick him, she had not seen him in weeks and had thought he might have gone back to New York. "I've not had a chance to thank you properly for saving Luke. Things could have been so much worse than they were."

"I'm glad I could help. Truly, Olympia, that's all I want to do." His eyes met hers, hot and clear.

Almost against her will she believed him. He gave every sign of sincerity, and unless he had changed even more than she thought, she would know if he was lying. Still, that didn't make him right.

She met his gaze and returned it with her own, willing him to understand.

A shout and a scuffle sounded somewhere over her shoulder, and Olympia realized abruptly that Teddy still held

her hand. She jerked it free and turned to face the fresh crisis. The rude man who had caused the mess pushed through the crowd, towing Jonathan by the elbow.

Olympia sighed. Jonathan was frequently up to mischief, but it wasn't like him to deliberately disobey her. "I'm sorry, he—"

"This little fiend tried to pick my pocket."

She gasped, at a loss for words.

Jonathan tugged on his arm, trying to wrench himself free of the man's grasp. "I was just trying to get what he owed us. He destroyed half our stock and he should pay for it."

"I will not. It was an accident, and if the plates hadn't been perched so precariously on the edge of the table, it would never have happened."

"That's not true," Jonathan howled, frustration and rage twisting his features.

"Stop it this instant, Jonathan," Olympia demanded. "You're not making things any better. And stealing? How could you?"

Angry tears welled in his eyes and he continued his vain struggle to free himself. "It's not fair that 'cause we're orphans we have to take whatever people want to dish out." He kicked the fellow who held him. The man grunted and shook him.

"Stop it and let him go," Olympia ordered the man.

"I will not. It's to the police for him."

"I said, let him go!"

Face mottled red, the man stepped closer. "And I suppose you're going to make me?"

"I'm going to make you." They both turned to look at Teddy. He had not raised his voice, but it cut through the squabble easily.

"I'd like to see you try," the man snorted, but he did stop shaking Jonathan.

Teddy's smile in response was slow and dangerous, with a wicked curl at the edges. Olympia hoped never to be the recipient of such a look.

Teddy's tone was conversational. "I can whip you if necessary, but I believe we can settle this without the need for violence."

"I think not." The man sniffed again and wiped his nose with the back of his other hand, which held a salesman's valise.

"Then I shall gladly beat you in a moment."

The man began to bluster and Teddy silenced him by pointing at his bag. "I see you work for Kulthorp's Kitchen Essentials."

"What of it?"

Teddy again smiled that awful smile. "Simply that I'm great friends with Bradley J. Kulthorp. We belong to the same clubs and we have dined in one another's homes. In fact, he lives a block from me."

The fellow's Adam's apple bobbed and some of the flush filtered out of his cheeks.

Teddy continued. "I would hate to describe to Mr. Kulthorp the scene I witnessed today, where one of his salesmen threatened, bullied, and robbed a young woman and several orphans. He's a family man, you know. I don't think he'd care for it."

"Of all the cheek! This brat tried to rob *me*, not the other way around."

Teddy gestured to the dustpan Olympia still held. "Destroying someone's wares and refusing to pay for damages

certainly qualifies as theft in my book. Wouldn't you say so, Ernie?"

The stationmaster had taken up a position by Teddy's shoulder. "Ayup, I'd say so, for sure. In fact, maybe we should get Officer Richards. He can sort things out for us right quick. Of course, his investigation may take awhile, and you'll need to stay put until a judge can hear the case." He scratched his head. "I'd say that'd be after the New Year."

"I need to see to my route." The belligerence had drained from the salesman's tone and he sounded only plaintive now.

Ernie and Teddy looked at one another, then Teddy shrugged. "I suppose there's one way we could settle matters without having to take things further."

"What?"

"You let go of the boy and offer him and Miss Paris here an apology. Then you pay for the damages and be on your way."

"That's outrageous."

Teddy stepped up until he was no more than six inches from the other man's face. "What is outrageous is the way you bully people who cannot defend themselves. You accept the terms now, or I will give you the beating you requested earlier."

"That would be assault."

"No, that would be coming to the defense of my young friend here." Teddy squeezed the man's wrist until he whimpered and released Jonathan.

The fellow pulled his wallet from his waistcoat. He looked at Olympia. "How much for damages?"

"Ten dollars."

The man grumbled but pulled two five-dollar bills from

his wallet. Instead of handing them to her, however, he flung them to the ground.

"That wasn't very polite. I suggest you pick it up."

"No. No, it's okay. I've got it." Olympia wanted the whole horrible scene over. She stooped and picked up the money. "Thank you. I know you don't like the gingerbread, but maybe you'd like a teacake to see you on your way?"

She offered the plate to the man, and after a grudging moment, he accepted one. Having been allowed to save face, he went on his way.

The rest of the crowd woke as if they had been the cast of *Sleeping Beauty* after the spell had been broken, and went about their business.

Olympia moved to embrace Jonathan. "Are you all right?"

He jerked away from her. "I hate you." Then he sprinted away from the station.

❧

Teddy's heart clenched. Olympia looked as if someone had punched her in the stomach. He touched her arm. "Let me go after him. I know how he feels all too well."

She nodded without looking at him and turned to her other charges, who were staring, unmoving and maybe even unblinking. "Come along, children. Let's pack these things up and head home."

Once Teddy had ensured that Olympia had gone without being molested again by the salesman, he trotted after Jonathan. He wasn't too worried about where he might have run off to. The kid was so much like himself that it wasn't hard to guess.

He branched away from the road and headed up the

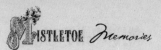

mountain. The exercise felt good. After that confrontation, he needed to work off some steam. The strength of his reaction had surprised him. All the old rage and impotence of childhood injustices had swamped him. Holding back his desire to pummel the man had made his shoulders and neck ache with tension.

Yeah, he knew how Jonathan felt all too well.

At the edge of the Graff property line an enormous old pine spread its boughs. Teddy smiled at the sight and a wave of nostalgia clogged his throat. His childhood here with Mrs. Graff, Olympia, and the others hadn't been so very dreadful. It had really been just a few in the village, like Karl, whose ignorance and cruelty had made him want to leave.

He had allowed them to drive him away.

This was a new thought, and he paused to catch his breath and revolve it in his mind. Was it true? Would he have stayed on the mountain?

No, not permanently.

He knew himself to be too ambitious. He would have struck out for New York eventually. But things could have been different. He could have left with Mrs. Graff's blessing and come back to visit her and Olympia. He wouldn't have been alone.

Teddy came to the tree and leaned his head back to see the top. It shivered ever so slightly. Jonathan was definitely here. He dropped to his hands and knees and crawled beneath the spreading branches and immediately found the magic that had embraced him as a child. The sense of finding a hidden place.

The tree's secret was that its mantle of pine needles didn't extend to its heart. The inner branches were denuded and the arching boughs created a circular space of some ten to twelve feet at the base, with the trunk in the middle. Fallen pine needles cushioned the ground and along with this, there was evidence of habitation.

Teddy smiled again and stood. This had been—was still—a marvelous fort.

He had scavenged packing crates and scraps of lumber from all over the village and used them to make ladders and ramps and walls until the tree had become a castle. Reaching to touch a piece of roughly sawn wood, he raised his head to look up.

A small face poked out of its hiding place and demanded, "What do you want?"

"I thought we might talk."

"Did Olympia tell you about this place?"

Teddy shook his head. "Are you kidding? I made this place. She found out about it from me."

"You did?" The question was less challenging now.

"Yep, and I can prove it. Did you ever find my safe?"

"Safe?"

"To keep valuables in."

Jonathan shook his head.

"Come down to the second platform. Look around the trunk to your right. Right about eye height press in, and you should feel the bark give some. You'll see the edges then and you can work the cover free if you get a thumbnail under it."

The boy's face disappeared and Teddy could hear his passage down the tree. A moment later there was an exclamation, a flurry of rustling, and then the boy was

shinning to the ground. He plopped down on the carpet of needles and Teddy joined him. Jonathan had plucked his shirttails out and wrapped his loot in them. When he let go, the treasures appeared in his lap as if by magic. A tiny compass, two pencil stubs, a tightly wound ball of string that smelled slightly mildewed, an arrowhead, and best of all, a brass spyglass.

"This was all yours?"

Teddy grinned in response. "Yours now."

Despite the longing in his eyes, the boy shook his head. "I don't want your charity."

"It's not charity; it's the laws of property ownership. I abandoned this fort and all it contained, and you found it and claimed it."

"Why did you leave?"

Heedless of the potential for sap on his suit, Teddy leaned back against the trunk like he would have as a boy. "I left because of fellows like that man at the train station today."

"It's not fair."

"You're right. It's not fair."

Jonathan barreled on. "And Olympia takes everyone else's side. She doesn't understand. I think she thinks everybody else is better than us, too. Wait. What did you say?"

"I said you're right: it's not fair." Teddy met the boy's eyes. "It's not fair that there are people who are so miserable that they let it spill out and splash all over people who they think aren't in a position to fight back."

Jonathan simply stared.

"That's a lot of misery inside a person. But see, the way they act says a lot more about them than it does about you. So now you get to make a decision."

"What?"

"You can choose to prove them wrong or not. No one has the right to define who you are but you and God. He says that you are His son. And you—well, you define yourself for people every day, by the actions you take, the words you say, and the choices you make."

Jonathan stared at his lap, a thoughtful frown on his face as his fingers traced the spyglass.

"As for Miss Olympia. She's trying to teach you to pick your battles. Some things are worth fighting for, but others. . ." Teddy shrugged. "I do know that she loves you a great deal and was hurt by what you said."

"She's gonna fight you for our house, I think."

Teddy refused to rise to the bait.

Jonathan swallowed. "I was just mad at that guy when I said that to her."

Teddy didn't say anything right away. "It's your choice, I suppose. You can treat people like that fellow at the train station if you think you'll feel better for it."

Jonathan started at that, his lips parting. "I'm not like that man!"

"No?" Teddy stood and brushed the back of his pants off. "I'm starting to get hungry. Coming?"

Frowning more deeply, Jonathan stood, too, and they crawled out from under the tree together.

They took their time walking back to the house. They'd come within sight of the kitchen lights when Teddy asked a question that had been nagging at him. "Jonathan, are you related to Miss Olympia?"

"Nah, not really."

"How is it you have the same last name?"

Jonathan looked up at him as if he were surprised. "I came to Graff House like she did. Somebody left me on the porch. We're the only two that ever didn't have last names. But see, when I started school I needed to have one, so she said I could share hers if I wanted. It was a nice thing for her to do." A thoughtful look came onto his face. "I wouldn't ever want a different name."

Jonathan picked up speed. He clattered up the back steps and burst into the kitchen. Olympia turned from the stove, and he ran to her, flinging his arms around her in a fierce embrace.

"I'm sorry."

She hugged him back and wiped tears from his cheeks with her thumb. "It's all right. I love you. I was worried about you. Are you okay?"

He nodded. "I love you, too."

"Good, then go wash up. We're about to have supper."

Teddy hung back, knowing he wasn't truly welcome.

Forgiven, and apparently feeling much more lighthearted, Jonathan ran off, shouting that he had something to show the other boys.

Olympia wiped what looked like already clean and dry hands on her apron. "Thank you for talking to him. And for intervening today. I don't know what might have happened if you hadn't."

"It was my pleasure, truly. He reminds me of myself."

She grinned at him. "More than you know. But then, he's grown up on stories about you."

"Me?"

"Of course. You figure prominently in most of my best childhood memories."

The statement cut like a flaying knife. Teddy swallowed hard. "I was wondering if you would come to lunch with me tomorrow to talk. I would like the opportunity to explain."

He could see reluctance warring with the sense that she owed him for his intervention, but she finally made a decision. "You can pick me up at noon."

He nodded and put his hat back on as he let himself out. "I'll see you then." But for the life of him, he didn't know quite what he would say when he did.

CHAPTER 5

Teddy appeared promptly at noon the next day, and having been unable to think of a sufficiently dire excuse, Olympia was dressed and ready. He had a cart and horse along, and she looked at him askance.

He scratched the back of his neck. "I had hoped that you would be willing to let me show you something."

She allowed him to hand her up into the cart. "What?"

"It's in Morristown. I thought there might be a better selection of restaurants there as well."

"Teddy, I don't know. I left Grace in charge of the children."

"I promise it won't take long. We can make the train if we hurry and be back before the children hardly realize you were gone."

Reminding herself of what he had done for Luke and Jonathan, she sighed. "Very well, but we cannot miss the afternoon train."

He flashed her a relieved grin. "You know how trustworthy I am."

"That's what worries me."

He shot her a hurt look and guilt blunted the edges of her righteous indignation. She cast about for a neutral topic of conversation. "I'd like to hear all about your adventures in New York and how you came to be a highfalutin business man."

"It's fairly dull, really."

"I don't see how it can be. You're like one of Alger's rags-to-riches stories."

"Nah. No unknown relative left me a big inheritance, and a rich widow didn't fall in love with me. I just worked hard and paid attention."

"But what do you do, precisely?"

"I started out as a clerk in an investment bank. Luckily, Mrs. Graff made sure we had good educations, so I had a foot up on Alger's hard-luck cases."

"I wish she could hear you say that. She feared she had driven you away by being too hard on you."

He looked at her. "What? No. I didn't leave because of her." He turned his focus to the reins, giving them a snap. Silence stretched between them. They passed out of the village before he cleared his throat and spoke again. "I loved Mrs. Graff. I thought she was done with me."

"Oh, Teddy, that's not true. She loved you dearly. I think you were always her favorite. She used to talk of you as if you were Peter Pan, or at the very least, one of the lost boys."

"If I was Peter, then you must have been Wendy."

Olympia laughed. "Well, I can tell stories. And darn socks. And even though I never had one, or—or maybe because I never had one, I know how important a mother is. But I'm surprised you know of the play or the stories, since you don't have children."

"I saw it in the city. I was trying to curry favor with my boss at the time and took his two boys to see it. I think I was more taken with the story than they were."

"I know what you mean. Adults value childhood more

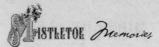

since it is no longer in our grasp. I took Mrs. Graff into New York for some doctors' visits, and we went to see it as a special treat. It captured her imagination completely."

"You were there? In New York? We might have been sitting within a hundred feet of one another and never known it."

"Life is strange." Olympia stared out over the valley as they rounded a curve in the road. "Do you think things might have been different if we had met then? Could we have changed all this?" She waved at the space between them as if it were a great chasm and not just a few inches of air.

Teddy didn't answer but smacked the reins again. The horses dutifully picked up speed, and in a scant few minutes they were pulling into the German Valley train station. The train was already chugging into the station, and after a few moment's mad scramble to secure the horses and buy tickets, Olympia found herself on the train and sitting beside Teddy. At least she had the window seat. She stared resolutely at the familiar scenery. It was his turn to offer a conversational gambit.

"You asked what I do." The words were quick, as if Teddy had seized on them and flung them out in desperation.

Olympia turned to him. "Yes." He looked flustered and boyishly uncertain, and she found herself having a hard time holding onto her hauteur.

"Well, I started as a clerk, then I became an investment officer. I saved up and started investing my own money, too, and what with one thing and another, I got pretty lucky. Now I invest in or buy businesses outright and help make a go of them."

The world of finance had only the vaguest outline in Olympia's mind. "Any particular sort of business? Like shops and things, or factories?"

He shrugged. "I could buy shops, but mostly I buy into companies that need investors to provide capital."

"Oh." Olympia did not try to hide her lack of comprehension.

"I like to find companies who are developing new technologies. Smart inventors aren't always very smart businessmen. So I team up with them. I give them money to develop their invention. They create it, and together we figure out a way to get it to people."

"What kind of inventions?"

"I'm working with one company now that has developed several improvements to Edison's moving picture camera, and another that has developed a better projection system."

"I saw one of his pictures at the county fair. It was amazing."

"I think there are going to be great developments in films over the next few years. People love them, and they are going to get better and longer. Soon we might even be able to hear what the people say."

"But if the camera has already been invented, what else is there to do?"

He grinned. "Well that's the question, isn't it? There are always ways of making something better. And somebody has to make new films for people to see. They will die out if the novelty wears off. And there's more. What about a place for people to go and see films, like the theater? Instead of having actors performing in person, you have a screen for the movie

to be shown on."

"You think people would pay for that?"

"Why not? You did when you went to the fair, didn't you?"

"Yes, I suppose I did."

The trip into Morristown went far more quickly than Olympia had anticipated. Somehow they managed to fall into conversation as if they had been apart a week, not years.

Teddy handed her down to the station platform and offered his arm. "Do you mind if we walk to the restaurant? It's not far."

Olympia agreed readily and hoped he couldn't hear her stomach growling. She hadn't had any breakfast. There hadn't been any left after the children had eaten.

They approached a fashionably ostentatious restaurant, complete with a red carpet in front and potted palm sentinels flanking the door. Her footsteps slowed and she smoothed her hand over her neat gray walking suit. It had looked smart when she had put it on in Schooley's Mountain that morning. Now it seemed dowdy and cheap.

"Teddy, I'm not sure I'm dress—"

He looked up. "You look beautiful, and you'd bring this place a dash of class, but we're not headed here. I'm taking you someplace where the food is better and the staff is friendlier."

They rounded the corner. Halfway down the block, Teddy stopped and opened a door with a flourish. The sign painted on the window read PASQUALE's. The warmth of the place was like an embrace after the cold of the December afternoon. Olympia closed her eyes and inhaled deeply of the fragrance-laden air and tried to name the different aromas. Garlic, and basil, and maybe oregano. She opened her eyes. All the tables that had been squeezed into the small dining room were full of diners chattering happily over their meals.

"Good, huh?" Teddy helped her off with her coat.

A short, stout man with darkly furred forearms showing below rolled-up shirtsleeves stepped from the back room. He threw up his arms at the sight of them. "Teddy, eh! You come for a visit!"

Teddy approached the fellow. "Salvatore, my friend, it has been too long. Do you think Sophia will feed us?"

"Of course, of course. Sit. Sit." He practically pushed a pair of studious-looking young men out the door to free a table for them. "I've never known you to bring in a young lady before."

Teddy slapped the fellow on the back. "Salvatore, this is Miss Olympia Paris. She and I grew up together. Olympia, this is Salvatore Landi. He operates the best restaurant in New Jersey."

Olympia smiled and extended her hand. "It's a pleasure to meet you."

Salvatore put a hand next to his mouth as if he were going to whisper, but his comment could be heard throughout the room. "You be good to Teddy here, okay? He's a good boy, but he needs a woman to take care of him."

Her cheeks flamed. "I—"

Teddy cut in. "Is Sophia making her famous spaghetti?"

"Does the day end in *Y*? Of course, she makes spaghetti. I'll bring two. And some bread."

He bustled away.

Olympia concentrated on removing her gloves.

"I worked here for a month on my way into New York

and earned enough to pay for a room for a week and a new suit."

"You must have made quite the impression."

"I've been back a few times since then to visit."

The pain in Olympia's heart was knife sharp and cold as ice.

Teddy must have noticed he'd said something wrong. He reached across the table and touched her hand. "I couldn't come up the mountain. I just couldn't. I wasn't ready."

She pulled away. His touch melted the ice edge of pain, but a dull ache remained. Luckily Salvatore returned, sparing her the need to respond.

He carried with him a basket full of steaming rolls. "Sophia's going to come out and see you when she can get free, but she can't take her eyes off the pasta at the moment."

Teddy replaced his frown with a bright smile. "I can't wait."

Salvatore looked from one to the other of them, an eyebrow going up. Then he moved away to take care of other customers.

"I'm sorry, Olympia—"

She waved a hand. "It doesn't matter now, anyway. I'm glad you were able to find friends who meant something to you." She tried on a bright smile of her own, but it didn't seem to fit right, too tight at the edges. "I understood that you wanted to talk to me today. I assume it is about the house?"

"I had hoped to save it for a little later. Just in case you get mad at me, I want you to have had a good lunch first."

She thawed in spite of herself. "Good grief, Teddy, you'd try the patience of a saint."

"I did try the patience of a saint." He pushed the basket

of rolls toward her.

Olympia selected one and took a ladylike nibble. Buttery and garlicky, it all but melted in her mouth. "Mmm."

"Sophia is an amazing cook." Teddy popped an entire roll in his mouth.

"What did you order for us?"

It took him a moment to answer, and she smiled in spite of herself as he chewed furiously then swallowed. "Spaghetti. It's an Italian dish. I guarantee you will like it."

"Or what?"

"Or I'll eat it for you."

"That doesn't sound like much of a bargain."

"I'll put it this way. I've tried to invest in this place so they could expand. They wouldn't let me, but I still come to eat. It's that good."

Salvatore appeared again bearing two huge, steaming bowls. Behind him came a short, energetic woman with her hair tied up in a kerchief. She kissed Teddy's cheeks and told him it had been too long and ordered him to eat before sweeping back to the kitchen.

Olympia stared into her bowl. It looked sort of like a stew, but there was something underneath. She picked up her fork and poked at the mass.

"It's pasta. It's like dumplings, but long and thin. The sauce is made of tomatoes and sausage and spices." He showed her how it was to be eaten, and she tried twirling the long strands around her fork.

It took her two tries and the bite she wound up with was huge, but she got it to her mouth without dropping anything. "Mmm."

Teddy waggled his eyebrows and shoveled another bite in his mouth. "Told you."

It took almost no time for them to clean their plates. At last, sated, Olympia pushed back from the table. "The children would love this. Maybe after I've paid off the taxes I will bring them here to celebrate."

Teddy leaned forward over clasped hands. "Can I ask you a question? How did you get in this bind? I can't believe Mrs. Graff left you the house with nothing to keep it up on. She knew what it took."

"She left me everything she had, but she was sick a long time before she passed. We tried everything. She had been in such good health until then. Nothing worked, and well, there wasn't much left when all was said and done. Then the roof needed to be replaced. And over the past five years the taxes have more than doubled. Somehow we've been stringing along until now though." She met his gaze straight on.

❧

Teddy refused to be drawn into an argument. Or to respond to the sense that he needed to defend himself. He hadn't even known Mrs. Graff had been ill. If he had, of course, he would have helped. "If you're done, we should probably go. We don't want to miss the train back to German Valley. And I want to show you something first."

Teddy took leave of the warm hospitality Salvatore always offered. Outside, the December wind felt twice as cold as he remembered. Luckily, they didn't have far to go. A couple of blocks later, he drew Olympia to a halt in front of a sturdy brick building with a short, wrought-iron fence in front and a concrete arch over a wooden door. Carved into the concrete were the austere words County Orphan Asylum.

"What is this?" Olympia hesitated.

"This is where the children would be brought. I've been assured that it is a first-rate facility. Come on, you'll see."

Deep creases scored her brow, but she followed him up the path and stood by his side as he clanked the heavy knocker against the solid door. A scrawny lad in a uniform of brown serge jacket and pants, hair cropped close to his scalp, answered the door.

"May I help you?"

Teddy smiled and doffed his hat. "We're here to see Mrs. Finch."

"Yes sir. Come in, please." The boy smiled and stepped aside.

The house was exceptionally quiet. The boy led them across the foyer and up a flight of stairs. The place seemed clean. The brass work on the gas lamps glowed with polish. There didn't seem to be cobwebs or dust lurking in the corners. There was a faintly institutional smell, however.

"Are there many children here?" Olympia asked, breaking the silence.

"There are twenty-six of us, ma'am. I'm Brian." The boy continued on, almost breathlessly. "I'm almost fourteen, and I'm really strong. I can work hard. I'm smart, too. I know my sums. I can even do some multiplication. I can read and write, too. If you were looking for a boy my age, I think I could make you real happy. I'd sure try."

Olympia's reproachful glare at Teddy made it clear that she blamed him for this mix-up. For everything in fact.

For the boy, she had only a Madonna's gentleness. "Brian,

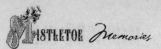

we're not here to adopt someone. If I were, I can promise I'd pick you right off. I can't imagine a smarter, better boy anywhere."

Teddy refrained from rolling his eyes. She'd pick them all and take them all home with her to that rundown old house, where she couldn't afford to care for them. It was lucky he'd come back when he had. Even if she wouldn't acknowledge it, the best thing for everyone would be if she were made to let go of the past and embrace her own future. To think of herself for once.

The boy smiled ruefully. "Can't hurt to try. I always hope that someone will want me one day. Even though nobody ever has."

Olympia put her arm around him like they'd known one another for years. "I'm an orphan, too."

"Really?"

She nodded solemnly. "I never knew my parents. Do you remember yours?"

"Oh yeah." A dreamy look came into his eyes. "My mom was the best cook. She could make soup out of a rock. And my dad taught me how to whittle and fish. They was killed by the cholera."

"I always wondered if it was harder to have parents and lose them, or never to have known them at all."

"I figure both ways are hard." The boy came to a halt in front of a closed door. "This is Mrs. Finch's office." He rapped at the door.

"Enter."

The boy moved to push the door open.

Olympia captured his hands in hers. "You are worthy

of love, Brian. I can tell just from what you said that your parents loved you. And if they loved you that much, so will another family."

"You think so, you think someone might want to adopt me some day?"

"I really do."

"Enter!" The voice from the other side of the door had grown impatient.

"Thanks, ma'am." The lad opened the door and announced the visitors.

Mrs. Finch looked a bit like her namesake. Dark, wide-spaced eyes took their measure dispassionately. Her gray shirtwaist drooped in a fashionable pigeon-chested pout. Her movements were quick but somewhat jerky, increasing her resemblance to a bird even further. "Thank you, Ryan. Run along to your chores."

Teddy would not have thought it was possible for Olympia to stand any taller than when they entered, but he would have been wrong. "His name is Brian."

"Excuse me?" Mrs. Finch looked like she had forgotten the topic of conversation.

"You called that young man Ryan. His name is Brian."

"Yes." Mrs. Finch made a shooing gesture at the boy, who had paused in the doorway. "Run along, Brian."

Teddy stepped forward. "Mrs. Finch, I'm Theodore Carstairs. I believe you were expecting us."

"Ah, Mr. Carstairs. I understand you are willing to donate generously to our home here."

"I am willing to make a donation, but there are also six children I am aware of who need your services."

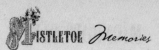

He glanced at Olympia, about to introduce her, but she stood rigidly, her mouth in a thin, tight line. He thought better of his plan.

"We were hoping you could show us your facilities. I understand they are excellent."

Mrs. Finch nodded with self-congratulatory pride. "We have received several commendations from the state auditors."

The place was clean and well-cared for, if austere. The children were all in uniforms of brown serge and the boys had identical short haircuts, while the girl wore two plaits down their backs. But there was something wrong. Teddy couldn't quite put his finger on it until they were nearly done with the tour. He straightened from looking into a big pot of soup that Mrs. Finch insisted he examine to see the chicken and vegetables it contained.

"Very fine, um, soup." He replaced the lid. "It's very quiet here," he observed.

"Yes, we are quite insistent on strict discipline." Mrs. Finch smiled with pride at her regime. "We insist that the children's chores and lessons be done with no dilly-dallying and no shirking."

"Is this a place for children or a monastery?" Olympia's tone was caustic, and Teddy winced, though he agreed with her.

Mrs. Finch seemed oblivious, however. It might not have occurred to her that anyone could have a different perspective. "Of course there are times when the children are allowed to play in the afternoons, but we find that allowing them too much free time is counterproductive."

"Does anyone ever break out?" Now Olympia's tone dripped sweetness.

Luckily, Mrs. Finch had no imagination. "Oh, no. We lock the doors very securely at night, and of course the windows are barred."

Teddy scrambled for something to say before Olympia could make her contempt plainer. "Are the children ever taken anywhere?"

"We go to church on Sundays, of course." They had come at last back to Mrs. Finch's office door. "I hope we can count on that donation?"

"I belie—"

Olympia cut him off. "How does one become a board member of this fine institution?"

Mrs. Finch glanced to Teddy and back to Olympia. "A board member?"

"Yes." She smiled brightly. "Surely you have an operating board that exercises oversight? I believe I would enjoy a position on such a board."

CHAPTER 6

The Morristown train station seemed a good deal stuffier than it had earlier in the day. Olympia had not spoken two words to Teddy since they left the orphanage. Now, as the train huffed into the station, she rounded on him. "Why did you choose our house, Teddy?"

"I told you." Teddy blew on his hands. "When I came to town, all I heard was people's hard-luck stories. I talked to Mr. Hunt and Mr. Skinner, and they welcomed the idea of another hotel. They say there are thirty men and thirty women who could use the work. It's a small village, Olympia. That's a lot of people. The folks on the mountain know all about running hotels, so it will be easy."

"Not that. I understand your plan, Teddy. I want to know why you chose our house as the site of your new hotel. Why not simply refurbish Heath House?"

He should have known she wouldn't be put off. "I truly didn't know you lived there still."

"Why, Teddy?" She used a schoolmarm's stern voice.

He sighed and moved out of the way of a disembarking passenger. "I don't know. There's the spring on the Graff property and I wanted a new hotel, not just to make over Heath House. With all new facilities and the latest amenities, we can attract the cream of society from New York and Philadelphia and Boston. I was thinking we could have a roller skating rink and a couple of bowling lanes." He had a new thought. "We could even have a cinema where the newest films could be shown for our guests."

"I don't think this is about what is good for the village. I think this is you showing everyone they were wrong about you being trouble."

He had had just about enough. "I don't deny that I want to show up people like Karl Krause. He treated us like dirt, and I'd love to make him eat a mouthful or two of dirt in return."

"Then you've become just like them. Wanting to show the world how much better you are than they. And you don't care who you hurt in the process, because you're thinking of nothing but your twisted vanity. You want to turn the very place they despised and mocked into a place they can't do without. So you didn't want to know who lived there. You chose to remain ignorant when a short walk or a few questions would have told you everything about the children and me."

Teddy forced his hands open from the fists they had curled into. "What's done is done. I am willing to buy the property from you outright. I'll give you ten thousand dollars for the house and land and I will pay the back taxes. You can decide whether you want to stay shackled to those orphans or not."

Olympia's anger burned white hot in her eyes for a minute then died down into what could only be described as a pitying smile. "That's what you don't understand, Teddy. You never have. I don't operate an orphanage. I have a family."

She climbed up into the train without waiting for him and took a seat, staring stonily out the window.

The trip to Morristown had been another terrible idea. Teddy sat across from a silent Olympia and let his head fall back against the seat. What more did she want from him? He couldn't make a fairer offer. He had hoped the trip would show her she had no reason for concern if the children were to go to the orphanage. But it seemed she would insist on stubbornly finding fault.

Although. . .

He couldn't imagine Jonathan thriving under the conditions there. Nor Luke, nor Alice, nor any of Olympia's other rascals. Had he still been young, he wouldn't have taken to Mrs. Finch's humorless discipline, either. He'd have schemed a way out at the first opportunity.

Still, it wasn't as if the children were mistreated, and structure was good for young minds. The image of young Brian's narrow face in his mind's eye brought a stop to his self-justifying litany. No. He had to admit it. The children would be better off with Olympia. Just like he had been better off with Mrs. Graff. She had treated him like a son, not a charge. When he heard the word mother, her face came to his mind. Warmth filtered down through his chest. She had loved him. He had no doubt about it. He'd had a family all along. He'd just let others' definition of family keep him from appreciating what he had.

He'd straightened up, ready to share his insight with Olympia, when skirts rustled past him and a plump figure trailing feathers took the seat next to her. Heidi Krause smiled broadly at him.

Teddy spat out the feather that had found its way into his mouth. "Miss Krause."

Olympia glanced at her new companion. "Hello, Heidi."

"It's so nice to have company on this trip. I find it so boring, but no one from the mountain ever seems to bother coming to town, and it's really the only place to find any halfway decent shops. Of course, I'd much rather go into New York, but Karl doesn't like to have me go so far on my own. But this time I won't just have to look at the same old scenery. I'll have friends to chat with."

Olympia surreptitiously rubbed her temple. But she managed to dredge up a smile. "What did you come to town to shop for?"

"Oh…" Heidi loved nothing more than an opportunity to talk about herself. "Karl thought we could do with some new furnishings for when we buy your house, Olympia."

Teddy's jaw went slack. "What?"

Heidi beamed. "Oh, you know Karl. Ever since we talked to you, he's been determined to outbid you for that old pile. I don't know why, but he's always admired it."

This could not be happening.

Olympia looked from one to the other of them. Her face had gone pale and her fingers clutched at the fabric of her skirt. Teddy stared at her, willing her to understand. He had never seriously thought Karl would make good on his threat to bid on the house. He had a house, for heaven's sake. A perfectly good house. Though not as fine or as large. Maybe Karl hadn't felt superior all those years, maybe he'd been envious? Teddy's view of the past shifted and crystallized. He'd been a fool, from the time he left the mountain, up to today.

But with God's help he was done being a fool. He was going to find a way to make things right, for everyone.

Olympia stared absently at the passing scenery. No matter how she had scrimped and saved and scrounged, she was still short of her goal by a hundred dollars, and it was Friday. The last Friday before Christmas on Sunday.

The last day to pay her taxes.

The thought of Karl Krause getting her house made her nauseated. His contemptuous drive to modernize everything would gut the house of everything that made it special. He would rip out its heart in order to turn it into a showpiece.

God, I don't know why You've let this happen. Help us trust You as we've always done. You haven't let us down; You've given us a new beginning. Help me to figure out what it is.

She blinked back useless tears as Heidi continued to prattle on about damask curtains and a new divan that was the latest in elegant furnishings. The train pulled into the German Valley station with Heidi still talking.

The woman stood and gave Olympia a hug. "I'm so happy you're not too upset about the house. I was afraid you would be, but Karl said no, and I see now he was right. I do think it will be better for you not to have to deal with all those children. You could even go to college. You used to want to do that, didn't you? Well, now you're finally free, and you can do whatever you like."

A part of Olympia thrilled at the idea of not being responsible for anyone but herself, but she knew that without the children her life would be incomplete. A little zing of realization, like a shaft of light, shot through her distress. *As long as the children and I are together, everything else can be managed.*

She laughed, and Heidi chuckled, too, delighted to have been witty enough to have made a joke.

It was true. While she loved the home she'd grown up in and her memories there, it wasn't the house that was important—it was the people who lived there. She felt as if she'd stepped from the dark of midnight into the clear light of morning. The doubt and fear had vanished, and she knew what was most important to her.

She and the children could find something smaller and more manageable. Not on the mountain perhaps, but down in German Valley. If she sold the house to Teddy, there would be money left over that she could put into savings for emergencies.

She sighed. Teddy would probably hire her to work at his new hotel if she asked him. He might make her eat humble pie, but she would eat worse if it meant keeping the children together.

She would take Teddy up on his offer to buy the house. She'd tell him as soon as they were alone. Only, when she had finally extricated herself from Heidi's good wishes, Teddy was nowhere to be seen.

Charles Oxley, who drove the touring coach up the mountain for the Dorincourt, hailed her. "Miss Olympia, Teddy asked me to take you on up the mountain if you've a mind to go."

She moved toward him. "Where did he go? He was here a moment ago."

"Dunno. He was in a tearing hurry to get back into town. Ran off to ask Ernie if he could borrow that crazy automobile of his. I guess he must've forgot something or other." He

hopped out to hand Olympia up into the carriage. "It must've been important."

"Yes." Olympia gazed back down the track in the way they'd just come. "It must have been."

CHAPTER 7

Olympia called at the Hotel Dorincourt later on Friday evening, but she was informed Teddy hadn't returned. Mr. Harmon shook his head and flapped at her to go away. "I don't know when he'll be back."

The next morning she was back. And then again in the afternoon. One of the housemaids, Lucy, confided in her that Mr. Carstairs hadn't come in at all the previous evening. But he'd paid in advance for his stay, and his luggage was still in his room, so Mr. Harmon wasn't put out.

Olympia used hotel stationery to leave Teddy a note. She had no idea where he had gone or why. Hopefully, he would come see her as soon as he could. And when he did, she would apologize for judging him so harshly. It hadn't been fair to jump to assumptions about his motives.

She stepped out onto the hotel's broad veranda. It had started to snow while she was inside. Fat white flakes floated down lazily and bunched together like landlocked clouds. She had been blessed to grow up on Schooley's Mountain. The mountain was beautiful, just like a picture postcard of Christmas. She pulled on her mittens and stepped off the porch, raising her face so the snow could kiss it.

She hoped Teddy's offer was still good, but it might be too late. She didn't know if Mr. Keckley would allow a last-minute payment on Monday morning or if he would insist

the county already owned it and she no longer had any right to sell it.

Whether Karl or Teddy bought the house, she hoped she could get them to allow her and the children to stay until the New Year. Then she could rent a small place for them all. She couldn't immediately think of anything that might work on the Mountain or down in German Valley, but she would ask around.

The money she had scrounged to pay the taxes would go toward rent. Even if the sale couldn't be completed, she had the funds they would need to set up housekeeping in a new home.

She picked up her pace. All the village children would be waiting for her at the church to practice the Christmas pageant. It was the same pageant they put on every year, so the children had a good idea what they were expected to do, but Olympia had found through the years that a few hours of practice made for smoother performances.

Tomorrow would be Christmas. It was hard to believe. She had been baking gingerbread and waiting tables and writing so furiously in the past weeks that the days had blurred together.

She would have to confess to the children that she hadn't been able to make the money they needed. Staying together was going to be their gift this year. It was all she could offer them. She hoped it would be enough.

꙰

Christmas morning arrived with a fresh wave of snow. Olympia watched from the window seat as the children bounded down the stairs and stopped at the bottom, eyes drinking in the tree. At the base, arranged carefully in neat packages tied with ribbon, sat two small gifts for each of them.

They ran to the tree and dropped to their knees, scrambling to find their presents. Olympia had knitted them each a new pair of mittens and tucked a candy stick inside. The second package contained a story she had written and illustrated especially for the recipient.

Olympia chewed her lip and watched them like they were a firing squad. If they didn't like the gifts...

Alice's tearing fingers revealed her mittens and her little shoulders slumped.

"I'm sorry, kids. I couldn't buy—"

Grace whirled and ran to her. "The books are beautiful, Olympia, and so are the mittens. More than we expected. We know how hard you've been trying to save."

It was time to confess. "I had hoped that we could stay in this house, but I wasn't able to raise enough money." Her throat hurt. "But even though we won't have the same house, we'll be together." She faltered, her voice breaking. "I'm sorry. I'm so sorry."

The children piled close.

"It's okay, Olympia." Jonathan put his head on her shoulder. "It's okay. We'll find another place to live."

"Yeah." Luke was still awkward with his cast. But he put his good arm around her waist and his head on her shoulder. "We'll be okay if we're together."

"That's right, we will."

The twins buried their faces in her shirtwaist and Alice clutched her skirts, while Grace retained her hold on Olympia's hand.

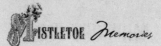

Olympia drew them all closer still, planting kisses on the tops of heads and upturned cheeks. "I love you all so much."

"We love you, too." It was a sweet chorus, and they clung together for a moment, knowing they could face the whole world as long as they were together.

Then the boys started jostling one another, and Olympia extricated herself from the scrum.

Grace pulled a small bundle from her pocket and extended it to Olympia. "This is from all of us."

Olympia accepted the little box tenderly. Careful removal of the wrapping revealed a handsome new pen. She gasped. "It's beautiful. How did you ever—?"

"We didn't steal it or nothing," Jonathan said.

"No, I didn't think you had." Olympia beamed at the scamp.

"We all found odd jobs around town to earn money and chipped in for it." Grace was proud of the accomplishment. "I picked it out. I thought you could use it to do your writing."

"Thank you. All of you. This is the best surprise I've ever gotten."

Jonathan led them all in a cheer.

"Now who's hungry?" She hurried to the kitchen and they trailed after her like baby ducklings. From the oven she pulled a big batch of cinnamon rolls, sending the warm, sweet scent swirling around the room. Whooping with delight, the children took their seats.

Olympia slathered the rolls with a sweet glaze then dished them up. The children laughed and talked, with no hint that they were disappointed over their lack of presents. She watched, misty-eyed, until they had finished and almost licked the pan clean. Watching them was sweet enough for her. The best present she could have asked for.

At last she forced herself to stand. "It's time to get ready for church."

"If I get ready quick, can I go ahead?" asked Jonathan.

On another day she might have questioned him, but he looked so angelic, and she couldn't think of any particular mischief he could get into on the way to church. "You'll go straight to the church, with no detours?"

He nodded solemnly. "Cross my heart."

"All right, then, you may go ahead of us."

Jonathan bolted upstairs and a few minutes later pounded down them again.

Olympia tied bows and buttoned buttons and straightened hats until everyone finally looked presentable. They found the snow still falling as if it meant to continue forever.

Hands safe from the cold in their new mittens, the boys immediately started a snowball fight, and they all joined in. Matt sent a corker flying at Olympia that knocked her hat clean off.

They shared identical open-mouthed shock and then laughed uproariously. Olympia started singing "Joy to the World" and the children boomed along. Raucous and laughing, they marched to church.

She swung through the doors of the church antechamber and finished her chorus, "And heaven, and heaven, and nature sing!" with a flourish.

Mrs. Strauss and the other ladies helping with the last-minute preparations laughed and applauded, while Olympia took a bow like she was on stage.

The usual mad scramble for costumes and props ensued as the children ran around, forgetting what they were supposed to be doing. Olympia was sewing up a ripped angel's wing, when Mrs. Strauss nudged her. "I think there's mischief afoot."

The room had grown unnaturally quiet. All the children were clustered in a tight knot, whispering furiously. Olympia set aside her wings.

At that moment, Pastor Jeffers entered the room with a broad smile and a "Merry Christmas" on his lips.

The children turned on him. At their fore stood Jonathan. "Pastor, I'm a-noticing you that we're going on strike."

The pastor's smile slipped. He blinked. "You're going on strike?" he glanced at Olympia.

She shrugged and shook her head.

Jonathan remained businesslike. "Yes, all us kids are on strike. We're not doing any old pageant until the auction of our house is cancelled. We don't want to have to move away from our friends. And they don't want us to move neither." *Lord, that boy would succeed marvelously at something one day.* Olympia hoped it wouldn't be crime.

"Well—you see, I don't think. . ." the pastor floundered.

Olympia, who had more experience dealing with Jonathan's particular brand of genius, stepped in. "Jonathan, what is all this?"

"You heard."

"I did, but this isn't the way to go about getting what you want."

"It works for the oppressed workers of the bourg-e-see."

Olympia stepped into the middle of the knot of children.

"I know you aren't happy about the auction. I'm not excited to be leaving either. But I can tell you this. God will take care of us no matter where we end up. We will try to stay close so that you can still see each other. But, and I want you listen to me very closely, even if we do have to go farther away, it doesn't mean that we won't be friends anymore. I will find work near here, maybe at the new hotel."

"But you can't do that. Mr. Carstairs is mean," piped up a childish voice.

Others chimed in.

"Yeah."

"He's the one who's kicking you out."

Olympia shook her head. "Ted—Mr. Carstairs isn't mean. In fact, he's trying to do something wonderful for our village. He's trying to make sure that the people who need jobs can find them here instead of having to move away to a bigger town." She looked over her little audience of upturned faces. "Donald Hecht, hasn't your father been looking for work since Heath House closed?"

The boy nodded and shrugged.

"And you, Robert James?"

Another nod.

"We may not like that our house is being auctioned. But it will be best for the village. If there were another way, Teddy would have found it." Her heart gave a little pang as she said the words. She had so hoped Teddy would come back. Even if it was too late for him to buy the house from her. She had itched to apologize. But it seemed he wasn't coming back. He must have grown tired of her accusations and decided that staying in Schooley's Mountain was more trouble than it

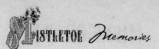

was worth. He had employees who could run such mundane errands as attending an auction or gathering his things from a hotel.

Maybe she could get his forwarding address from Mr. Harmon. Then at least she could send him a letter. She'd probably never see him again. That thought made her chest ache and her eyes sting.

❧

Teddy was bursting to talk to Olympia. One of the good folks in the church informed him that she was in the back with the children, and he made his way there. Visions of his own years as a shepherd or wise man and on one memorable occasion a donkey, attended his progress.

He pushed through the antechamber door but drew up short. The cheerful chaos he recalled was absent. The children seemed upset, the adults bewildered. When it became clear that he was the cause of the upheaval, Teddy backed through the door, but then he paused.

Olympia waded in among the children. She was so beautiful. Her slender figure stood tall and straight as she addressed them. Treating their concerns as gravely as if they had been voiced by adults. Then he realized she was defending him. She didn't hate him.

He felt suddenly like his feet didn't quite reach the ground. He was floating.

There was a chance for him yet.

He withdrew, his intention of attending the pageant discarded. He needed to talk to Mr. Harmon. And he needed to call in a favor. Several favors. He suddenly had a lot to do.

When Olympia got home that afternoon, tired but satisfied that the pageant had been a success, she found an envelope on the floor where it had been slipped under the door.

"What's that?" asked Grace.

"I don't know." Olympia opened the envelope to find seven tickets to the Hotel Dorincourt's annual Christmas party. She hadn't been in several years because tickets were too dear.

Grace gasped and clasped her hands in ecstasy. "The Dorincourt Party is the biggest event in the whole village. It's even bigger than anything they have in German Valley. I've heard it is ever so elegant."

Olympia stared at the tickets. Stay in and soak up the last few hours in their home, or go to a party? A glance at Grace's rapturous expression and the decision was easy. "I guess we're going to a party."

The children cheered. If it was a real party, there would be cake.

Grace's rapture turned to despair. "I don't have anything to wear." She raced upstairs to search through her meager closet. Olympia followed and suggested they go up to the attic. There they found old trunks and boxes bursting with beautiful, if old-fashioned, gowns. They scavenged some ribbons and lace.

In the bottom of a trunk lay a dress of evergreen-colored silk with fine gold net overlay, wrapped carefully in tissue paper. Olympia fingered the fabric and wondered who might have worn it. She pulled the gown out and held it up to the light. No moth holes that she could see.

"Oh, Olympia, it's beautiful. You should wear it tonight."

"Me? Tonight?"

"Yes, that straight silhouette is so fashionable now. And it will look beautiful with your hair."

They carried their bounty downstairs, and after a quick lunch, Olympia set to updating one of Grace's dresses. While Grace pestered her to wear the green dress.

"If I agree to try it on and see if it is suitable," Olympia said, "will you be satisfied?"

"Will you wear it if it is suitable?"

"If it is suitable."

"And let me dress your hair?"

Olympia rolled her eyes. "Why are you so concerned about my appearance?"

Grace shrugged. "Maybe a handsome knight will come and sweep you off your feet tonight."

Olympia doubted it. The only fellow she wanted sweeping her off her feet had fled to New York and she couldn't blame him.

❧

The Dorincourt's windows shone and its halls rang with laughter and warmth.

In the corner of the ballroom, an enormous Christmas tree stood bathed in a golden glow from dozens of candles perched in its boughs. Tinsel sparkled and on the top a star gleamed.

Mrs. Strauss greeted them with a broad grin and open arms. "Merry Christmas! You look stunning."

Olympia laughed. "I think this dress is about a hundred years old. But Grace insisted I wear it. Would you happen to know anything about the tickets that were pushed under our door?"

Rather than the knowing wink Olympia expected, Mrs. Strauss shook her head and sounded surprised. "I don't know a thing. I'm so glad to see you though. You all deserve a night of festivity."

The children scattered to the four corners of the ballroom, having immediately spied friends upon their arrival. Grace huddled with a group of girls her age who giggled and peeked over at a group of boys doing essentially the same thing.

Olympia smiled indulgently. It hadn't been so very long ago that she had been one of those girls. Though truth be told, she'd only ever had eyes for Teddy. None of the other boys had ever held a candle to him. The need to make things right between them burned in her stomach.

Mr. Harmon seated himself at the piano and began playing. Several couples scooted out onto the dance floor. One of the boys shyly approached Grace and she accepted his offer to dance. He took her hand and escorted her onto the dance floor while she glanced back over her shoulder at her friends, panic-stricken.

Alice sighed, and Olympia looked down to see her gazing enviously after Grace. Jonathan reappeared, and with the kindness that was his redeeming grace, held out a hand to the little girl and solemnly escorted her onto the dance floor.

Enormous platters of cookies and cake, thinly sliced beef, cheese, and tiny tea sandwiches studded a long buffet table that was punctuated by an enormous punch bowl. Olympia spotted Mark popping from beneath the table to collect another plateful of goodies and then disappearing again

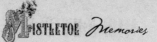

beneath the tablecloth. It was a good bet Matt and Luke were hiding out underneath there as well.

Ernie appeared and asked her to dance. More than happy to give herself over to the joy of the moment, she accepted.

Sometime later, Mr. Harmon heralded a fanfare on his piano. Olympia looked up with the other guests as the ballroom doors were opened. Framed in the door, complete with white beard, long cloak, and sack of toys, stood Father Christmas.

Cries of delight came from the children and they ran closer—stopping short of touching this apparition, however.

"Ho, ho, ho!" The figure moved through the crowd and took a seat in a large wingback chair that had materialized in front of the tree. "I understand that there have been some very good children in this village."

It was Teddy. Olympia's heart gave a little thrill. He'd come back. She would have a chance to make things right between them.

In answer to his statement, small heads bobbed up and down all around the room. He opened his bag and began to draw out gifts for the children. Calling each by name.

They came to him and collected their gifts with shining eyes. Toy airplanes for Matt and Mark, a real artist's watercolor set and paper for Grace. For Jonathan a penknife and for Luke a baseball and glove. And finally, for Alice, the handsomest porcelain doll Olympia had ever seen. She laughed out loud at the reverent wonder in Alice's eyes as she accepted the doll in gentle arms and clasped it to her chest.

She had to thank Teddy from the bottom of her heart. His gesture was so kind. The other children at the party got gifts, too, until the bag looked like a deflated balloon.

Father Christmas reached inside one last time. "It looks like I have just one gift left. Who can it be for?"

The partygoers looked around curiously. It was a good question. All the children had gifts already.

"Miss Paris."

Olympia gasped. "Me?" Blushing furiously, she stood rooted to the spot. The people around her motioned her forward.

"Go on."

"Get your gift."

Olympia walked forward uncertainly. Teddy, that is, Father Christmas, held out a small white envelope. She accepted it and pulled open the flap with trembling fingers. She pulled out the paper inside then stared. Then she stared some more.

"What's in it?" Whispers came from all sides, growing more insistent. "Tell us."

Olympia clutched the paper tighter as if it would try to take wing if she relaxed her grip. "It says. . ." The hubbub settled down. "It's a receipt. The back taxes on our house have been paid in full."

There was a cry of delight and the partygoers surged toward her. Tears streamed down her face. She was engulfed in a tide of well-wishers patting her on the back, embracing her, laughing with her and for her. The children wormed their way through the crowd, jumping up and down, they were so excited. They nearly knocked her over in their rush to hug her and get a look at the magical slip of paper that meant their house had been saved.

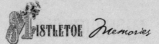

Alice tugged at her skirt until Olympia bent to pick her up. The little girl threw her arms around Olympia's neck. "I knew Father Christmas wouldn't forget us. I knew it."

When at last she was allowed space to breathe, Olympia looked around for Teddy, but Father Christmas had disappeared.

Heidi Krause drew near.

Olympia didn't know what to say. "I know you were excited about getting a new house—"

"Dear me, no. I'm happy for you." Heidi gave her a hug. "You belong in Graff House. I don't know if I would ever have felt like I belonged there. But now that Karl brought up the idea of moving, I can get him to build a new place. I've already got plans." She hooked her arm through Olympia's and drew her along, filling her in on all her interior design schemes.

Olympia looked futilely for Teddy but allowed herself to be pulled along, feeling obscurely that she owed Heidi and doing her best to listen.

But her heart wasn't in it. Her heart was with Teddy— wherever he was. She wanted, no, needed, to talk to him.

CHAPTER 8

Teddy raised his head to look at the sky through the branches of his old tree fort. It had been a long time since he'd had this view. But he remembered it perfectly, and as he watched the stars spin through the night in their stately midnight dance he felt more at home than he had anywhere in the last ten years.

A branch cracked and there was a rustle from below. Teddy propped himself up on an elbow and looked over the edge of the platform. "Who goes there?"

"It's me."

Olympia. His heart quickened and his throat turned dry. "What's the password?"

"Really?"

"You have to know the password."

He could almost hear the rolling of her eyes as she answered. "Girls stink."

Chuckling, he lowered a rope ladder for her. "I can't believe you remember that."

"Send the basket, too."

He lowered a second rope that had a basket tied to the end. She piled in several objects then began climbing.

At last she came level with him and he helped her onto the platform.

"Whew. I haven't done that in years." She sat on the side,

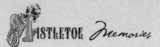

her legs dangling over the edge.

He settled beside her and began hauling up the basket. "But you remembered the password."

She grinned back at him. "Yes, I remembered that horrible old password."

"How did you know I'd be here?"

"A hunch. This place was always your sanctuary." She reached for the basket and pulled it toward her. From inside she pulled two blankets, a Thermos and mug, and a plate of gingerbread cookies.

She handed him a blanket and drew the other around her shoulders. Then poured out a steaming mug of coffee and handed it to him. They sat for a moment watching the stars and eating gingerbread, the warm scents of coffee, ginger, and cinnamon vying with the cool of the pine and the open sky above.

"You gave us the tickets to the party, didn't you?" Her voice was hushed like they were in a cathedral.

"I wanted to make sure you would be there."

She turned to him, her face shining in the moonlight. "Teddy, I can't thank you enough. I never expec— I will pay you back over the next year."

"There's no need, Olympia. I wanted to make things right."

"I need to make things right, too. I owe you an apology for the things I said. I shouldn't have judged you and your motives. You have every right to be hurt and furious."

Teddy's chest felt tight. "But you were right about me, Olympia. I wasn't thinking about the good of the town as much as I was thinking about satisfying my own pride." He took her hand. "You helped wake me up to the blessings I took for granted because I was so focused on what I considered unfair."

"You were right, though, Teddy. Once I set aside my attachment to Graff House and thought about it more clearly, I realized there's just no way I can keep up with it. Between the maintenance and the taxes and all the things the children need, I can't do it. I'm afraid I'm going to be right back in this position in another year. It might be better to let it go. As long as the kids and I are together, I can be content wherever we are."

He opened his mouth, but she continued on.

"And there are folks in town who could really use the jobs a new hotel would create. I don't want other families to go hungry either."

"Ah, well I've had a brainstorm about that. Remember I told you about the moving picture company I bought into?"

"Yes."

"They do most of their filming around New York City, but there are some scenes that need the great outdoors. Edison has been filming some at Cuddebackville in upstate New York. But I think Schooley's Mountain would be perfect. We're close enough to the city for them to come and go again in the same day if they needed. And when they are here, they will need food, help with costumes. If they are doing a whole picture, they will need places to stay and people to do laundry and all the things that go into supporting a film crew. There will be jobs aplenty."

Olympia exhaled and a puff of steam blossomed in the air between them. Her eyes were bright. "That's such a relief.

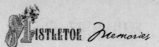

The folks around town will be so excited. I bet a cinema in German Valley would do well."

"That's a great idea, and it would mean even more jobs." Teddy couldn't take his eyes off her face. Rosy-cheeked from the cold and vibrant with hope for the future, she'd never looked more beautiful.

She pulled her knees up to her chest and wrapped her arms around them. A shiver went through her and she pulled the blanket tighter around her.

Teddy held his blanket open. "We'll be warmer if we share."

She hesitated for a fraction of a second then acquiesced. His arm settled around her shoulders, and he pulled her close, reveling in the joy of her presence.

There was nowhere else in the whole world he would rather be. "Since you don't have a pop I can ask, I guess I'll have to ask you if I can court you." The words sounded awkward, full of forced lightness. If she said no, he didn't— there would be no way he could go back.

Once again she turned to face him directly, her wide eyes luminous in the moonglow. "There's never been anyone else, Teddy. Not ever. I've loved you since I was fourteen years old, and I'll love you until the day I die."

He lowered his mouth toward hers. Her lips were soft and warm. Tentative at first and then more urgent. He pulled her closer to him, his free hand tracing the line of her jaw, the arch of her temple. She was the most lovely, the most precious thing God had ever placed in his life. He wasn't going to ever let her go.

After a long moment they pulled apart, and she leaned

her head against his shoulder. "Do you think you will be able to handle a ready-made family?"

"It's all I've ever known." He grinned at her. "And I wouldn't dream of trying to separate you from those kids. You belong together, just like you and I do." He paused. "But I think six is enough."

She grinned back, a twinkle in her eye that he knew all too well. "Is that negotiable? There's this boy named Brian—"

Laughing, he tilted her chin up for another kiss. "You drive a hard bargain, Miss Paris. But you're more than worth it."

COMFORT AND JOY

Jennifer AlLee

CHAPTER 1

The sun shone bright on Schooley's Mountain, melting the earlier freezing rain and turning the ground into a slushy, muddy mess. Carefully placing her rubber boots in the least treacherous-looking spots, Joy Benucci picked her way from the SUV to the front steps of Comfort House. She peered over the warehouse-club-size package of toilet paper in her arms, making sure nothing was left on the stairs. An unexpected trip on a skateboard would be bad enough in good weather. The last thing she wanted was to land in this slop.

"Hang on, Ms. B." The deep voice was followed by heavy footfalls on the stairs, and then the bulky package was lifted from her hands.

Joy smiled. "Thanks, Leon."

He shrugged. "Glad you stocked up. Dana's making dinner tonight, so we'll probably need it."

Joy knew she shouldn't laugh, but there was no stopping it. Leon was still settling in after joining Comfort House a week earlier. That he'd started calling her Ms. B. instead of using her full last name was a step in the right direction, although she doubted she'd ever get him to just call her Joy. But at least he felt comfortable enough to kid around.

"Don't let Dana hear you say that." She shooed him back to the house with a wiggle of her fingers. "I'll meet you inside."

He turned quickly, but not before she caught the lift of his

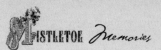

mouth. Every young adult that came into the program had a defense mechanism. For some, it was in-your-face bravado. For others, an out-of-proportion sense of humor. For Leon, it was a tough, protective shell designed to keep people out. But that shell of his was showing cracks.

Joy returned to the SUV, grabbed the last few bags, and slammed the hatch. When she turned around, Leon was waiting for her in the doorway.

"Almost forgot. There's a man here to see you."

Before she could ask for more information, he walked inside. Joy scrunched her nose. Had she forgotten an appointment? This time of year was always a crazy blur of fundraisers, donor appointments, holiday party networking. . . . Calendar mishaps weren't all that uncommon. But she was sure her schedule had been free this afternoon.

Once inside the house, she went straight to the kitchen. Dana must have convinced Leon to help with dinner, because they sat at the breakfast table, hunched over a worn copy of *The Betty Crocker Cookbook*. Joy dumped the bags on the counter with a thud and they both looked up.

"Any luck coming up with a menu?"

Dana frowned. "Kinda. But this would be a lot easier if you'd let me search the Internet."

Joy laughed. "The point isn't to make it easy, it's to teach you something. Meal planning is one of those vital but underappreciated life skills."

"Like cleaning toilets and changing light bulbs." Ben, the current king of comedy in their group home, brayed with laughter as he strode into the kitchen and straight for the refrigerator.

"Hold it." Joy raised her voice to get his attention. "Since you'll be in and out of the fridge anyway, put away these groceries, would you?"

Without waiting for his reply she headed for the living room, where she expected the guest was waiting.

He stood in front of the fireplace, back to the doorway, looking at the framed photos on the mantel. Joy took a moment to size him up. The perfect fit of his dark gray suit spoke of money, but his slightly-too-long hair brushing the top of the collar told her he wasn't preoccupied with appearances. Which was a good thing, considering Joy's casual getup of blue jeans and a bulky sweater.

Before he could find her ogling him, she cleared her throat. "May I help you?"

He turned and nearly stopped her in her tracks with a smile straight out of a toothpaste ad. "Only if you're Joy Benucci."

"I am." She pulled her stare from his lips, making herself look him in the eye. *Oh my.* Such frosty-blue, amazing eyes.

"Glad to meet you. I'm Evan Lancaster."

Joy took the hand he extended. His shake was firm but not bone crushing. So far, this man appeared perfect, which put her on guard. Nobody was perfect. . .especially people who showed up unannounced.

"What brings you to Comfort House, Mr. Lancaster?"

He removed a card from inside his suit jacket. "I represent the estate of Mr. Samuel Fowler."

Joy frowned. Sam Fowler owned Comfort House. Why would he send a lawyer. . . ? Wait a minute. "Estate? Did something happen to Sam?"

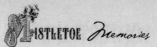

"Perhaps we should sit."

An invitation to sit was rarely a good thing, but she still settled onto the big brown sofa under the window. He sat on the other end and reached for a briefcase she hadn't noticed by the side of the coffee table.

"I'm sorry to have to tell you, Sam passed away."

He had to be wrong. "I just talked to him last week. He sounded fine."

Mr. Lancaster put the briefcase on the cushions between them and snapped open the lid. "It was quite sudden. His heart."

"How awful." Joy's shoulders slumped. "Sam was a wonderful, generous man."

"Yes. Generous to a fault." He pulled a sheaf of papers from his case.

Joy's heart thumped faster. There was only one reason a lawyer would be here with papers after poor Sam's passing. He'd left her something in his will.

He'd left Comfort House to her.

The dear, sweet man. He knew how much the house meant to her, how important it was to the people who passed through it. Joy took a deep breath and a weight lifted from her chest. What a relief it would be to not worry so much about funding.

"Miss Benucci."

Evan's voice cut into her thoughts. She blinked against the tears filling her eyes. "I'm sorry. My mind wandered."

"I noticed." He cleared his throat. "Miss Benucci, I'm not just Sam's lawyer, I'm his nephew."

She would have said how sorry she was for his loss, but he barreled on.

"I've come to tell you that Sam left this house to me."

Nothing moved in the room. Not air, not sound waves, not even her heart. A terrible possibility blossomed, pushing away the earlier sense of relief. "I don't understand."

The lawyer set his mouth in a grim line. "I'm the new owner of this building."

"What are those?" She pointed at the papers he still held.

"These are eviction papers, Miss Benucci. You have thirty days to vacate the premises."

CHAPTER 2

The boulder of worry became a landslide, burying Joy. "You can't." A hundred thoughts crowded her mind at once. Finally, a semicoherent protest made its way out. "I have a lease."

"I'm aware of that." Evan handed her the papers. "Here's a copy. The clause on page four states that in the event the owner, that's Sam, is deceased, then the new owner, that's me, has the right to terminate the lease."

She flipped to the page in question and read, becoming a little bit colder with every word. She'd never taken the time to go over the fine print in the contract. All that mattered to her had been that Sam had believed in her cause, and because of that, he'd arranged a monthly payment she could afford.

Evan leaned forward as though trying to look over the top of the papers. "You'll see it only requires the new owner to give the lessee fourteen days' notice. But this close to the holidays, I thought thirty was more appropriate."

She looked at him, eyes narrowing into slits. "While I appreciate you not throwing us out right before Christmas, an extra sixteen days hardly solves my problem."

"I'm not throwing you out," Evan said. "I'm giving you ample notice to find a new place to run your. . .charity."

The way he spoke told her just how little he thought of the work she did and made her want to tell him just what she thought of him at that particular moment. But if there was any chance of changing his mind, she needed to keep her cool.

"Comfort House is *not* a charity."

He raised an eyebrow. "Perhaps I misunderstood. Do the residents here pay rent?"

"No. This is a transitional house. The young adults that come here are fresh out of the foster care system. We work on life skills and they learn how to function on their own."

"I see." Evan didn't seem impressed. "No matter what you call it, you will have to move your enterprise elsewhere. I have other plans for this house."

"What plans?"

"I'm sorry, Miss Benucci, but it's not appropriate to discuss that with you." With a glance at his watch, he stood. "I need to get going."

Joy followed behind him, muttering under her breath, "Probably has an orphanage to foreclose on."

Evan stopped short. "What was that, Ms. Benucci?"

"Uh, just. . .be careful out there. The roads are slippery, you know."

She hurried around him and led the way down the hall. Opening the door, she put on what she hoped was a convincing smile. "Have a good day, Mr. Lancaster."

"And you."

As soon as both his feet crossed the threshold, she shut the door softly behind him and leaned against it. What was she going to do now?

"Is it true, Ms. B.?" Leon walked out of the kitchen, followed closely by Dana. Ben brought up the rear and for

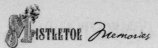

the first time she could recall, he wasn't smiling.

"Do we have to leave?" Dana, usually tough as nails, teetered on the verge of tears.

"No." The word pushed past all the worry and fear and logic in the moment.

Ben hitched his thumb toward the door. "That lawyer said we have thirty days to leave."

Joy nodded. "Yes, he did, but I don't for a moment believe it's going to happen. I don't know how, but God will keep us in this house."

Dana rolled her eyes. Ben stared at his feet. Only Leon's expression mirrored her own determination.

"Can we have a house meeting tonight?" Leon asked.

"Great idea." Joy looked into the kitchen, checking the time on the microwave. "Tanya gets home from work around five thirty. We'll have our meeting after dinner. Cool?"

"Cool." All three answered in unison.

"Great." They would talk it over later. For now, they needed the distraction of doing something normal. She rubbed her palms together. "What did you guys come up with for dinner?"

જી

Evan Lancaster had an afternoon full of meetings to prepare for, but he couldn't keep his mind on any of them. Every time he tried to read the brief in front of him, the image of Joy Benucci floated through his mind.

He'd expected to deal with a slick operator who would try to manipulate him. He hadn't been prepared for a sweet, fresh-faced young woman who looked like she'd just trotted off a college campus. The only trace of the gold digger he knew she was came with the look in her eyes when he said he was the executor of Sam's estate. He'd seen that look before, when people realized they'd been left an inheritance. But then he'd crushed that idea, and her shock had been obvious.

Leaning back in his chair, Evan pinched the bridge of his nose. Legally, he had every right to evict the woman and her gang, but he actually felt guilty. For one crazy moment, he had the urge to take it all back and tell her she could stay. But common sense prevailed. He was having an emotional reaction, and that's what her kind excelled at: manipulating emotions. He wouldn't allow himself to be played like that. Not again.

A knock sounded, and before he could answer, the door opened. His secretary, Claire, stuck her head in. "Not going out for lunch again?"

He shook his head. "Too much to do here."

"That's what I thought." She walked in carrying a white Styrofoam container and a bottle of water. "I ordered Chinese."

The aroma wafted his way, drawing a grumble from his stomach. "Beef and broccoli?"

"Yes."

"Two spring rolls?"

"Yes."

"Extra plum sauce?"

"Of course."

"Claire, you spoil me."

She set the food on his desk then planted a fist on one ample hip. "It's purely selfish. If you get dizzy and pass out

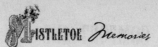

in court and cause a mistrial, it creates all kinds of headaches for me."

His eyes shot up. "I don't have court today, do I?"

"No. I was speaking in generalities." Her tough veneer fell away, and a motherly smile took over. "Besides, I like taking care of you."

Claire's son was in the military, stationed somewhere overseas. Evan knew very little about what he did, except that it was so secretive, even his mother didn't know where he was. In his absence, Evan had been happy to let Claire adopt him as a surrogate.

He unwrapped the wooden chopsticks and opened the container. Chopsticks poised over the still-steaming beef, he looked again at Claire. "Anything else?"

"How did your meeting go this morning?"

Ah. Perhaps there was more than one ulterior motive behind her luncheon offering. "Just fine."

"You had no problems telling that poor woman you're closing down Comfort House?"

Evan gritted his teeth. "I did not close it down. She's free to keep it running as long as she wants. She just has to do it somewhere else."

Claire crossed her arms and frowned.

"What?" He snatched up a piece of broccoli and popped it in his mouth.

"Evan, you're the smartest man I know. But right now. . ." She shook her head and turned to leave. "Enjoy your lunch."

The click of the door latch came as he swallowed his food. He forced himself to eat a few more bites then flipped the lid shut with a snort of disgust. First that Benucci woman had taken up his morning and now she'd ruined his lunch. The sooner he was done with her, the better.

Thirty days. In thirty days, she'd be out of his life and out of his head. And not a minute too soon.

CHAPTER 3

The house meeting started off badly. The teens went from worried to upset, loudly voicing their opinions of Evan and his eviction notice.

"Hold it, guys." Joy held up her hands, warding off the verbal barrage. "Mr. Lancaster is a lawyer, not the devil himself."

"He's kicking us out of our home," Ben said. "If he's not the devil, he's at least a minion."

"Why's he doing it, anyway?" Dana twisted a strand of dark, coarse hair around one finger. "What does he have against you?"

Joy shrugged. "I have no idea."

"Maybe you spilled punch on him at a benefit," Ben suggested.

"My clumsiness makes that entirely possible. But, since I've never met the man, it didn't happen."

Ben snorted. "It still could."

That brought on a flurry of ideas about how to inflict nonlethal harm. And while filling his car with shaving cream or rigging a bucket of eggnog to fall on his head had a certain delicious appeal, Joy forced herself to remember that she was the in-charge adult in the room.

"How about we channel all this energy into some constructive, practical ideas?"

Silence fell on the room. Apparently, no one had anything constructive or practical to say.

"I'll go first. Dana, your question of why he's doing this is a good one. I need to get that answer."

Dana nodded. "How are you going to do that?"

"We could hack into his computer."

Joy didn't want to know if Ben really could do that. "That's a little much, don't you think? I'll start with the direct approach. Go right to him and ask."

"And if he won't answer?" Leon asked.

Ben shot a finger in the air. "*Then* we hack into his computer!"

"No. Then we try a different tactic."

"We don't have a lot of time, Ms. B.," Leon said.

"What can we do?" Tanya asked.

Joy looked at the four young people around her. Each had developed their own way of handling stress and dealing with bad situations. She'd known them long enough to know they were all scared to death of being without a home.

"Right now, the best thing we can do is pray."

The reaction was a mixture of eye rolling and nods of agreement. Interestingly, the guys were more open to prayer than the girls were.

"No offense, Joy," Dana said, "but we want to do something real."

"I know you do. But we don't have enough information. Anything we decide to do now might make matters worse. Prayer may seem like a waste of time, but believe me, it's not. And it will help you find some peace. If you like, think of it as meditation."

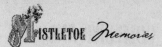

Tanya and Dana still looked skeptical, but at least the eye rolling had stopped.

"All right." Joy slapped her palms on her knees and stood up from the couch. "Tonight's meeting is adjourned. We'll meet again tomorrow night and I'll tell you what I find out."

Now alone in the room, she released the worked up, positive outlook she'd put on for their sake and let the desperation of the moment fall back on her.

They were being evicted. Her dream was being torn out from under her, and there was nothing she could do about it.

No. Not nothing. Joy pulled back her shoulders. They had a plan, after all. Not a very detailed plan, but a plan nonetheless. She would go to Mr. Evan Lancaster's office in the morning and demand to know why he was so determined to shut down Comfort House.

And once she knew, she'd find a way to stop him.

❦

Evan glanced at his watch as he bounded up the courthouse steps. Nothing had gone right that morning. His alarm hadn't gone off and his coffeemaker refused to work, making him late and grumpy. Then, when he'd finally gotten through unusually heavy traffic, it had taken fifteen minutes to find a parking spot. He'd be cutting it close, but he'd make it.

"Mr. Lancaster!"

They'd only met once, but he'd recognize that honey-sweet voice anywhere. "Ms. Benucci." He only half turned, hoping to translate his desire not to stop.

She either didn't notice or didn't care. "Mr. Lancaster, we need to talk."

That was the last thing he needed. "This isn't a good time."

"I just need you to answer one question."

The woman was determined, he'd give her that. "How did you know where to find me?"

"Your secretary said you'd be at court."

Of course she did. Evan would have to talk to Claire about taking sides, especially when the side she chose wasn't his. "Look, I'd be happy to talk with you, but it will have to wait."

He turned and continued up the steps, only to be stopped short a moment later when Ms. Benucci trotted ahead and blocked his path.

"I'm sorry if this is inconveniencing you, but I find being evicted inconvenient."

If he wanted to get inside, he would have to hear her out. "Fine. What is your question?"

"Why are you shutting down Comfort House?" She crossed her arms tightly over her chest.

He'd really hoped to avoid this conversation, especially in public where anyone might be listening. The longer they stood there, with her looking like smoke might come from her ears at any second, the more people were taking notice.

"There's no other way to say it." He lowered his voice, hoping to keep the next bit between the two of them. "I don't trust you."

She couldn't have looked more shocked if he'd slapped her in the face. "How can you say that? You don't even know me."

"No, but I know your kind."

"My kind?" Her voice rose, making it obvious she didn't care who overheard them. "What kind is that?"

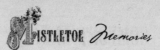

Evan sighed. "You conned my uncle into signing a lease with monthly rent far below what the property is worth. And now you've got those foster kids living there."

She lowered her arms to her sides, hands fisted. "I have never conned anyone in my life. Sam understood what I'm trying to do at Comfort House, and he knew how hard it is to fund something like that. So he arranged low rent payments as a way of supporting the House."

With her cheeks glowing bright red and her eyes snapping with fire, Evan wondered if she was in danger of spontaneously combusting. The effect was disarming, and for a moment, he almost believed her.

"You asked me your question, and I answered it. Good-bye."

He stepped to the side, but she stepped with him and poked a finger at his chest. "Listen to me, buddy." Now she was shouting, and a group of serious onlookers had gathered. "I don't know where you got your warped idea of who I am, or what you have against foster kids. But there is no way I'm giving up Comfort House without a fight." She glanced away from him for a moment and then added, "Especially when you want to evict us at Christmas."

The gasp from the crowd confirmed they saw him as a Scrooge who hated foster kids, hated Christmas, and hated this adorable, irritating woman.

In the court of public opinion, Joy Benucci had just made a compelling case.

CHAPTER 4

He has a problem with foster children?" Joy's best friend, Bernadette, leaned over her double-bacon cheeseburger, eyes narrowed. "Did he say why?"

"No." Joy jabbed a limp french fry into a glob of ketchup. "To be fair, I didn't really give him a chance."

Once the crowd had gathered, Evan had totally shut down. He'd given her a stern admonition to call his office and make an appointment to discuss the situation further then pushed his way past her and stalked into the courthouse.

"One good thing came out of it," she said.

Bernadette waggled an eyebrow. "Oh, I can't wait to hear this."

"There was a reporter there, covering another story, obviously. But she overheard everything. She wants to talk to me about my side."

"Print or broadcast?"

"I'm not sure." Joy dug in her purse. "She gave me her card and said to call her. Here it is."

She handed the card to Bernadette, who immediately let out a low whistle. "You met Alex Faraday and didn't recognize her?"

"Who's Alex Faraday?" Joy took a sip of her iced tea.

Bernadette shook her head. "Girl, you are refreshingly naive. Alex Faraday is probably the most popular morning

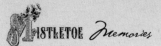

news anchor in New Jersey."

Joy's inhale of shock unfortunately interfered with her swallowing. She sputtered and coughed, and waved away her friend's hand as Bernadette moved to slap her on the back. After a moment of breathing into a napkin, she looked up, her eyes watering.

"Morning news?"

"Yep. It's exactly the kind of thing you need." Bernadette polished off the last bite of her burger, licked ketchup from her fingertips, and pushed her plate aside. "You, my friend, are fighting a war, and the more people you can bring over to your side, the better."

Warring with anybody was the last thing Joy wanted to do. The only thing she liked less was being forced to shut down Comfort House.

"I guess I don't have much of a choice." She sighed and took the card back, tucking it safely in her wallet. "But I'm going to try talking to the lawyer again." At Bernadette's scowl, Joy hurried on. "It's only right to get all the information I can before I talk to a reporter. If that doesn't work, then I'll rip him apart on the air."

Bernadette smiled. "That's the spirit. I think you need a little something to celebrate your courageous decision."

"What do you have in mind?"

Bernadette waved at their waiter. "Dessert."

❧

Some days, Evan found court to be exhilarating. Today, it had beaten him down. He turned his head against the wind blowing through the open framework of the parking garage and pulled his camel hair coat closer around him. So far, today had been miserable in every way possible.

"What's the matter, counselor? Lose a big one?"

Evan looked up and groaned. A woman with a sleek blond bob leaned against the driver's-side door of his car, arms crossed, lips curled up in a smug smile.

The day had just gotten worse.

"Hello, Alex." He pushed the button on his key fob, hoping the pop of doors unlocking and the flashing headlights would give her a hint. No such luck. "Is there something I can help you with?"

"I overheard the conversation you had with that woman outside the courthouse earlier. I thought you might want to tell me your side of the story."

Evan held back a growl. "Why would I want to do that?"

She jerked one shoulder in a half-hearted shrug. "Because this is the kind of human interest story that brings in ratings. Imagine how many of my viewers might be potential clients of Lancaster and Associates? Or maybe they already are." Alex looked him over, from his Italian loafers to his silk tie. "People are going to wonder why a man like you feels compelled to throw a bunch of orphans out into the street right before Christmas."

"They're not orphans," he spit out in exasperation. "They're foster kids. Former ones, at that."

Alex waved her hand in his direction. "Foster kids, orphans. . .same thing. They have no parents looking out for them. All they have is Joy Benucci, the David in our little drama, battling to save their home from the rich, powerful, heartless Goliath."

Evan was far from rich, and the extent of his power was

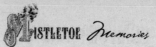

determined entirely by the circumstances of the moment. As for being heartless, there were days he thought he could function better without one. Nothing she said was true, but none of that would matter once she got done spinning her story.

"You're not going to let me off the hook, are you?"

The spark in her eyes told him everything he needed to know. She was enjoying this a little too much. Undoubtedly, it had more to do with the two months they'd dated and the way their one-sided romance had ended than it did with the story.

"Fine. Call Claire and have her set up a time for us to talk tomorrow." He reached into his inner coat pocket for a business card, but she stopped him with a shake of her head.

"Don't bother." She pulled her phone out of her pocket and waggled it at him. "I still have your office on speed dial. Your home number, too."

She stepped away from his vehicle and walked toward the elevator. There was an extra sway in her step, as if she hoped he was watching.

"That'll teach me to date a reporter," he muttered as he got into the car. Before he started the engine, he took his cell from his briefcase and called the office. He'd better warn Claire there'd be two angry women calling.

CHAPTER 5

I got a job!"

Dana dashed into the house so full of excitement that Joy let it slide when the girl forgot the rule about not slamming the front door.

"Where is everybody?" Dana's voice sounded in the hall.

Joy pushed the chair away from the computer desk and rolled across the room, leaning her head out the door. "I'm in the office. No idea where everybody else is. Come tell me all about it."

Joy rolled back into the room to avoid a collision. A moment later, Dana burst in, tossed her purse on the end of the loveseat shoehorned into an open space on one wall, and shrugged out of her coat. Then she flopped down herself, let loose a huge sigh, and broke into a smile bigger than Joy had ever seen on her face. Dana was a lovely young woman, but that smile transformed her.

And it was as contagious as a yawn. Joy grinned right back. "Details. I want details."

"Well, I did what we talked about. Went in and told them how much I wanted the job."

"This is at the veterinarian's office?"

Dana nodded. "I told them I'm taking classes at the community college and working toward vet school, but that I really want the experience of working in a vet's office."

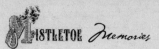

"Very good." Maternal pride swelled within Joy, despite the fact that Dana was only ten years younger than she. "And they'll be able to schedule you around school?"

"Myda, that's the woman who hired me, said it wouldn't be a problem. She wants to start me in the main office, see how I work with people and the animals. If that goes well, I might get to assist with simple things like vaccinations." Dana threw her head back, dug her toes into the carpet, and let loose a squeal. "I can't believe I actually got the job!"

Joy laughed. "Why are you so surprised? You worked hard to get ready for that interview." They'd both worked hard, polishing Dana's résumé, which was heavy on goals and ambition but almost empty of practical work experience.

Dana's face grew serious. "I'm still not used to people giving me a chance. To have a professional in the field I want to work in talk to me, take me seriously, and see my potential. . . ."

"I know exactly what you mean." Joy had seen it, time and again. That moment when one of the young adults at the house realized they could exceed the limitations they always thought were part and parcel of being a foster kid. It was one of the main reasons she'd started Comfort House. And why she couldn't let Evan Lancaster shut it down.

Now that the conversation had turned to emotions, a subject that made Dana uncomfortable, she obviously wanted to move on to something safer. She looked past Joy to the computer monitor. "What are you working on?"

"Going over the books." She frowned before she could stop herself.

"How bad is it?"

She could fake a positive attitude and essentially lie to Dana about the state of things. Or, she could treat the young woman like the adult she was and give it to her straight.

Joy sighed. "It's bad. I was hoping if I contacted some of our bigger supporters, they could help me sway Mr. Lancaster."

"You mean convince him he doesn't really want to evict us?"

"Exactly. But then I started calling people. Turns out, most of them have decided not to support Comfort House after the first of the year."

"What?" Dana jumped up off the couch. "Why would they stop all of a sudden?"

Joy shrugged. "The economy, wanting to focus their altruism elsewhere... I have no idea. Nobody really wants to tell you why they won't give you money anymore."

"It's that lawyer." Dana paced the floor, although the open space was so tight, she could only take three steps before she had to pivot and go the other way. "He got to them."

The thought hadn't even occurred to Joy. "No. He wouldn't do something like that." *Would he?*

"Why not? He wants the house. He wants us out. He's a lawyer with power and influence. Makes perfect sense to me."

Dana had little respect for lawyers, and from what Joy had learned of the girl's past, she knew it was with good reason. Still, the idea that Evan Lancaster would be so unfeeling, to not only throw them out of the house but also see to it that she couldn't start again anywhere else... it was a bit too much to swallow.

Joy put up her hands, palms out. "Dana, stop pacing. You're making me dizzy."

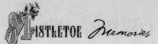

"Sorry." She picked up her purse and coat. "I'm going to my room. But if you need help taking care of the lawyer, just yell. I know where I can get my hands on horse tranquilizers."

She winked and fled the room before Joy could remind her that pocketing meds would not help her advance in her new job. Still, she laughed to herself. Dozens of aged-out foster kids had lived at Comfort House over the last four years. All came with their own baggage, their own stories, their own unique personalities and coping mechanisms. But there was one thing they all had in common: a perverse, dark sense of humor. It was more pronounced in some, but they all had it. As though joking about all the bad things that had happened or could happen would somehow protect them from pain.

Joy squared her shoulders. There was nothing funny about this. Evan Lancaster was trying to destroy her work, but it was more than that. Everyone who passed through Comfort House needed the experience. They all left stronger and more independent. Evan was messing with the lives of people who had a home one day and were out on the street the next. There was no way she would let him confirm their already-strong conviction that they couldn't trust anyone but themselves.

She grabbed her purse and pulled the business card from her wallet. She'd tried to talk to the lawyer, and it hadn't worked. There was no reason to think he'd give her more information if she tried again.

Joy picked up her cell phone from the desk and dialed the number, tapping her foot against one of the chair's casters until someone finally answered.

"Hello. This is Joy Benucci calling for Alex Faraday. She's expecting me."

"Any calls?"

Claire looked up at Evan as he leaned over her desk. "Tons, but not the one you've been waiting on for the last two days."

He took the pink stubs of paper and shuffled through them, his frown deepening every time he saw a name that wasn't hers.

"If you want to talk to her so much, why don't you call her yourself?"

"I don't *want* to talk to her, but she was so insistent on talking to me. It just doesn't make sense that she hasn't called."

Claire fussed at her desk, straightening a stack of already-straight files. "I never did think that woman was stable. Why you dated her as long as you did is beyond me."

"What? I never dated Joy Benucci."

"Joy Benucci? I thought you were talking about Alex."

"No. Although, come to think of it, Alex was supposed to call, too."

"Yet you're obsessing about a practical stranger." Claire leaned her elbows on her desk and rested her chin on her clasped hands. "What is it about the charming Ms. Benucci that has you so distracted?"

Evan snorted. "Charming? She accosted me on the courthouse steps and made me sound like an ogre. I can think of a few words for her, and *charming* isn't one of them."

"Whatever you say, boss." Claire wiped the smile from her face, but her eyes still held a spark of mischief. "What I said still applies. If you're bothered that you haven't heard from her— from Joy, I mean—then you should make contact yourself."

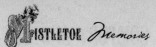

As much as he hated to admit it, Claire was right. Ignoring the problem wouldn't make it go away. He turned and walked to the door.

Claire called after him. "Aren't you going to call her?"

"No. Going to do something better."

He would have to deal with Joy Benucci sooner or later. It might as well be on his terms.

CHAPTER 6

As soon as Evan spotted the news van in front of the house, he knew coming there had been a mistake. Unless the local media had taken a sudden interest in this little story, Alex had to be doing an on-site interview.

The temptation to do a U-turn in the middle of Schooley Mountain Road and flee was great, but he fought it. Maybe this could turn into a good thing. By talking to both women at once, he could get his point across with a minimum of redundancy.

By the time he parked behind the van and walked up to the front door, Evan had convinced himself this was a blessing in disguise. He was almost whistling when he pushed the doorbell.

The door opened and a young man with short blond hair glared at him. "What do you want?"

"I'm here to see Miss Benucci. I'm—"

"I know who you are." He stepped back from the door but didn't invite Evan in. Instead, he turned toward the hall and yelled, "Joy! That lawyer is here."

It wasn't the first time Evan had heard someone say the word *lawyer* with the same emphasis as they'd say the word *maggot*. He pushed the door farther open and stepped inside. When the young man glared at him again, he merely smiled. "Thank you for announcing me."

A moment later, Joy came down the hall. "Mr. Lancaster. I wasn't expecting you." She stuck out her hand to shake his, but her movements were stiff, as was the forced smile on her lips.

"Please, call me Evan." Maybe if they used first names, she'd relax and listen to what he had to say.

"Why are you here, Mr. . .Evan?"

"Our earlier conversations didn't go very well. I was hoping we could try again."

She crossed her arms and pursed her lips, thinking for a moment. "Have you changed your mind about evicting us?"

"Miss Benucci—"

"Joy." She interrupted, her tone condescending. "Please."

"Joy, this isn't about—"

"Because if you haven't changed your mind, then I really don't see how this conversation can go any better."

She was a piece of work. "We'll never know if we don't try. What do you say?"

"Tell him where he can go," the blond-haired guy muttered.

"Ben," Joy snapped, and jerked her chin at him. "Go join the others, okay?"

Ben obviously didn't want to go anywhere, but after a moment of hesitation, he nodded and walked away.

"I'd be happy to talk to you again," Joy said. "But we're in the middle of something right now. Maybe you could come back later."

"Evan?" That polished voice came from the hall, and Alex walked toward them. "I thought I heard you."

Joy looked from him, to Alex, and back again. "You two know each other?"

"Evan and I go way back." Thankfully, Alex didn't go into further detail. But the tilt of her head and the gleam in her eye said she'd come up with an idea that involved him, and he'd be smart to leave while he still could.

"You're right, Joy. I'll come back tomorrow."

"Oh no you don't." Alex linked one arm around his elbow and the other arm around Joy's. "Now that I have the two of you together, it's the perfect opportunity for a little he-said-she-said."

Wrinkles creased Joy's forehead. "I don't want to turn this into an episode of *Jerry Springer*."

Evan bit his tongue to hold back a laugh as Alex's face flushed pink under a thick layer of makeup.

"Of course not," she said, walking toward the living room and dragging Evan and Joy with her. "It won't be sensational. Promise. I simply want to get both sides of the story."

He didn't trust Alex any farther than he could throw her, but maybe the situation was turning in his favor. Joy obviously needed to keep up her sympathetic image and didn't want to chew him out on camera. If they talked about their situation with Alex as a mediator, perhaps he could make his point.

He looked past Alex and caught Joy's eye. "I'm game if you are."

Joy sighed. "All right."

She pulled her arm away from Alex and led the way into the living room. Several portable lights and a reflector screen were set up, and a cameraman was adjusting knobs on some fancy equipment Evan didn't recognize.

"What's *he* doing here?"

The question drew his attention. Two girls and two guys

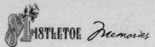

sat shoulder-to-shoulder on the sofa. Evan recognized the one who asked the question as Ben, the rude kid who'd opened the door.

Joy touched her forehead with her fingertips, as though trying to push back a headache. "Mr. Lancaster is going to tell his side of the story."

From the unhappy responses, Evan knew these kids weren't going to cut him any slack. Going toe-to-toe with Joy was one thing, but he wasn't prepared for five against one.

Maybe this hadn't been such a great idea, after all.

❧

"Is this really necessary?" Joy pulled away from Brandi, the overly enthusiastic, stick-thin makeup woman jabbing at her face with a fat powder brush.

"Oh yeah." Brandi's heavily black-rimmed eyes widened. "The lights will wash you out, the camera will distort your image. What I'm doing is just to counteract that. Most people have no idea how much work it takes to look natural for the camera."

"You're the professional."

Brandi smiled. "Don't worry. The powder is just to keep down the shine. Now close your eyes and relax."

Closing her eyes was one thing, but Joy didn't think it was possible to relax. Last week, her biggest concern had been whether she could find a way to squeeze one more kid into the house. Now, she was trying to save the home for the ones who already lived in it, and she was desperate enough to go on television to do it.

A few minutes later, after poking and swiping at Joy's face with unknown makeup implements, the woman stepped back. "All done. You can open your eyes."

Joy took the mirror Brandi held out and inspected her work. She half-expected to look like she'd stepped out of a tacky Las Vegas review, but true to her word, the makeup woman had kept it low-key and natural.

"Thank you."

"No problem." Brandi shooed her out of the chair. "Next!"

Tanya plunked herself down in the open spot and looked into the nearby makeup case. "I sure hope you've got something with a little more color in there. Olive is not going to do it for me."

Brandi waved her hand in the air. "No worries. I can mix and match enough shades to take care of the United Nations."

Joy laughed as the two bantered about models and stereotypes. Tanya was one of those rare people who could talk to a stranger and within a minute or two have them feeling like they were lifelong friends. The skill had served the girl well as she'd bounced her way through the foster system.

Joy went to the couch and sat next to Leon. "You ready for this?"

He shrugged. "I guess. What's up with those two?" He pointed across the room to where Alex and Evan were standing in the corner, having an animated conversation.

"I have no idea." Well, she had a *bit* of an idea. Alex and Evan had a history, no doubt about that. But what kind? Professional? Personal? Both? For some reason, she didn't like the thought of them involved in a personal way. And she really didn't like the fact that she didn't like it. So she shrugged the thought away. "They're probably just talking about the interview."

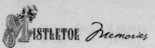

Leon snorted. "Shouldn't you be in on that conversation?"

He was right. Whatever they were talking about, they were in her home. Alex had invaded with her mini film crew, and Evan just happened to show up at the same time. What if they'd planned this all along? They could be standing right there, discussing their scheme to shut down Comfort House, right under Joy's nose. She had every right to know what they were talking about.

"Excuse me," she said to Leon.

Thanks to the network of cords and equipment scattered about, Joy was forced to take the long way around the room. As she drew closer, she finally made out some of the conversation.

"Don't you dare make me look stupid," Evan said.

Alex laughed. "Whether or not you look stupid is entirely up to you."

"I just don't want you using this as a chance to get even with me."

Her eyes narrowed into a decidedly unfriendly glare. "Nothing I could do would make us even."

Uh-oh. The conversation was more personal than Joy expected. No way did she want to get in the middle of that. With a quick pivot she tried to go the other way, but her foot caught in a cable. A high-pitched shriek left her lips as she twisted back around, trying to stay upright. But it only made things worse.

Everything moved in slow motion. Her foot yanked on the cable and a tall light stand wobbled and tipped. Joy pitched forward, arms flailing, searching for something to break her fall. For a split second, there was no noise in the room, and Joy squeezed her eyes shut, bracing for the fall. Then pandemonium broke loose.

Everyone was shouting and moving at the same time. Something broke Joy's fall. Something warm and sturdy. No, not something, but someone. Someone who let out a grunt when they collided and then wrapped strong arms around her to hold her up.

"Are you all right?" The concern in Evan's voice was sincere, but Joy was distracted by the way it made his chest rumble beneath her cheek.

She opened her eyes and looked up at him, trying to catch her breath. "I tripped."

He grinned. "I noticed."

Joy realized that in her desperation to keep from falling, she'd clutched onto Evan's neck. Letting him go, she took a step back, but almost tripped again on the cable that was still tangled around her ankle. Off to the side, Ben tightened his hold on the light stand he'd kept from falling over.

"Hold on there, Indy," Evan said. "One wrong move, and you'll trigger this here Burmese tiger trap."

Joy tilted her head. The man had a sense of humor. That was a point in his favor. Not that she was making a list of pros and cons. But if she were, humor would definitely go in the pro column.

Holding one of her hands to steady her, Evan hunkered down beside her. "Okay. Lift your foot. Slowly."

Joy did as he said, teetering as he pulled the cord off her foot. Once she was untangled, he stood up and put his hands on her shoulders. "Think you're steady enough to try this on your own?"

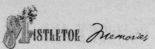

She smiled at him and nodded, but he didn't move his hands. Just smiled back at her.

"Oh please." Alex's disgusted tone broke into Joy's head. "If you two are done groping each other, I'd like to finish this interview before all the equipment is destroyed."

Evan took a step back, his expression turning serious. "Ready any time you are."

Joy turned and carefully walked back to the sofa, keeping her eyes on the ground and navigating around cables. Once she was sitting, she looked over at Evan. He leaned against a wall, arms crossed, jaw set. His change of mood gave her emotional whiplash. How could he be laughing and joking with her one second, sullen and withdrawn the next? Maybe it went along with being a lawyer. Or maybe he was a moody guy. That would go in the con column. If she were weighing the pros and cons. Which she most certainly wasn't.

CHAPTER 7

There was an old adage about never working with children or animals, because they'll upstage you every time. As the interviews continued, Evan began to understand why. Even though the former-fosters were all eighteen or nineteen, making the term "children" nonapplicable, they were running away with the show. Worse than that, they made him doubt his own motivations.

Alex interviewed all four of the teens at the same time. Despite Evan's initial concerns, she was completely professional. Her questions were insightful and avoided sensationalizing the issue. Still, there was no denying their stories were heart wrenching.

Tanya entered the foster system when she was nine. Ben and Dana had been in it even longer. Leon's mother died when he was fourteen. He entered the system when the manager of his apartment complex called social services to report that the teen was living alone and behind on the rent. Between the four of them, they'd been in over thirty-five different homes over thirteen years.

Alex leaned forward slightly, her gaze sweeping from one to the other. "Why is Comfort House so important to you?"

"People don't get it," Ben said. "Once a foster kid turns eighteen, he doesn't exist anymore. Which means no more money for the foster parents. When they stop getting their

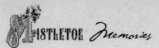

money, you're out of a home."

Evan wanted so badly to jump up from his seat and counter what Ben said. That wasn't always true. There were times when the foster parents loved the kid just as much as their own flesh and blood. And sometimes, the foster kid took advantage of that love.

"Did that happen to all of you?" Alex asked.

They nodded. Dana clutched the edge of her seat, hunching her shoulders and hanging her head. When she looked back up, the pain in her eyes was unmistakable.

"I turned eighteen one month before high school graduation." Her voice shook, and she stopped. Tanya patted her knee, encouraging her to go on. "The morning of my birthday, my guardians told me I was on my own. The mother took me to the room I shared and watched me pack my things. You know, to make sure I didn't steal anything. Then the father told me to give him my house key. And that was that."

As good a reporter as Alex was, even she couldn't keep her emotions from showing. "They threw you out? Just like that?"

"They wished me luck. Oh, and they told me God would take care of me." Her laugh was bitter. "What a joke."

"What did you do?" Alex asked.

"There's no way I wasn't going to graduate. So I went to someone I trusted. My English teacher. She let me stay with her, finish out the year. And she helped me get in here."

Dana looked across the room and finally, a real, hopeful smile lifted her lips. Evan followed her gaze and saw Joy, hand to her mouth, tears rolling down her cheeks and ruining all of Brandi's work.

There was no way that woman was acting. She cared about these kids. She really cared. And they cared about her.

What had he done?

❧

Evan looked extremely uncomfortable.

After a quick makeup repair job, Joy joined him in the chairs set up in front of the camera. She looked at him out of the corner of her eye. He adjusted his tie, shifted in his seat, crossed his ankle over his knee, then uncrossed it and let his foot thump back down to the floor. If she didn't know better, she'd say he was as nervous as she was. But he was a lawyer. Surely he was used to making his case in front of more imposing people than her.

Joy smiled at him, hoping to alleviate both their nerves. "I'll be glad when this is over."

He didn't smile, but he wasn't frowning anymore, either. A step in the right direction. "It won't be bad."

"If you say so. I'm used to public speaking, but I've never been filmed before. It's a little intimidating."

Now he fiddled with his hands, rubbing his fingers absentmindedly. "Joy, I need to tell you something. I—"

"Sorry to keep you waiting." Alex breezed back into the room. "Had to check in with the station, but now I'm all yours." She settled into the chair across from them, and the sound man adjusted her mic pack as she placed an earpiece and fluffed out her hair to cover it. "Are you two ready?"

"Yes," they answered together.

"Wonderful. Here we go."

Alex eased them into the interview with some simple background questions. Gradually, the questions became more personal.

"Joy, we heard from the people who live here how much Comfort House means to them. But I must admit, I'm still not entirely sure what its purpose is."

You can do this, Joy told herself. *You've answered this question dozens of times.* "Not all foster kids have the same experiences. Some are prepared for life on their own by their foster parents. Others become part of the family they've been placed in. But too many are cut loose and set adrift as soon as they hit eighteen. Comfort House is a transitional home. It's a place where they learn basic skills they may not have mastered, like balancing a checkbook, making a budget, and planning nutritious meals. And it gives them a safe place to be until they're ready to go out on their own."

"I see." Alex nodded. "And how do you know when they're ready?"

"Every person is different, but when it's time, they know and I know."

Alex smiled. "It takes a special person to dedicate her life to helping others like you have."

"I'm not special. I just know how important a place like this is. I'm only sorry that space limits me to four kids at a time."

Alex leaned forward. "It sounds like you have personal experience with being on your own."

Joy's back stiffened. Did Alex already know about her past, or was she just fishing because of what Joy said? Either way, it didn't matter. There was no shame in where she came from, especially if it would help people better understand how important her cause was.

"My mother died when I was four, and my father went

to jail when I was eight." A cold flush ran through Joy at the thought of those years alone with her father. She hadn't thought things could be any worse after he was gone, but she'd been wrong. "There were no relatives to contact, at least none that would admit being related to those two, so I was put in foster care."

Joy felt as if a thousand eyes were boring into her, and not just because of the camera. She turned to see Evan looking at her as if seeing her for the first time.

She pushed forward. "My experience was similar to Dana's, except that my best friend, Bernadette, took me to meet the youth pastor at her church. The youth group kind of adopted me and helped me out."

Alex had the knowing look reporters often wear following a big reveal. "No wonder this home is so important to you."

Joy nodded. "Funny how God works. The darkest day of my life actually opened the door to my future. I can't imagine doing anything else."

"But now, you just might have to." Alex turned her body sharply in the chair and focused on Evan. "Mr. Lancaster, now that you own the building, you've decided to evict Miss Benucci and effectively shut down Comfort House. What's behind that decision?"

Evan glanced at his hands, which were clasped in his lap, took a moment, and then looked back up at Alex. "It was never my intention to shut down Comfort House. Miss Benucci is free to continue her work. She just needs to do it in another building."

"I can't afford to do it in another building," Joy shot at him. "Especially now that you've scared away most of our supporters."

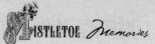

"What?" Evan's brows drew together.

"Miss Benucci, are you saying that Mr. Lancaster has used his influence to pull your funding?"

Evan's previous discomfort had turned to anger. "I did nothing of the sort."

Joy stood, even as the steady-cam operator motioned for her to stay in the shot. "Then why did people who've supported us for years suddenly decide to put their money elsewhere? All of them at the same time? Seems like an awfully big coincidence, don't you think?"

"Yes, it does." Evan jumped up and glared at her. "But that doesn't mean I had anything to do with it."

"Then who did?"

"I don't know!" His shouted answer brought a squeal of feedback shooting through the sound system.

Alex cursed as she yanked the earpiece from her ear. "Cut!" She pointed at Joy. "And that's only because I promised you this wouldn't turn into the *Jerry Springer* show. The way you two are going at it, I wouldn't be surprised if chairs started flying."

"I'm sorry." Evan removed the mic from his lapel, unclipped the pack from his belt, and set them on the chair. "Joy, I did not strong-arm your supporters. But I think I might know who did."

"Who?" Alex and Joy asked in unison.

Evan sighed. "I can't say right now, but I'm going to find out. Alex, I know I'm asking a lot, but please don't air this interview."

The reporter raised her eyebrows. "You've got to be kidding. Why not?"

"Because I don't want the person I suspect to catch wind of it. I promise, if you hold off, I'll give you an exclusive when all this is done."

"I don't know. . . ."

"It will be worth the wait. Trust me."

Joy followed the conversation, not at all sure what was going on. Who else was involved? Why would anyone other than Evan want to run her out of her home? And why did he want to stop them?

"All right." Alex extended her hand. When Evan shook it, she grinned at him. "But if your exclusive isn't juicy enough, we may have to renegotiate our deal."

A muscle in Evan's jaw twitched, then he nodded sharply. Without another word, he left the room. A moment later, the front door slammed.

"I guess we're done," Alex said to Joy. She turned to her people and made a circular motion in the air with one finger. "Wrap it up. Let's head out."

While the organized chaos of the crew took over the room, Joy moved out of the way. Ben came up beside her. "What the heck just happened?"

Still in a state of semi-shock, Joy shook her head. "I have no idea."

And she wasn't entirely sure she wanted to find out.

CHAPTER 8

Show me the file."

Evan burst into the office, his father's secretary hot on his heels.

"I'm sorry, Mr. Lancaster," the woman said. "I tried to stop him."

Robert Lancaster shook his head. "It's all right. There's no stopping this one when he gets an idea in his head."

The secretary left the room, and as the door clicked shut, Robert looked serenely at his son. "Now, what is it you want?"

"The file you said you had on Joy Benucci."

Robert leaned back in his chair and laced his fingers over his stomach. "Why don't you have a seat so we can talk about this like gentlemen?"

Evan took a deep breath and told himself to calm down. He wished they could sit and have a conversation like father and son, but that hadn't happened in a very long time. Sitting on the other side of the desk, he felt more like a student sent to the principal's office than one successful lawyer talking to another.

"The file," Evan repeated. "I want to see it."

"Why?"

"Because I'm having second thoughts."

Robert nodded slowly. "Ah. Let me guess. You talked to the woman, and she got you to buy her sob story."

"Yes, I talked to her. And it's not a sob story. She wants to help people. She and those kids care about each other."

"Of course they do." Sarcasm tinged Robert's voice. "Just like Sean cared about your mother and me."

Evan couldn't blame his father for being bitter toward his foster brother. His parents had loved Sean like he was their own, and he'd taken advantage of them. His mother's heart had been broken, but his father's had been hardened.

"You can't judge everyone in the foster care system by the way Sean acted."

Robert let the comment slip by without a response. Instead, he picked up his cell and began tapping and sliding across the screen with his thumb. "I have a meeting in twenty minutes. We can talk about this later."

"No. We will talk about this now." Evan wasn't about to be dismissed. "You told me you dug into Joy's background—"

"Oh, it's Joy now, is it?" Robert shook his head. "You should know better than to fraternize with the enemy."

"She's not the enemy. She's a warm human being, and frankly, I don't think you found anything worse in her background than the fact that she used to be a foster kid."

"I don't like what you're implying."

"Then show me the file."

After several long moments of staring each other down, Robert looked away.

Then, Evan knew. "There is no file, is there?"

"Of course there's a file." His father yanked open a desk drawer. "When I found out about the idiot deal Sam made with her, I hired a private investigator. Your uncle was ruled by his emotions, just like your mother, God rest her soul."

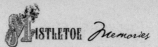

Your uncle, your mother. . . .Robert was doing everything he could to distance himself. But Evan wouldn't let him. "What did you find out?"

"Take a look." He tossed the file on the desk. "Her father went to prison for dealing drugs, and her mother killed herself. That's why Joy Benucci went into foster care."

The fact that her mother committed suicide made Evan's heart ache for Joy, but it didn't change his opinion of her. "What does any of that have to do with the kind of person she is?"

"It has everything to do with it. That's the stock she comes from. An unstable mother and a junkie father."

"She isn't a show dog. Her pedigree doesn't determine how she'll turn out."

"No, she's more like a pit bull," Robert sneered. "You can raise them to be friendly, but they still have that killer instinct. The minute you cross them, they'll go for the jugular and never let go."

Evan bit back a harsh retort. If Sean only knew how much damage he'd caused. But after a year of unsuccessful searching, Evan had given up. It was a waste of time, especially since he doubted Sean cared.

He opened the folder and looked over the six pieces of paper inside. Four pages contained detailed background information about Joy's parents. A quick scan of those made him wonder how she had turned out as normal and sweet as she did. The other two pages were about her: birth records, where she'd gone to school, a list of previous addresses and jobs, her credit history, and her police record.

"She got a parking ticket," Evan said dryly. "That's the

worst thing you could find on her?"

"Just because I couldn't find anything doesn't mean there's nothing to find. It just means she's good at hiding it."

Evan sighed and shut the file. "Why did you coerce her supporters to pull their funding?"

At least this time, Robert didn't try to deny anything. He even looked like he might be the tiniest bit ashamed of his actions, or at the very least, he regretted Evan finding out.

Frustration bubbled up, propelling Evan from his chair and setting him pacing the room. "By going to her contributors, you stopped her from continuing her work anywhere else."

"Exactly." Robert shook his finger at his son. "How can I let her do to anybody else what was done to us?"

"She's not a con artist." Evan walked up to the desk and leaned over it, his palms on the edge. "Trust me enough to trust my judgment."

His sincere request had the opposite effect he'd hoped. Instead of softening toward him, Robert stiffened, his lips pressed so tightly together the skin around them tinged white. For a moment, Evan thought the conversation was over. But then Robert stood with slow deliberation.

"Sean asked me to trust him, and I did. Then, when I wanted to cut him off, your mother begged me to trust her, and I did, even though I knew better. I gave him another chance, again and again. If I'd listened to my gut in the first place, our savings wouldn't have been wiped out and your mother wouldn't have died with a broken heart." He shut his eyes tightly against the images that assaulted him.

Evan had the urge to rush around the desk and embrace him, but that would just make his father feel more

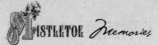

uncomfortable. "Dad, I understand how you feel. But this isn't the way to deal with it."

Robert opened his eyes, and they were cold as flint. "It's my way."

"No." Evan shook his head. "I'm not going to evict Joy and the people who live at Comfort House."

"You don't have to, because I am."

"You can't."

"Oh yes I can. You signed that house over to me. I own the property now." He pulled his shoulders back and buttoned his suit jacket. "Now, I really do have a meeting to get to."

Evan stared at him as he walked to the door. "Dad, please. Don't do this."

His father turned, and for a moment, Evan had a glimmer of hope. But it was dashed by the smirk on Robert's face.

"By the way, you might want to tell your girlfriend that the conditions of the original lease still apply. She has fourteen days from the time you spoke to her to vacate the premises."

Evan was doing the math in his head as Robert walked out of the office, leaving the door open behind him. Fourteen days. . .his heart sank.

Now Joy and her kids would be without a home as of December twenty-third. Two days before Christmas. And he was the one who had to deliver the news.

❧

The house was wonderfully still after Alex and her crew left. Joy wandered into the kitchen and took a bottle of water from the fridge.

Evan certainly had taken off in a hurry. He thought he knew who was behind the loss of her funding, but what exactly did that mean? Could he reverse things? Even if he did, it would hardly matter unless she could negotiate an affordable rent on another house. Or unless he changed his mind about evicting her.

Joy shook her head. There was no use speculating and getting her hopes up. She would find out what was going on soon enough. For now, she needed to do something positive and uplifting. They all did.

She walked into the living room where Dana, Tanya, Ben, and Leon were huddled together in an animated conversation. "What's going on?"

"We're trying to figure out why that lawyer is so hot to kick us out," Ben said.

"He said it was because Sam charged too little for monthly rent."

"Then why didn't he just raise the rent?" Dana asked. "If he's going to rent the place out to someone else anyway, it makes sense that he'd try to keep the renters he already has."

Leon nodded in agreement. "And if he's not renting out the house, then he wants it for something else."

Joy's mind went back to the day she'd met Evan. "He said he had other plans for the house, but he wouldn't tell me what."

"If we can figure out why he wants the house and what he wants to do with it, then maybe we can save it." Dana was uncharacteristically optimistic.

The last thing Joy wanted to do was dampen their spirits, but she didn't share their enthusiasm. "I think it's great you're trying to save Comfort House. But right now, I want to do something a little more festive." They looked at her blankly.

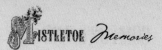

"Let's get the Christmas decorations up."

She laughed at the positive response as they all jumped to their feet and headed out into the hall. Just as they were going up the stairs, the doorbell rang. "I'll be up in a minute. The boxes are in the attic, near the door. They all have *Christmas* written on them."

Ben jogged ahead of the others. "That sure narrows it down."

Joy chuckled to herself. A good dose of Christmas was exactly what they needed. When she opened the front door, she smiled at her next-door neighbor. "Mrs. Clifton. So good to see you. Come in."

Snow was falling in soft, slow flakes, but Mrs. Clifton shook her head. "Oh no, dear. I don't have a lot of time. I came across this while George and I were packing, and I wanted to return it."

Joy took the vase Mrs. Clifton held out. It was inexpensive glass, the kind you'd buy at a discount store. Joy had taken flowers to their house one day when Mrs. Clifton was laid up with a broken arm. "Thank you. Did you say you're packing?"

She smiled broadly. "Yes. Now that George and I are retired, we're migrating to Florida."

"I had no idea. I never saw a FOR SALE sign on your house."

"That's because we never put it on the market. A nice lawyer came to us and made an offer on the property." Mrs. Clifton leaned in closer and lowered her voice. "It was too generous to pass up."

Joy smiled sweetly, even as the muscles in her shoulders tightened. "How lovely. Um, that lawyer. . .his last name wouldn't happen to be Lancaster, would it?"

Her eyes widened. "You've met him? Such a nice fellow. And handsome, too."

"Mmm. Yes."

"I should have known he would have talked to you, too. It seems he's been buying up a lot of property in the neighborhood."

"He has?"

"Oh yes. The Ryans and the Schumachers have closed their deals. And the Johanssons are waiting for a response on their counter offer."

Joy wasn't sure how much longer she could keep up her pleasant veneer, and she didn't want to take out her frustration on her neighbor. "I'm sorry, but I have some work I need to get back to. Thank you for the vase. And many blessings in your new home."

"The same to you, dear." Mrs. Clifton wiggled her fingers at Joy before heading carefully down the porch steps.

Joy leaned against the closed door, tightly clutching the neck of the vase. Mrs. Clifton thought Joy was moving, too, and no wonder. Comfort House was surrounded by all the neighbors who'd already sold their homes. That explained why Evan was evicting her. He needed the house, or else there would be a great big hole in the middle of whatever he had planned.

The doorbell rang again. Mrs. Clifton must have forgotten something. Joy pulled the door open and froze.

Evan Lancaster stood on her porch.

"Joy, we need to talk."

CHAPTER 9

I don't want to hear anything you have to say."

She tried to slam the door in his face, but he stopped it with his palm. "Trust me, you want to hear this."

"Trust you?" Joy snorted and, since shutting him out was impossible, she threw the door open and gestured wildly. "How can I? Every time I turn around, I find out another secret about you."

"I'm sure you have every right to be upset, but I honestly don't know what you're talking about." He leaned to the side and pointed. "Would you mind putting that down?"

Joy looked at the vase she'd been swinging like a club. "Sorry. I don't make a habit of answering the door with a blunt object in my hand." She was being ridiculous. As angry as she was, she still needed to find out exactly what he was up to. And sending him away wouldn't get her any closer to the truth. "Come in."

Instead of going to the living room, with its comfy couch and cozy fire, she led him to the kitchen, with its harsh florescent lights and hard, backless stools at the center island. No point in making him comfortable.

She pointed at a stool. "Have a seat."

Evan sat. They looked at each other. He seemed nervous. Why would the man who held all the cards be anything but confident? "What did you come here to tell me?"

"It's so complicated, I don't know where to start."

Joy was losing her patience. "Then let me start. I found out you've been buying up property all around me. When were you going to mention that?"

"Never," Evan said. "Because I haven't bought any property."

"My neighbor just told me that you paid her and several of my neighbors a visit. She's packing right now because you bought her house."

"Look, I'd know if I bought a house." Evan stood up so quickly he knocked the stool over. "She's made a mistake."

Joy jammed her fists on her hips. "Oh, really? She sold her home to a lawyer named Lancaster. How many of you can there be?"

Evan groaned. "Two."

"What?"

"There are two of us. My father is a lawyer, too. It had to be him."

"Your father?" Not knowing what else to do, Joy walked around the island and righted the stool as her brain processed this new information.

"He's the one I went to see."

"You think he's the one that talked to my contributors?"

"I don't think, I know."

From the look on his face, Joy could tell that Evan felt as betrayed and blindsided as she did. He'd just earned his way out of the kitchen.

"Come on." She crooked a finger at him. "Let's move this conversation to somewhere more comfortable."

She had a feeling it was going to be a long afternoon.

Evan was thankful Joy had let them move from the kitchen into the living room, even though it was filled with boxes marked *Christmas* and three very sour-faced teenagers.

"Where's Ben?" Joy asked.

Tanya pointed toward the ceiling. "Still in the attic. He said he found something important and he'd be down soon."

"All right, then. Everybody have a seat. Let's hear what Evan has to say."

The girls and Joy sat together on the couch while Leon settled on the loveseat. Evan sat in a wingback chair that was too close to the fireplace, making it a literal hot seat. He stood up, shrugged out of his coat, and decided to stay on his feet.

"I didn't even know Comfort House existed until Uncle Sam passed away. When I was going over the will, I called my father to ask him about it. He gave me the impression that, well, he gave me the wrong impression." Now that he could move, Evan began to feel more at ease, almost like he was giving a summation to a jury. "I thought the whole thing was a scam. Just a way to squeeze money out of soft-hearted people."

Joy flinched, as though she'd just been slapped. "Why would anybody think that?"

"My family has a history with the foster system." Evan paused. He didn't want to insult the young people in the room, but they needed to hear the truth. "My brother, Sean, was a foster child. My parents treated him like he'd always been part of the family. They loved him. And he knew exactly how to manipulate their feelings."

They all looked at each other. Leon was the first to speak

up. "What did he do?"

"What didn't he do? He started off small. Cut school, shoplifted, stuff like that. Then he moved on to bigger things. He always had a sob story, was always able to make my parents feel guilty so they'd bail him out." Evan stuffed his hands in his pants pockets.

"He managed to get through high school and then enrolled in college. For a while, it seemed like he was getting his life straightened out. But then he came to my parents with a crazy business idea. My father refused to invest any money in it, but my mother. . . She couldn't say no to Sean. She slipped him money without telling Dad. Somehow, Sean gained access to their banking information, and he cleaned out their accounts."

"That's terrible," Joy said. "I'm so sorry."

Evan nodded. "When Mom found out, it crushed her. She called, told me everything, and begged me to help her find Sean and the money before my father found out."

"Did you?" Leon asked.

"I looked everywhere, talked to all his friends, but there was no trail. I don't know how he did it, but he vanished. We never heard from him again."

Evan's heart clenched. All those years, he told himself he was over it, that he'd put the ordeal with Sean behind him and moved on. But now, the pain was still so sharp, he knew he'd been lying to himself. He hadn't forgiven Sean. He'd just buried his anger and hurt. That's why it had been so easy for him to believe his father's accusations about Joy.

"I'm so sorry." He sank into the chair, elbows to knees, head hanging. "You all shouldn't have to suffer because of my family drama."

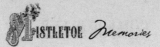

"At least now it makes sense."

His head jerked up at Joy's words. "What does?"

"Why your father doesn't trust me, for one thing. But also, why Sam rented me this place so cheap. I think it was because of Sean."

That hadn't occurred to Evan. "Go on."

"Well, when I first talked to him, he was extremely interested in what kind of work I did, and that I'd been a foster child myself. He kept saying stuff like, 'You turned out so well.' Like he couldn't believe someone who grew up in the system could have a good, productive life."

Evan nodded. "He always said he wished he could have done more. That he could have helped Sean. But honestly, I don't know what any of us could have done differently."

"There may not have been anything you could have done. He might have been too emotionally scarred before he came to you. Or, he could just be a bad person. Even in fully functioning, loving families, there can be an aberration. Doesn't happen a lot, but it does happen."

Evan opened his mouth to speak, but no sound came out. Instead, tears pricked the back of his eyes, and he blinked hard against them. He'd never cried over Sean, and he certainly wasn't about to start now.

Joy stood from the couch and came to him. She hunkered down beside his chair and put her hand on his arm. "You can't blame yourself, Evan."

Leon jumped up from his spot on the loveseat. "Wonder what's taking Ben so long." He hurried from the room, followed closely by Dana and Tanya.

"Thank you." He put his hand over hers. "I didn't even

realize I was blaming myself until now."

"It's hard not to take everything personally when your family is involved. But you had no control over the choices Sean made. For your own peace of mind, though, you have to forgive him and let him go."

"I don't know how."

Joy smiled. "Like anything else, you do it one step at a time. Can I ask you a personal question?"

"At this point, you can ask just about anything."

"Do you believe in God?"

He hesitated, then nodded.

"Then pray. Ask for His help. Forgive Sean in your heart, and the next time you find yourself thinking about him, forgive him again. God forgives us once then forgets our sins, but we usually have to forgive each other multiple times before it sticks."

Heat rose in Evan's cheeks. "It's been awhile since I prayed about anything. I doubt He remembers me."

"He never forgot you, Evan." She squeezed his hand. "Trust me."

He looked into eyes so sincere, so guileless, there wasn't any question. He trusted Joy, and he would trust God to help him with his brother and show them how to save Comfort House.

CHAPTER 10

By the time the teens came back in, Joy and Evan had moved their conversation to the couch.

"What did you find?" Joy looked up with a smile, letting them know it was safe to reenter the room.

"There's a bunch of old stuff up there," Ben said. His clothes were covered in dust, and a cobweb clung to the side of his head. But he was grinning and holding a cardboard box. "You're going to love this."

Joy motioned for him to set it on the coffee table and they all gathered around. He pulled an old album out first. "Look." He flipped carefully through the pages until he found the one he was looking for. "Right there."

They all leaned in to get a better view of the picture he pointed to. "Oh, wow," Joy said. "It's this house." She squinted to make out the faded, handwritten caption. "The Graff family, 1869."

Evan turned a few more pages then stopped and let out a low whistle. "The entire album is full of the people who lived here."

"Look at this one." Joy put her finger below the image of a man, a woman, and several children. Beneath it was written, *Opening day at the Graff House Orphanage.* "I had no idea this house served as an orphanage. It's almost like its purpose is to help children and young people."

"That's so cool." Dana peered over Ben's shoulder. "What else is in the box?"

"More photos, advertisements, stuff like that."

"Advertisements for what?"

"Looks like this place used to be a spa," Ben said. "There's a mineral spring somewhere."

Evan shook his head. "Actually, the spa was up the road, but this was probably one of the resort homes. And the spring is gone. The source was destroyed back in the forties when they were doing road work."

"How do you know that?" Joy asked.

"I'm full of surprises." Evan waggled an eyebrow.

Joy pulled a handful of papers and photos out of the box, put them in her lap, and carefully examined them. "This is amazing. This brochure claims the chalybeate waters from the spring could cure colic and the vapors, reverse melancholy—" She couldn't hold back her laughter any longer. It burst from her, doubling her over.

"Are you okay?" Tanya asked.

Joy nodded, but the laughter made her so jerky, she was sure she looked like a bobblehead doll in an earthquake. All she could do was point to the brochure in her hand.

"Now you have to share." Evan chuckled.

She waved her free hand in the air, took a few deep breaths, and finally stopped laughing long enough to read the next two lines to them. "Dry the over-moist brain and loosen the clammy humors of the body." She barely got the last word out before everyone in the room started laughing.

"How can something dry a wet brain and loosen clammy hummus at the same time?"

"Not hummus, *humors*!"

"Are you sure that spring is gone?"

"How will I reverse my melancholy?"

"This is doing a pretty good job."

The jokes came so fast, Joy wasn't sure who said what. But when she looked at Evan, his eyes crinkled at the corners, a deep, rumbling chortle spilling from his open lips, her heart skipped a beat. And when his eyes met hers, there was a connection so strong it felt more like a collision.

The laughter faded away, and Joy took in a deep, steadying breath. "Well, we all needed that."

"Yes, we did." The jovial ease slipped from Evan's face as his brow creased in concern.

"Don't worry." She smiled at him. "We know so much more now than we did just yesterday. We know that your father has some kind of plan that involves more than just this property. And we know this house has quite a history. There has to be some way to use that information to our advantage."

"I'm afraid there's one more thing you don't know," Evan said.

Ben glared at him. "Here it comes."

"Here what comes?" Dana asked.

"The one more thing. There's always one more thing." Ben closed the photo album and plopped it back in the box. "They lull you into a false sense of security, then they drop it on you."

Joy frowned at him. "Don't assume the worst. Evan wants to help us. He's on our side." She looked at Evan, hoping that now she wasn't assuming too much. "You *are* on our side, aren't you?"

"I am." His words were positive, but his tone was grim.

"And if it were up to me, I'd renew your lease for another fifty years."

"I thought it was up to you, since you own the building."

Evan shook his head. "Not anymore. I signed the deed over to my father. Now he's the landlord."

"Oh." Joy pushed down the panic that tried to crawl out through her skin. "Well, that makes things more challenging, but not impossible. We've still got three weeks to change his mind."

Evan scrubbed his face with his palm, a sure sign something was wrong.

"We don't have three weeks, do we?" Joy asked.

"No." He looked her in the eye. "Now you have the original two weeks specified in the lease."

Joy's mind whirled. She tried to picture the calendar, to remember what day it had been when she found Evan in this very room and he'd altered the course of her life.

"The twenty-third," Evan filled in for her. "You have to be out on December twenty-third."

"And the other thing drops." Ben stood up and brushed his hands on his jeans. "Come on, guys. We've got a week to get packed and find new digs."

There must be something positive she could say, but as Joy watched the four of them trudge from the room, she couldn't think of a thing. They'd trusted her, and she'd let them down.

What a merry Christmas this would be.

❧

"I'll do whatever I can to help you," Evan said. "We can look for another house. In fact, we might even be able to locate a short sale that you could purchase."

"I don't have the financial resources to buy a house." Her smile was sad and resigned. "Especially now that I have no funding to speak of."

He'd forgotten about that. "You may not have the old contributors, but that doesn't mean we can't get you new ones."

"In seven days?"

A plan began to formulate. "Let me check something." He took his phone from his pocket and pulled up the calendar. "How are you at schmoozing?"

"I hate it," Joy said. "But I'm really good at it."

Evan smiled. "Tomorrow night the Long Valley Historical Society is having its annual Mistletoe Ball. There are bound to be people there wanting to contribute to a good cause so they can claim it on their taxes next year."

Joy laughed. "That's a rather mercenary way to look at it."

"Not so much mercenary as practical. It's a one-hand-washes-the-other proposition."

"It's a good idea, but I haven't been invited."

"Sure you have. By me." He set his phone on the table, put his hand out, palm up, and grinned. "Miss Benucci, would you do me the honor of attending the ball with me?"

She slipped her hand into his. "It would be my pleasure."

He was about to say something else when his phone rang. He looked down at the screen and then back at Joy. "It's Alex."

She pulled her hand away. "Go ahead and answer it."

He snatched it up. "Hello, Alex." His eyebrows drew together as he listened. "Uh-huh." Listened some more. Nodded. "I think we should both come. Hold on." He lowered the phone and spoke to Joy. "Alex dug up something. Do you have time to go meet her now?"

"I guess so. Sure." Things certainly were moving quickly.

Evan put the phone back to his ear. "Alex, we'll be there in about thirty minutes. 'Bye." He ended the call and stood. "Things may be looking up after all."

CHAPTER 11

For the second time that day, Joy sat across from Alex Faraday. But this time, there were no lights, no cameras, no mic packs. This time, they met in a local restaurant, sitting in a cozy, high-backed booth in a corner that offered a bit of privacy. Alex had arrived first and ordered coffee for all. As soon as Evan and Joy sat down, Alex jumped into her story.

"I was doing some background research for the story about the two of you—"

"The story you promised to hold off on," Evan reminded her.

Alex picked up a clean coffee stirrer and pointed it at him. "Yes that's the one. Anyway, when I did an Internet search on you, I uncovered something interesting about your father."

Beside her, Alex felt Evan stiffen. No doubt he was concerned that Alex had unearthed some information about Sean and what his family had gone through.

"What did you find?" he asked.

"I was searching on your name, but when you look for one Lancaster, attorney-at-law, you end up with both. Your father's name came up as counsel for Prescott Development. When I saw that, it reminded me of an article I read last month." Alex opened the file that lay on the table beside her place setting. "Look at the highlighted section."

Evan took the printed page she handed to him. He held it so Joy could see it, too, but still read the marked section out loud.

"While the location has not yet been disclosed, a spokesperson for Prescott Development says the project will be a combination of high-end condominiums and luxury resort accommodations. It will far surpass the resorts that used to be such a fixture on Schooley's Mountain."

Evan looked at Joy. "This must be what he wants the houses for."

"Wait," Alex interrupted. "Houses? As in more than one?"

Joy wrapped her cold fingers around her coffee mug. "According to one of my neighbors, Mr. Lancaster purchased her home and several others."

"It makes sense they'd need some serious acreage for this kind of project." Alex tapped one manicured, pale pink fingernail on the table. "I just thought he was starting off with Comfort House. I didn't realize he'd gotten so far already."

"So the idea is to tear down the existing homes in order to build a new resort?" Joy shook her head. "That's nuts."

Alex lifted her coffee cup. "That's progress."

"That's not going to fly with the Historical Society." Evan took a pen from inside his jacket pocket and made notes on the article.

"What's he talking about?" Alex asked Joy.

"We found a box of old photos and documents that tell all about the history of Comfort House. It was one of the original resort homes. And it was an orphanage."

Alex nodded. "You know, the society is having its annual ball tomorrow. If we went together—"

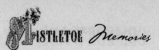

Evan held up his hand in a stop gesture. "I'm going and taking Joy."

"Don't flatter yourself," Alex said with a chuckle. "I already have a date. When I said *we*, I meant all of us. We could definitely get some people on our side."

Joy let out a deep sigh. Not only did she have to look for new financial supporters, she had to convince people that the house she lived and worked in should be preserved as a historical landmark. This was going to be the busiest Christmas ball ever.

❧

By the time Evan brought Joy back home that night, it was dark, which made it easy to see the multicolored lights outlining the first-story eaves of the house.

"Looks like the kids have been busy." She turned to Evan. "Would you like to come in?"

One side of his mouth tilted down. "I would very much like to, but I can't. I have work to do before we storm the barricades tomorrow night."

Joy laughed. "Now I don't know whether to wear an evening gown or something out of *Les Mis*."

"An evening gown, please."

She had one hand on the door handle, but her body was turned toward Evan. The look in his eyes, the tightness in her chest. . .it was like something out of a movie.

"Joy."

She could barely breathe. "Yes?"

"We're being watched."

He pointed to the house where a curtain had been pulled back and at least two faces were close to the glass. She laughed.

"I guess that's my cue to go."

Evan nodded. "See you tomorrow."

Walking from the car to her front door, Joy told herself it was ridiculous to wish he'd kissed her good-bye. They hadn't even been on a date yet. And their date the next evening was more of a business proposition than anything else. Evan was a powerful attorney who wore expensive suits and dated glamorous reporters. She was a social worker who rarely had a reason to wear anything but jeans and hung out with troubled teens. They were worlds apart.

"I'm home!" she called out to anyone within shouting range as she stomped the snow from her boots and removed them just inside the doorway. Ben and Tanya, the two who had been looking through the window, came out of the kitchen. Leon and Dana entered the hall from the living room.

"I have lots of news," Joy said. "But first, the Christmas lights. Very nice."

"But wait, there's more." Dana turned and motioned for Joy to follow.

The living room had been transformed into a festive, cozy gathering place. The artificial tree—purchased at an after-Christmas sale three years prior because it was easier on the budget than buying a new tree every year—stood in one corner, covered with lights and an assortment of mismatched ornaments. Garland hung on the mantel, and a small Christmas village was arranged on the coffee table.

Joy felt like the Grinch when his heart grew two sizes. "This is so great. But what changed your minds? Before I left, you'd all headed off to pack your things."

Ben, Dana, and Tanya looked at Leon, who apparently

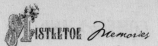

had been appointed the group representative, whether he wanted to be or not.

"I realized we can't give up." Leon looked away, as though he didn't want anyone to see what he was feeling. But when he turned back, his eyes blazed with conviction. "I've never given up in my life. None of us have. If we did, we wouldn't have ended up here."

Dana took a step forward. "We're here for a reason. Whether it's God, or the universe, or fate. . .I don't know. But we won't give up without fighting."

Tears brimmed in Joy's eyes, but she didn't care. She didn't care if she blubbered like an idiot. "I'm so proud of you. All of you. And I'm glad you're up for a fight, because we've got one ahead of us."

Ben picked up a box of Kleenex from a side table and handed it to Joy. "We've got a bunch of ideas."

Joy narrowed her eyes as she took the box of tissue. "None of them involve buckets of eggnog, do they?"

"Not anymore." Ben grinned.

Tanya chucked him in the ribs with her elbow. "We seriously have some good ideas."

"Evan and I came up with some ideas, too. We need to sit down and go over all of it." She pointed to Tanya and Dana. "And then I need to see you two in my room."

They exchanged worried looks. "Us?" Dana's voice squeaked. "What for?"

"I need your opinion about an outfit." Joy spoke with what she hoped was an air of mystery. "I have a ball to attend."

❧

Evan was used to working long days. But the stress of doing a good job and winning a case wasn't usually paired with such a strong emotional component. In the week that he'd known her, Joy Benucci had become extremely important to him. He didn't want to let her down, or her kids.

After poring over legal precedence, Evan was certain that Comfort House met the requirements to be classified a historic landmark. That would keep anybody from tearing it down. But his father still owned the house, and he had the right to evict Joy if he wanted to. Somehow, they had to convince him that Joy wasn't hiding anything, and that her cause was one worth supporting.

His cell phone let out a high-pitched *ding*, signaling that he'd received a text message. It was from Joy.

CHECK YOUR E-MAIL.

Short, sweet, and to the point. Just like the woman herself. Except for the short part.

Her e-mail made him smile. The teens were with her, ready to fight to save their haven. Ben and Leon had already created "Save Comfort House" pages on all the major social media sites. Dana and Tanya had initiated a tell-all-your-friends chain of texts, tweets, and instant messages. And then the girls had helped Joy pick out a dress for the Mistletoe Ball.

The idea that Joy was concerned enough about what she wore to enlist help told him this was more than just an opportunity to try and save her cause. She wanted to look nice, and he liked to think she wanted to look nice for him.

Evan went to enough black-tie events that he owned his own tuxedo. He just hoped the shirt was clean. With a frown, he pushed away from the desk. He'd take a look in the closet, then grab some more coffee, and then hit the computer again.

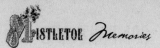

He found himself whistling as he walked into his room. It was a ball, so there would be dancing. Would Joy dance with him? He imagined they'd move gracefully together, her delicate hand enclosed in his fingers, his other hand resting lightly on the small of her back.

Mixing business with pleasure was something he never did. But in this case, there was no way to separate the two. The best thing he could do was concentrate on completing their business. Then, he and Joy could get to know each other better. He hoped, much better.

CHAPTER 12

$\mathbf{A}$re you sure it's not too much?"

Joy turned in front of the mirror and let the midnight-blue silk swirl around her legs, drawing sighs of admiration from the young ladies sitting on her bed.

"You're going to something called a *ball*," Tanya said. "I don't think anything in your closet could be too much."

"It's perfect," Dana said.

They were right. It was perfect. Joy had forgotten she even owned the dress. She'd found it at least a year ago at an overstock shopping outlet for less than what she'd pay for a pair of jeans. She'd bought it on the off chance she'd be invited somewhere very fancy. Once again, God had provided for her needs before she even knew she had them.

The pealing of the doorbell made all three of the women jump.

"He's here." Dana bounced off the bed, followed by Tanya.

"Am I ready?" Joy took one more look in the mirror. Thanks to the girls, her hair was swept into a casual yet sophisticated updo. Her makeup was more dramatic than she was used to, but it fit the occasion. They'd done everything they could to make her presentable for the evening. Now if only someone could do something about the swarm of butterflies in her stomach.

"You look beautiful." Tanya held out her beaded clutch

331

purse. "Time to make your entrance."

The girls were already thundering down the stairs when Joy took a deep breath and convinced herself to step out of her room. She made her way slowly down the staircase, one hand on the banister, the other holding up her skirt slightly. *Do not fall,* she repeated over and over in her head. *Do not fall.*

She concentrated so hard on staying upright that she didn't even notice Evan until she descended the last step. When she saw him, her breath caught in her throat. He was gorgeous.

Evan seemed a bit at a loss for words, too. Finally, he smiled and said, "You look beautiful."

Her eyelids dipped as a flush warmed her cheeks. "Thank you."

"Before you go, we need to get pictures." Tanya ran forward, camera in hand. "How about in front of the tree?"

As they moved into the living room, Leon and Ben flanked Evan and took turns grilling him.

"Turn your cell phone off when you get in the car," Ben said.

Leon nodded. "No texting and driving."

"And have a designated driver."

"Better yet, no drinking for either one of you."

Joy laughed as Dana posed her and Evan by the twinkling lights of the plastic tree. "I don't drink."

"Neither do I." Evan's arm was around her back, his fingers snug against her waist. He leaned down, pulling her close to his side, and whispered in her ear, "We may be perfect for each other."

She looked up at him at the moment Tanya snapped a picture. "That was cute. Now both of you look at me and smile."

A few minutes later, her vision blurred by white spots, Joy held up her hand. "I think that's enough." She turned to Evan. "We should get out of here before we go blind."

"Agreed."

They made it as far as the porch before they were stopped again, this time by Ben. "Hey, take a picture of them out here. It'll be like the one of the Graff family."

"Good idea." Tanya hurried down the steps and looked up at them. "This is a great tie-in with the history of the house."

Evan pulled Joy close again. "We can't say no. It's to save the house, after all."

A shiver went through her, more from his fingers brushing her arm than the chill in the wind.

"Is that wrap going to be warm enough?" he asked with a frown.

Joy smiled. "It'll be fine, as long as we don't have to walk too far."

Three pictures later, they finally made it to Evan's car. He held the door open for her, helped her in, and then went around to the driver's side. When he opened his door, Joy heard Leon call out one more admonition. "Have her home by midnight!"

Evan gave him a two-fingered salute then shut the door. He chuckled as he fastened his seat belt. "They certainly are protective of you."

"They're a good group of kids."

"Yes, they are." He grew serious. "I'm sorry I ever thought otherwise."

Joy reached out and squeezed his hand. "I understand why you did. Now, we just need to get your father to see us the way you do."

Evan nodded. "Buckle your seat belt, Joy. We've got a Christmas miracle to pull off."

❧

Evan had been to his fair share of formal shindigs, but never had he felt as proud as when he entered the banquet hall with Joy on his arm. Unlike most of the women, she wasn't dripping with sparkling costume jewelry designed to make everyone wonder if it was real, and her dress didn't scream out that it just might be an original. Joy was a vision of simple, unpretentious elegance.

"Everyone looks so beautiful." Her voice was low, and her fingers tightened on the crook of his elbow.

He patted her hand. "As far as I'm concerned, you're the most beautiful woman in this room."

She beamed at him. "That's good enough for me."

"Are you ready to schmooze?"

Pulling back her shoulders, she took a deep breath. "I'm ready if you are."

"Let's go, then."

For the next hour, Evan led her from one cluster of people to another, making introductions and starting conversations. After the fourth time he and Joy were offered drinks, he fetched them glasses of ginger ale from the bar. Joy looked pleased to have something to hold besides her purse. But if she felt any discomfort talking to so many new people, she certainly didn't show it.

They had just finished talking to Mrs. Gaebler, a widow

with a heart for architectural preservation and a substantial financial portfolio, when Joy motioned across the room. "Alex is here."

Alex raised her hand and wove her way through the crowd, pulling a tall, muscular man along behind her.

"Hi, you two." Alex stopped in front of them, automatically striking a pose with her weight thrown back on one leg, the other extended with toes pointed so it peeped through the slit in her sequin-covered, strapless crimson dress. "Evan, Joy, I'd like you to meet Derrick Watson."

Evan shook the man's hand. "Nice to meet you."

Beside him, Joy's mouth had dropped open in shock. "Derrick Watson? Of the New York Giants?"

The big man laughed, and her hand virtually disappeared when he engulfed it in both of his. "That's me. Nice to meet you."

Evan frowned. The main point of this evening was to gain support for Comfort House, and having a retired pro-football player on their side could only help. But he didn't like the way the man looked at Joy like she was dessert. And worse, Joy didn't seem to mind.

"Come back to earth." Alex put her hand on Evan's shoulder to get his attention. "Fill me in."

"Excuse me?" Joy was laughing at something Derrick had said, and Evan had a hard time paying attention to anything else.

Alex rolled her eyes. "Who've you talked to? What kind of reaction are you getting?"

"Good. Very positive so far."

"Wonderful. Now, there are a few people I think you and

I should speak to together." Before Evan could stop her, Alex had linked her arm around his. "Joy, I'm going to borrow your date for a few minutes so we can buzz in a few ears."

At least Joy looked surprised, and none too happy, to see Alex hanging onto Evan. But she didn't protest. "Sure. I'd like to talk to Derrick, too. If nobody minds."

"Great by me," Derrick said, grinning a toothpaste-commercial smile that didn't seem like it could have survived years of pro ball.

"I don't mind," Alex said.

Evan minded. A lot. But he couldn't very well say it. "I'll come find you in a few minutes."

Alex tugged him in one direction while Derrick put his hand on Joy's back and led her toward an hors d'oeuvre- and dessert-covered table, saying something about how he was always hungry. Joy's laughter made Evan want to turn around and tackle the man, but instead he moved forward. There was work to be done. He'd figure out his personal life later.

&

Evan had promised to find her in a few minutes, but that had been more than an hour ago. Joy's talk with Derrick had gone extremely well. She had his phone number in her purse and an invitation to call him. When people started recognizing the football player, Joy excused herself before she was crushed by the crowd. She'd spoken to more people and had several good leads to follow up on. Now, the crowd was beginning to thin out. She sat by herself at a round table, resting her tired feet and nursing a tall glass that looked like champagne but was actually sparkling cider.

Where was Evan?

Finally, she spotted him, coming back into the ballroom with Alex. Where had they been? Alex pulled him to the side, leaned in close to say something, and then kissed him on the cheek. The next moment, she dashed away and latched on to Derrick. Evan rubbed at his cheek as he scanned the crowd.

Joy raised her hand to get his attention. When he saw her, a smile lit up his face and he hurried to the table.

"I didn't expect to find you alone." He settled in the chair beside her and leaned close. "Where's Derrick?"

"Surrounded by fans. We finished talking awhile ago."

Evan hesitated. "Did you have a good time?"

"Oh yes, he's a real sweetheart." She patted her purse. "I've got his number and he told me to call him and work out the details."

Evan pulled back, his eyes narrowed. "Details?"

"Yes." From the storm clouds brewing in Evan's eyes, Joy knew something was wrong. She just had no idea what. "That was the whole idea, right? To find people who would help support Comfort House."

"Oh. The details about. . .oh."

"Of course. That's why I was so excited when I realized who he was. Derrick's been very open about the fact that he was a foster kid. He had a great experience; his foster parents even adopted him. But he knows how important a place like Comfort House is." The more she talked, the more Evan's mood lightened, and finally it dawned on her. "You thought I was interested in him, *personally*?"

Evan shrugged. "Well, he's a famous athlete."

Joy laughed. "And I was worried when I saw you come back in with Alex and she kissed you."

"You were?"

"A little bit."

Evan chuckled. "What a couple we are."

A couple. Hearing him call them that felt good. It felt right. She reached for his hand. "There's one thing we haven't done yet tonight."

"What's that?"

"Dance."

Evan stood and pulled her to her feet. "We need to take care of that right away."

They stepped onto the dance floor to the strains of "Moonlight Serenade." And there, with her hand in his, his arm around her, her cheek resting above his heart, Joy felt something she'd never felt before. A sense that this man could be her family, her home. Whether they saved Comfort House or not, God had brought Evan into her life. She knew that like she knew her own name.

The song ended, but before she could say anything, the band leader made an announcement.

"Ladies and gentlemen, just a reminder that complimentary portraits are being taken in the gazebo outside the west exit. Don't miss the opportunity to commemorate the evening."

Evan looked down at her. "What do you say?"

Joy smiled. "I say we shouldn't miss the opportunity."

They walked through the double doors and out into the chilled night. A lovely gazebo had been set up a few feet from the door, along with heat lamps for those who were waiting.

When their turn came, Joy stood close to Evan, her smile impossible to erase.

"Wonderful," the photographer said. "Now how about a traditional pose under the mistletoe?"

"What?" Evan asked.

The photographer pointed above their heads. "This is the Mistletoe Ball, after all."

They looked up to see a fat sprig of dark green mistletoe tied with a piece of red velvet ribbon hanging above their heads.

Joy swallowed and summoned up all her courage. "What do you say?"

Evan cupped her jaw with his palm, his thumb caressing her cheek. "I say we shouldn't miss the opportunity."

His lips lowered to hers, and the world burst into a flash of light.

Then the photographer took the picture.

CHAPTER 13

The next few days, Joy alternated between floating on a cloud and being weighed down with worry.

She was in love. Giddy, sappy, unexplainable love. And best of all, Evan seemed to love her back in the same giddy, sappy, unexplainable way. The only thing putting a damper on their new relationship was the fact that his father wanted to run her out of town.

The closer they got to the twenty-third—or E-day as the kids called it—the more she worried about what they would do. Finances weren't as big a problem as they had been. Many of the new contacts she'd made said they wanted to support Comfort House, including Derrick Watson, who could likely fund the entire thing for the next twenty years if he was so inclined. The problem was, whenever Joy thought about leaving, something in her heart twisted. She was certain they were supposed to stay in this house. And that somehow, God was going to use the situation to heal Roger Lancaster.

Alex had run her story, but she'd left Evan out of it. Instead, she focused on the development company, the historic angle of the properties in question, and the fight to save Comfort House. Between her report and the social media exposure, they'd been inundated with e-mails, snail mails, even phone calls. Public support was on their side.

For the moment, the house was blissfully quiet. Ben, who

had appointed himself the official recorder of the house's history, was busy cataloging the contents of several more boxes he'd recovered from the attic. The others were out, either at work or college.

Joy sipped a cup of tea and moved things around in the pantry. She needed to step away from fighting and planning and strategizing. She needed to make cookies. If they had the right ingredients.

She pulled out baking soda, sugar, a bag of chocolate chips. . . . It was looking good. She leaned farther in, digging behind a canister. The doorbell rang and she jumped, smacking her head on the pantry doorframe.

Joy rubbed the sore spot on her head as she went to the door. "You'd better not be a solicitor."

She yanked the door open. A man stood on the porch, hands jammed in his coat pockets, shoulders hunched forward. He was probably in his late thirties, but it was hard to tell for sure. "Can I help you?"

"I hope so." The man looked up at her, and now she could see a thin scar running down his cheek to his jaw. "Are you Joy Benucci?"

"I am." Joy's fingers tightened on the door, just in case he turned out to be trouble. But from the tortured look in his eyes, she guessed he was more in need of help than out to hurt anybody.

"I'm looking for my brother, and I hope you can help me."

Joy opened the door a little wider, and even though she already knew the answer, she asked him, "Who's your brother?"

"Evan Lancaster." The man looked at the ground and said so low she could hardly hear him, "I'm Sean."

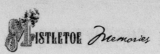

Evan pulled up in front of Comfort House, braking a little too hard and skidding on the snow-covered driveway. Joy's text had been cryptic to say the least: COME OVER AS SOON AS YOU CAN. IT'S IMPORTANT. Evan didn't know if it was good or bad, personal or business. He and Joy were going to have to talk about the finer points of clear communication.

She must have been watching for him, because the front door opened before he left the car. Bundled up in a heavy jacket, mittens, and scarf, Joy looked more like one of her teens than the person who ran the place.

"What's the emergency?" He jogged up the steps and dropped a kiss on her cheek. Normally, that would have brought out a smile, but her cheeks were flushed, her eyes worried, and her smile was nowhere in sight. "What is it?"

"Evan, I. . ." Joy looked behind her at the house then turned back to him. "There's someone here to see you. And I don't know how you'll react."

"Who is it?"

"Your brother."

He'd heard her wrong. She couldn't have said what he thought she said. But when he didn't speak, she put her hand on his arm.

"Sean is here."

Anger bubbled up inside him. He tried to push past her, but she stopped him. "Let me go inside, Joy."

"No. Not until you promise me you'll stay calm and hear him out."

Evan felt sick. "How long was he here before you texted me?"

"About an hour."

"He had an hour to fill your head with lies, and you believed them."

Joy frowned and crossed her arms over her chest. "You should know me better than that. Yes, he talked, and yes, I listened. But I don't know him. Not like you do. I only want you to hear what he has to say and make up your own mind."

"I'm sorry." Evan reached for Joy and hugged her close. "I'm just in shock."

"I understand." She pulled back and looked up at him. "Are you ready?"

Evan nodded. Joy opened the door, and they walked in together.

Sean sat on the couch in the living room. As soon as he saw Evan, he shot to his feet.

"Evan. It's good to see you."

He nodded. "Sean." Time hadn't been good to Sean. He was gaunt, scarred, and looked far older than his twenty-nine years.

Joy sat on the loveseat and motioned for Evan to join her. Then she looked at Sean. "Sit down. You two have a lot to talk about."

Evan settled beside her and took her hand, grateful that she realized how much he needed her to stay with him. She would support him, encourage him, and if he lost his temper, she would keep him from throttling Sean.

Sean fidgeted with his hands, picking at the skin around his nails. "I've wanted to talk to you for so long," he finally said. "You have no idea."

"No, I don't. Because you vanished with our parents'

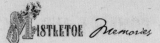

savings and we never could find you."

"I'm sorry." Sean buried his face in his hands, and a sob tore from him. "I'm so sorry. I made huge mistakes. Messed everything up. I never deserved to be part of your family, and I don't deserve your forgiveness now."

Evan's first instinct was to go to Sean and comfort him, but he held himself back. Mom trusted Sean, and it had devastated her. Evan looked at Joy, hoping she could tell him what to do.

He didn't need to ask. "Follow your heart," she whispered to him.

Evan looked at Sean, crying from the depths of his soul. Pain like that couldn't be worked up. Evan knew, the same way he'd known about Joy, that Sean was sincere. His brother had done terrible things to their parents, and heaven only knew what he'd done in the years he'd been gone. But like the prodigal son, he'd come home. He was broken and damaged, but he was home.

With a silent prayer for help, Evan stood and moved to the couch, where he sat beside his brother. He opened his arms and, as the sobs continued, Sean turned and collapsed against his chest.

❧

Joy was back in the kitchen, but instead of making cookies, she was putting together sandwiches. Sean looked like he hadn't eaten in days, and Evan had a bad habit of working through lunch. They could all use a snack. Besides, it had given her an excuse to leave the two brothers alone to talk in private.

It was a miracle Sean had found his way back. From what he'd told her, he'd gone to California and used the stolen money to invest in some shady, not entirely legal operations. He'd lived the high life for a while, but then the business went south, the money dried up, and all the friends he thought he had dropped him. For the last two years, he'd been living on the streets, making his way back home.

Joy opened the fridge. Where had the mayo gone? She moved aside a jug of milk and there it was, pushed all the way to the back. She reached in just when the doorbell rang, making her jump and hit her head. Again.

"You've got to be kidding." She rubbed the back of her skull. Now she had two sore spots. "If one more person comes to visit, I may end up with a concussion."

She wiped her hands on a towel and went to the front door. Even though she'd never met the man who stood on the other side, she knew immediately who he was. He was a near-perfect older version of his son.

"Mr. Lancaster. I'm Joy Benucci."

"I'm aware. I've seen your picture quite a lot lately." He motioned behind him at Evan's car. "I see my son is here. May I come in?"

She stood back for him to enter then pointed away from the living room. "Let's go in the kitchen."

How was she going to break the news to him? "Uh, can I offer you something? Water, coffee, tea"—she looked at the food-laden counter—"a sandwich?"

"No, thank you. I came to talk to you, actually."

"Me?"

"Yes. I may have been too hasty in my assessment of your character." He cleared his throat. "Several people whom I respect very much have told me that I'm being a jerk."

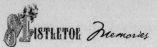

Joy burst out laughing, bringing a shadow of a smile to Robert's face.

"They said it more tactfully, but the meaning was clear."

Joy was a swirl of emotions. She wanted to know what this change of heart meant for Comfort House, but right now, there was something more important to address.

"Mr. Lancaster, I look forward to having a long talk with you, but there's something you need to know." Joy took a deep breath. "Evan is here. And so is Sean."

His face paled and he gripped the edge of the counter. "Sean is here?"

"Yes."

"How. . ." He swallowed, blinked, and then gave his head a hard shake. "How did you find him?"

"I didn't find him. He found me."

Robert Lancaster, hard-boiled attorney-at-law, looked as if he might keel over right there in her kitchen. Joy took hold of his arm. "Are you all right?"

He looked down at her, his eyes wide with shock. "I don't know what to do."

"It seems to me that God wants you to talk to Him." From the way his brow creased, he wasn't convinced God had anything to do with the situation. "Think about it. What are the odds that the very first time you come to this house, both of your sons are here?"

"Joy!" She heard Evan calling her name from the hall. "Are you okay? I heard the doorbell, and—" He stopped in the kitchen doorway. "Dad."

Robert was barely holding it together. Only one word came out. "Sean."

Evan nodded. "Yeah." He went to his father and put his arm around his shoulders. "Come on."

The two men left the kitchen together, and Joy exhaled the breath she'd been holding. *O Lord, You truly do work in strange and mysterious ways.*

A moment later, Ben strode into the kitchen. "What is going on? Why are there three grown men crying in the living room?" When she turned and Ben saw the tears rolling down her cheeks, he threw his hands up in exasperation. "Not you, too."

Joy laughed and caught him in a bear hug. "It's a Christmas miracle, Ben. You don't fight it, you just go with it."

CHAPTER 14

Comfort House was bursting at the seams on Christmas Day. The usual residents were there, all of whom were able to celebrate without the impending doom of losing their home, thanks to the withdrawal of the eviction and the fact that the house was on the fast track to being dubbed a historical landmark.

And all three Lancaster men were there. Sean looked better than he had that first day, but there was still a long road ahead of him. The reunion with his father had gone better than expected, considering the circumstances. But there was still pain and distrust to be worked through. Evan had opened his home to his brother, willing to give him a chance to prove himself.

Joy excused herself from the crowded living room to refill the cookie plate. Between Leon, Ben, and Sean, the cookies were being consumed faster than seemed physically possible. Maybe if she used a larger platter they would last longer. Crouching in front of the island, Joy opened the cupboard door. Of course. . .it was way in the back. She leaned in, reaching as far as she could.

"Sweetheart."

Evan's voice was right behind her. She jerked up, but at the same time she felt his hand on her head. The next second she heard him grunt as his fingers were pinched between her head and the cupboard.

Joy stood and put her arms around his neck. "My hero."

His hands settled gently on her waist. "I hope you appreciate the depths of my love for you."

"Oh, I do."

"As much as I want to spend some time alone with you, we better get these cookies to the people before they revolt."

Joy sighed. "You're right. But I'm taking a rain check on that alone time."

He chuckled as he followed her out of the kitchen. "You better believe it. A rain check, a snow check, a sunshine check. . ."

As they walked into the living room together, all the teens yelled out, "Stop!" Dana pointed at the ceiling.

They stopped in their tracks and looked up.

Mistletoe.

Evan raised an eyebrow. "What do you think?"

Joy handed the platter to Robert, the person closest to her, then turned back to Evan. "I think this is a tradition I can get used to."

ABOUT THE AUTHORS

Carla Olson Gade has been imagining stories for most of her life. Her love for writing and eras gone by turned her attention to writing historical Christian romance. She is a member of American Christian Fiction Writers and Maine Fellowship of Christian Writers. An autodidact, creative thinker, and avid reader, Carla also enjoys genealogy, web design, and photography. A native New Englander, she writes from her home in beautiful rural Maine where she resides with her "hero" husband and two young adult sons. You may visit her online at carlagade.com.

RWA-FHL Chapter President **Gina Welborn** worked in news radio scripting copy until she took up writing romances. *Mercy Mild* is her third Barbour novella. A moderately obsessive fan of *Community* and *Once Upon a Time*, Gina lives in Oklahoma with her pastor husband, their five Okie-Hokie children, a rabbit named Hobbit, and two Lab mixes that don't retrieve much of anything.

Lisa Karon Richardson is an award-winning author and a member of ACFW. Influenced by books like *The Little Princess*, Lisa's early books were heavy on creepy boarding schools. Though she's mostly all grown-up now, she still loves a healthy dash of adventure in any story she creates, even her real-life story. She's been a missionary to the Seychelles and Gabon, and now that she and her husband are back in America, they are tackling new adventures—starting a daughter-work church and raising two precocious kids.

Jennifer AlLee believes the most important thing a woman can do is discover her identity in God—a theme that carries throughout her stories. She's a member of American Christian Fiction Writers and RWA's Faith, Hope and Love Chapter. When she's not spinning tales, she enjoys board games with friends, movies, and breaking into song for no particular reason. Jennifer lives with her family in the grace-filled city of Las Vegas, Nevada. Please visit her at www.jenniferallee.com.